STREET FOOD AND LOVE

H.A. Enri

Martin Sisters Publishing

Published by

Martin Sisters Publishing Company

www. martinsisterspublishing. com

Copyright © 2014 H.A. Enri

All rights reserved. Published in the United States by
Martin Sisters Publishing, LLC, Kentucky.
ISBN: 978-1-62553-068-4
Young Adult/Contemporary
Printed in the United States of America
Martin Sisters Publishing Company

To my First Reader: You take in my first drafts like crème brûlée even though the words on those pages are really more like rat tartare.
Thank you for your exceptional literary palate.

CHAPTER ONE

Anybody who believes that the way to a man's heart
is through his stomach flunked geography.
~ Robert Byrne

They say you can't choose your family, but you can your friends. Personally, I think whoever created humans left a serious flaw in the design. We should all have a say in what kind of family we're born into *before* the birthing process. Who wouldn't want that? Of course, no one cares about my idea which is why I got stuck with Cedro, aka my father.

I finished my study packets earlier in the morning, so now I do what I normally have been doing the last few months: work the food truck with Cedro. I figure that if I help Cedro make money then I, in turn, can regenerate part of the college fund he *stole* from me (Yes, I said *stole*. I realize some may think *stole* is a strong term, but oh well, that's just the way I see it) since he usually divvies out a small portion of the profits to me. However, the way sales have been going there typically isn't much of a profit for either of us. Still, there are some benefits. I don't have my own car yet, so helping Cedro out keeps me in his graces, such that he lets me tote around his Jeep Wrangler Rubicon. I've learned a little quid-pro-quo never hurt anyone.

The L.A. lunch rush near La Cienega Boulevard, where Cedro has parked on a narrow Hollywood street called San Vicente, also lends to some good sightseeing, particularly those sights that have puckering red lips, a set of Colgate -white teeth, and a mask of perfectly tempered makeup applied as if Michelangelo were hired to prep her for a magazine shoot. She's in line and waiting to buy something from Eaby Baby's Edible Crazies. Her figure is demure but swirled in all the right spots. With arms akimbo, she is engaged with someone on her cell phone, an involved expression arresting her dynamic features. This young woman seems to be a professional, not an artist or an actress or trying to be either one. The green heals at the bottom of her legs and the cream skirt suit fitting her like a book cover say as much. She looks almost twenty-five, but I'm hoping she can't be more than nineteen or twenty, tops. From what I gather, most likely this hottie is into or trying to get into the business side of either the music or movie industry, wanting to be a producer maybe. In other words, if I made it as a comedian, I would be the talent and she would be my boss who owns the talent. *I like the sound of that. I play good little comedian; she plays seductive boss lady.* Just a few more customers and said boss lady will be at the window where I will be the host taking her order from one of the newest food trucks to hit the city boulevards.

The new rig, ideally, should be—but isn't—getting a nice draw. It's all trigged out, a fully loaded kitchen-on-wheels complete with a smoker, broiler, chef's grade range, flat griddle and rotisserie so that Cedro can prepare any kind of meat any way he wants.

"Come on over to Eaby Baby's," I call out of the window to passersby, stealing a glance at the magnetic enchantress. Of course, she still doesn't notice me.

A notepad in hand and a skullcap over my head so that my shoulder-length hair doesn't wind up in any of the food, I wonder how anyone could *not* notice me framed in this blur of brightness, its vibrant dapples of neon and pastels grotesquely woven into the design. *Yuck!* I haven't admitted it out loud because that would be way too harsh for Cedro, the *budding businessman extraordinaire*, but the graphics on his sidewalls are just plain horrid. I know he wanted to draw attention to the truck, but repulsing would-be consumers with colors that look like they came from the Crayola Reject Department is not the way to go. I'd even go so far as to say that if I were a starving stranger and I saw his truck rolling down the street, I would check myself into a mental ward thinking I have time warped to circa 1965 and woken up in a psychedelic nightmare.

Van Morrison? Are you there? Is that you?

Cedro is a novice in the street food scene and doesn't have the best marketing ideas, thus his business hasn't exactly left the runway yet, and I can't say I am disappointed. Not in the least. The whole I-spent-your-college-fund-on-my-midlife-crisis-capitalist-venture is just not an easy thing to soon forget. Couldn't he have purchased a less expensive truck and started off slowly? Instead he bought a top-of-the-line, 2013 Armenco GVWR 18-foot Utilimaster. The total cost of his mobile catering unit (MCU) was around $90,000. That's right. Ninety G's, and, by the way, this is before the $7,500 custom paint job he had splashed on it and had the words EABY BABY'S EDIBLE CRAZIES stenciled on its sides. That's $97,500 he spent on a business he knows absolutely nothing about.

Way to go, dad. I love you, too.

I take an order from a man in a suit and hand him his ticket, my eyes shielded behind my Bollé shades. "About five minutes and your order will be up," I assure him before reaching to the counter at my left and grabbing a piping hot pork slider that I pass out to an overweight, middle-aged lady in Wrangler jeans. "Thanks for coming to Eaby Baby's. Enjoy." I endorse her with a grin so as to seem to be paying attention to her even though I'm actually interested in what's going on behind her, namely that sizzling charmer who is not only getting closer, but is not at all aware of how ever more seductive she is becoming with each step she takes toward the ordering window.

"How we looking?" Cedro asks from the kitchen behind me, his colorful, inked out arms (that look ridiculous by the way, at least to me. I mean the guy is over forty-years-old and hasn't been in prison. This whole wannabe badass persona is getting way out of control) flashing me under his short sleeved chef's garb.

I turn away and can't help but notice that the line outside our ordering bay, compared to the other trucks shouldering the street by us, is painfully small.

"Eh," I add, not daring to put words to the slow-growing line.

By "slow-growing" I mean it in the sense of the growth rate of a Canadian White Cedar tree: about four inches for every one hundred and fifty-five years. For Eaby Baby's, a new customer trickles over only after realizing that the other trucks shouldering the street, the trucks they really wanted to purchase from, will take longer to serve them due to the extravagant lines pouring from their sides. For example:

A half a block down is the Cali Food Grill, which serves a variety of proteins that—surprise, surprise—are all grilled.

Grilled steak, chicken, fish, pork, veal, et al. That's what you get at CFG. Not too original, but they are established and always seem to gather a crowd, two positive signs of a good business.

Too Corny, a big yellow beast on four rubber cylinders, has one claim to street food fame: corn. They mash it, mix it, grill it, fry it or whatever it. A little sugar here, some butter and oil there, then throw in some kid of rich bread and that's Too Corny. It's really just overemphasized baby food, but apparently that's what people are going for these days. It must be the mush factor that people like because it somehow takes them back to their childhood.

Darn you, Nostalgia.

"Hi," I address the young business lady who's finally made it to me and whose neck is craned so that she is looking up to me from ground level. "First time here?"

"Hi," she says, continuing to scan the menu. "Um, yeah. Can you recommend something?"

"We have a lucky customer special," I begin. "It's for customer number forty-eight." That's an absolute lie. We haven't had more than twenty patrons all day. "I think you're it."

"Really?" She smiles the smile I was hoping to provoke when I formulated the lie.

Why this face before me isn't on the big screen, I have no idea. The way she has utterly taken the light from the air, absorbed it, and wrapped it around her is pure talent.

"Well, we'll have to see. You'll have to place the right order."

I turn around to see Cedro's expression. He's well aware that there is no real daily customer giveaway. The combination of rancor and confusion all tangled on his face and meeting at the center emphasizes this point. The center is never a good place for facial features to meet. Happy expressions expand outward

9

on the face and stretch to the ends; displeasure always crashes in on center, like missile lock on a jet when it's about to blast an enemy plane out of the sky.

"Dad," I urge through clenched teeth and wave my head quickly a few times. "Look."

Cedro, assembling the orders on the food line, pauses to take a quick peak over my shoulder. "Oh, okay. I see." He approves of the pretty girl and then turns back around and tears apart some pork. "But don't even think about comping her out."

"You really think I would do that?"

Cedro turns back around and looks down at my pants, then back up to my eyes. "I really don't know what you'll do. I've never seen you in action with the ladies." Again he scans me up and down.

Naturally, I check down my legs to see what he sees. "What are you looking at?"

"To see if you got a pair. And if so, how big that pair is. Because no real man would ever give a girl anything for free *before* getting what he wants from her. That's called a chump, and chumps live in Loserville. Is that where you're from?"

"So now you're the resident expert on women?"

"Between the two of us, yes. I am, in fact, our default expert. And as the default expert I can most honorably say this: never let a woman clip your *cajones*. If there is one thing I can teach you about a woman, it's that getting to a woman has got nothing to do with a woman. It's all about you being a man. After that, getting the girl takes care of itself. You just worry your little self with keeping your *cajones* right where they belong. There isn't a lady out there who doesn't have a pair of scissors waiting to snip away at you." He's using the tongs in his hand to illustrate his point. A few seconds after opening and closing the tongs, he turns back to the metal cutting slab and carries on with pulling apart a roast of tender pork.

I don't know why my mom left, so I have no evidence whatsoever regarding the success rate of Cedro's philosophy on girls. Right now though, I can understand how his approach to women would not exactly agree with all types, and I have no conclusive stance on the issue of manhood and women and *cajones* either, so I'm obligated to remain silent on the matter.

"Wow, Dad, thank you for this enlightening Jedi talk in the middle of some random, midweek lunch push. You really opened my eyes to some rather important things in life." I bow a few times and chant a couple of times, "You are so gracious, Oh Wise and Powerful Default Master of Manhood. Thank you eternally."

With his back to me, Cedro scoffs, not bothering to stop the rhythm he's creating with the pork and bread and sauce.

I turn back to the girl. Her finger is to the corner of her mouth, bouncing and tapping, keeping the pace of her thought. The scarlet polish on her perfectly manicured hands is a shade lighter than her lips. "So I have to order a certain thing to win?"

I nod. "It's the way it works. When you're the lucky customer, you don't automatically win. It just makes you eligible to win, *if* you order the secret order of the day."

"Like a mystery menu item?"

"Yep."

"Hmm. So what do I win?"

"Well, you'll have to try to find out."

This gets the other four customers involved, trying to instigate what the girl should order. I can see some heads turn from people in the other lines at the nearby food trucks. They, like me, are watching the pretty girl below me to see what she's going to do. She evaluates the handwritten menu listed on a dry-erase whiteboard that's hanging next to the service window. From the line, an anxious man and woman guess out loud.

"Pork belly sliders," the man boasts.

"Chicken with bacon melt," the lady attests.

The young beauty, in her sugary and irresistible tone, strikes with a sweet command. "Tell me what I win."

This is the moment of truth. I will either, as Cedro says, give her my *cajones* and lose my manhood by giving her a free meal, or I will fabricate some prize, one that will include a date with me. This may lead to potential and outright rejection, but I'm willing to take that risk as long as I can retain my manhood. No way is she getting me to give in that easily.

"You're probably thinking the prize is lunch on the house, right?" She nods, which I expected. "But that would be too shorthanded. What we do for you is...well you see, we here at Eaby Baby's Edible Crazies are into personalized customer service."

"Personalized customer service?"

"That's right. What you get if you win is me." I gave in. Guess that makes me a chump.

The pretty girl's expression sinks, going from hopeful anticipation to the way she is looking at me now, as if she just saw the Titanic go down.

I think this is the universal expression for rejection.

"Really. It's true," I remove my shades, trying to salvage a date. "I come to the location of your choosing and cook for you and, if you want, a host of your closest friends." I wink after this last detail.

Her head juts back as if she is dodging a punch, then her features reassemble into that the-Titanic-just-sunk look. "Like a private sampling?"

"Exactly!"

"Oh," the beauty expresses, her entire sheen now completely gone. It's like the sun has reached down and yanked back its light that was around her a few seconds ago, the same way a child does their toy from someone when they want it back immediately. "I thought...never mind. I'll just try the pork belly sliders."

"Ding, ding! You're the winner," I continue with the same, lame lucky customer routine even though she blew that line up already.

The girl reaches into her wallet and stands on her tiptoes, extending her arm and handing me the money. "No thanks." She smiles when she says this just to rub it in. "I'll just take the sliders. You can save the lucky customer prize for someone else."

Ouch.

The stain in my tone leaks through. "What kind of bread do you want for those sliders? Hawaiian or wheat?"

"Can I get one of each?"

Now I'm agitated. "That's fifty cents extra." It's not, but I tell her that because I got rejected.

"No problem."

I take her twenty-dollar bill and change it out, still charging her the extra fifty-cent rejection fee.

"You're number seventeen," I say, handing her the change before turning around to tell Cedro the new order. "Pork belly sliders, one Hawaiian and one wheat."

Hearing the lull in my tone, Cedro, without turning around, "But at least you still got a pair of *cajones.*"

CHAPTER TWO

Ask not what you can do for your country.
Ask what's for lunch.
~ Orson Welles

Stand-up comedy is my personal pursuit of choice, not food. I have been fortunate to land a twenty-minute spot tonight at The Laugh Factory among a lineup of what I call middle class comedians. The comedy circuit in Los Angeles is really nothing but a huge clutter of hacks who think they are funny but really aren't. That's the kind of quasi-talent anyone trying to break into showbiz as a stand-up comic has to get around. If I'm going to make a name for myself, I have to take the good with the bad until I prove myself to be better than the rest.

Right now I'm stuck in the greenroom waiting my turn next to some of the other supposed comics who are also trying to cut their performance umbilical cord. *We'll see who's got the mojo*, I think to myself.

"Bring your funniest stuff or you'll never get another chance," the booking manager told me when he called me. His words are a warning echo in my mind.

I know that getting a spot on the Hollywood strip at this zygote stage of my career is nothing to take for granted. Forget the bayonets and swords, my first strikes in showbiz have to be nuclear, so I've laced my jokes with some serious comedic uranium.

"Sole Eaby," a caffeine-saturated voice calls to me.

I glance toward the direction of the voice. It's one of The Laugh Factory's hosts. He's wearing a slim black tie over a teal shirt that is tucked into a pair of green Dockers. Setting the outfit's foundation is a pair of Converse. The guy is the epitome of urban. He must think I am completely out of my league, perhaps from the planet of No Style Whatsoever wearing nothing but jeans, a t-shirt, and a pair of blue Nike sneakers with white soles[1].

"Go crush it," one good-natured comedian calls out from the greenroom as I leave and file through the threshold to the backstage area.

I can hear the host on stage, spieling through the microphone to the audience. He's introducing me, explaining how the expected comedian that the crowd came to see had to cancel and, lo and behold, they get me. "Now, for kicks and giggles, we have a brand new comic for you tonight," he continues. Anytime an

---

[1] My name *Sole* has nothing to do with the bottom of a pair of shoes. Cedro, when he gave me the name, said that he'd meant it in its purist definition: *one of a kind*, that *I'm* one of a kind. These days, however, I'm not so sure about that. Every time someone calls my name or I write it on a piece of paper or I hear the word *sole* or *soul* sung in a song, I am supposed to be reminded of how unique I am. Whatever. No one who truly thought I was his one-of-a-kind would blow my future on his capricious new adventure.

MC starts my set by mentioning that I am "brand new," it's usually a big hint for them that means "not funny."

Great, I think. Just great.

Suddenly a large hand presses down on my shoulder. "Hold up, kid." The hand is accompanied by a Godlike baritone voice that sounds like it's rained down from heaven.

I turn around to see a hulking, thick-bodied man who is the proud owner of the bass voice and Sasquatch grip. There isn't much to say to such a giant of a man, so I opt for general silence and a helpless look on my face.

"ID?"

It isn't surprising that security is questioning my legal ability to perform. The minimum age is eighteen. Nevertheless, I am prepared. Cedro signed a notarized form that states I have his full permission to perform at over-eighteen and twenty-one clubs. At the latter, I am obligated only to the stage and greenroom, far away from the booze. This letter also means that Cedro gets the check written out to him. *Ek. Vomit.* That's his fee for helping out his son: somewhere around twenty-five percent, which is "a pretty good rate" according to Cedro because he is technically "the manager." I agree that the rate is good. I don't agree that my flesh and blood progenitor stealing any bit of his progeny's hard-earned funds is somehow a pretty good anything. Thievery is always thievery at any rate.

"Huh," the security guard grunts upon scanning the notarized parental note.

"It's authentic," I claim.

By the expression he gives me, I figure I should just nod in silence and speak only if he asks me a question, but he doesn't ask. He merely dips his head and returns my notarized consent form back to me with a sly gruff. "Good luck."

"Let's give a warm hand for Sole Eaby!" the MC roars.

His charge is followed by little enthusiasm from the crowd: hollow applause and quizzical stares, their way of letting me know that they are unwilling to offer me their approval without me validating my worth. Their respect is something I am going to have to earn. It's fine by me. I'm ready for the challenge.

The MC's brisk pace generates a cool breeze as he passes me stage left. Before I appear from behind from the curtain, he forewarns me, "Remember, kid, each joke you tell is another step up the mountain." I must have a quizzical expression about me, so he clarifies. "In other words, don't take any mike time for granted." I can't tell if that was an exhortation or a death sentence.

My approach to the microphone is a peppy jog. When I get there I can see before me an expectant audience. I take a bow, holding the posture for longer than a bow usually lasts. This exaggerated hold is intentional and meant to cause some confusion. The audience has no idea that this is part of my routine tonight. For a few more seconds, I allow my wavy, opal hair to drape down from my head like a waterfall. I can feel the crowd get restless. This is my cue.

Here we go, I charge myself with the task of making people laugh.

Standing upright, I remove the mike from the clutch. "I guess you're wondering 'What the hell,' right?" I open. "I can respect that. I mean, seriously, who am I? Here I am, a total stranger to you all, and the first thing I do is come on stage and bend over. You're thinking, 'What does he mean by this? Is he going to fart? Does his stomach hurt? Is he hitting on me? Did his appendix burst?'"

The audience starts to loosen up with some huffs.

"Well, let me tell you what I mean by my bowing. *Ouch!*" I scream into the mike like the late-great Sam Kinnison would have. "My fuggin back hurts![2]"

Spits of laughter blaze the house.

"It's true," I roll on. "I know, I know, you didn't come here for the truth. But oh well...you're going to get it anyway." I snicker, chiding the audience in a playful manner. "But while we're on the topic of truth, let me say that, have you realized that we live in a generation that lies more than any other in history?" The crowd claps.

"I don't believe anyone really hates the truth. We're just too afraid of what will happen to us if we say it."

More cheers and applause. Though I'm here to generate laughs, audience approval in this form is also acceptable during an act.

"So as our social defense, we adopt the practice of *Tolerance*. That's *Tolerance* with a capital T. Let me explain.

"When I told you that my back hurt, you were most likely thinking, 'There's no way someone my age can have back problems. That's not true.' If you were thinking that, you'd be right. I'm way too young for that. Something in your mind knew I wasn't telling the truth. But still, you let me get away with it. Have you noticed how often that happens? How often people

[2] According to Cedro, my mom had a garbage mouth. Being Spanish and thus Catholic, Cedro feels that swearing should only be used to express a strong emotion when extreme, ideally hostile, circumstances occur. Comedy wouldn't be one those *extreme* situations. Since I thoroughly hate my mom (even though I don't really know her) and everything she was, is, and does, I think it best to practice Cedro's rule since it separates me from having anything in common with my mom, wherever she is today. Thus I say words like *fugg* instead of the profane alternative. Some think I might as well say the bad word or that I am swearing. To them I say, "*Fugg it!*" because I don't consider it cussing.

lie to you and you just *tolerate it*!" I scream the last two words in to add emphasis.

"Let's look at the average middle-aged family. Let's say they live in a not-quite-so-rich neighborhood—no, no, that's another lie. Let's say they're sinking hard from the middle class almost to downright poverty. In this house there's a dad, a mom, a couple of kiddos and probably a few relatives poaching off of them." The crowd laughs.

"Come on, work with me. I'm Spanish. You know how we do it? Anyone in the house tonight Latino or Hispanic?

Over half of the audience members clap.

"See, you know what I'm talking about. There's no such thing as a single-family home in Hispanic culture. One of these days when I buy my first house and the agent asks me, 'So, are you looking for a single family home?' I have to say, 'Uh, hello. Look at me, Holmes. I'm looking for an *entire* family home."

For a moment, I let the crowd enjoy the taste of the mini joke embedded in the thematic one that surrounds it. "So, let's look first at the mom in that house. I'm going to call her the *post-child-bodied* mom. And, by the way, post-partum depression is not just for women. When a man sees that his once-hot wife takes on that post-child body, he too suffers from post-partum."

The audience thinks about that while I pause. A slow, steady growth of laughter flares up along with some booing. I guess a handful of people are offended, which is fine by me. Their clashing response tells me they're listening to the twists and turns in my delivery. That's acceptable. Sometimes negative reactions are just as good as laughter. Being controversial is not such a bad thing if you can handle it, and I know I can.

"Yes, people, you know it's true. You know that body, the wife whose body constantly screams 'Leave-me-alone-I've-had-a-kid!' That's such a lie. Her body doesn't have to scream that. She can change the tune—make it say something else. A good diet and some exercise and a lot less laziness and, presto, instant makeover." I say. "It's called *science*. But fat moms don't want to hear that word. That's too much truth. And yes, I said *fat*.

"They want to say..." I use my whiny girl voice. "'My metabolism's slow,' or 'Nothing I do works,' or the best one yet, 'You know when women have kids their bodies change forever.'" For effect, I look around at the empty stage, acting as if anyone else nearby can hear the absolute absurdity of that claim even though no one is next to me.

"That's just ridiculous. Just look around. Plenty of Hollywood mommas are looking pretty good, and it's not because 'they're special.' Like I said, it's called *science*."

The audience chuckles.

"But no, we let women walk around and lie to all of us—*right to our face!*" My signature scream floods the room with mock anger.

"They say, 'I can't lose weight. My body just won't...nah, nah, nah.' How many poor guys are out there suffering with a woman who is about as appetizing as last week's leftovers? It's just tragic."

In return, I get a hail of laughter and some crows of disbelief, the crossfire meeting right in front of the stage.

I grind on with my joke. "See, some of you think this is funny, and some of you still can't believe I'm saying this. Why? Like I said: no one wants truth. They just go on tolerating the lies and poor guys are suffering out there.

"Well, I can tell you this: there's no way the mother of my kids is going to pull that one over on me." And, in homage to

Sam Kinnison, again I warp into a yelling tirade, "I'M NOT GOING TO TOLERATE IT!"

Like a canon firing, the crowd discharges a boom of bliss. I let them laugh this way until it gradually fades. During the right moments, it's important to allow the listeners time to marinate in the humor for a bit. By hearing themselves laugh, they're encouraged to laugh even more at my next joke—just a little psychological trick I noticed that the greats, like Dennis Miller, Eddie Murphy et al, do during big gaffs.

I carry on. "Now, before you think I'm a misogynist, I'll prove to you I'm an equal opportunity guy. So let's look at the middle-aged family guy. You all thought I forgot about him, didn't you? Don't you worry. I'm fair.

"This guy is probably medium build and height, a couple of six packs away from becoming astronomy's new celestial body, and, to boot, has no idea how to raise a kid. You all know the kids I'm talking about. In school we're forced to sit in classes with them. They're the loud ones that make very bad jokes and *won't* stop telling them no matter how many times people *don't* laugh..."

The audience gets my dry humor and is completely gripped. I could practically say something like, "*Hey, that wall is white. Look. Ahh!*" and they would probably think it's the most hilarious thing they've ever heard.

"I mean, seriously, this dad is not only clueless as a parent, here's the worst part: He's all tatted up." I pause, letting the listeners think about that. "And he probably has the words spelled wrong."

I use a male skit voice. "'What's that say?' Someone asks."

For the dad I use a gravelly voice, trying to sound steely and rugged. "'It says *pro-found*. Pretty cool, no?'"

Back to male skit voice. "'Uh, no. Not exactly. There's no hyphen in the word *profound*, dude.'"

My normal voice. "Then the schmuck will try to justify it."

I return to my wannabe-tough-guy dad voice. "'No, fool, it's *pro* like *pro*fessional. I'm, like, a professional found.'"

Male skit voice. "'Uh...what?'"

After a collective burst of amusement, I bellow, "Come on. Now really, why the hell does this guy need a tattoo? He can't spell and it's not like he's ever done time or killed anyone."

I change my tone, creating a deep-voiced male character. "'Hey, why'd you get those tats, bro?' Somebody else will ask him."

I make my raspy, wannabe-tough-guy dad voice. "'Because I'm hardcore, bro.'"

Back to deep-voiced character. "'Bro, aren't you, like, *married*? With kids?'"

More laughter and clapping from the audience.

"See, people, it's just not tough guy status when you show up at McDonald's with a little five-year-old while trying to look like some bad-to-the-bone dude who'll kill anyone who tries to stop him on his mission of getting the cheeseburger Happy Meal.

"I think Tolerance at certain levels should be a crime. Letting people believe things about themselves that just aren't true should be a penal code violation. I don't care if it's a misdemeanor—whatever. But we have to stop encouraging this whole Tolerance idea and start encouraging truth," I rhapsodize to the delight of the crowd.

Every famous comedian has a brand, a signature piece to their routine, an anchor that they can be known for. Howie Mandel had Bobby. Robin Harris had Bebe's Kids. Jim Carey had Fireman Bill and all of his other impersonations. I'm experimenting with a) creating little skits to illustrate my punch lines b) Tolerance with a capital T, which is good because I can constantly fill new material into this topic and c) my screaming rants of certain phrases.

The digital clock on the back wall indicates my time is almost up. I begin the dismount to the routine. "But just remember, gang, it's not their fault. It's ours. It's ours because we're the ones tolerating their delusions.

"By the way, I have to say one more thing about tattoos: aren't they expensive? I mean, this middle-aged family guy sure isn't that rich. What does he tell his kids when they ask for a good dinner because they're tired of burritos with only beans, rice, and cheese? What if they want some meat in that thing for once?"

I hike up the pitch in my voice to sound like a whiny child. "'Dad, we're hungry. Can we put some chicken in the burrito tonight?'"

In response I imitate a gruff, wannabe-tough-guy, deep-voiced father. "'What? Heck no. Get out of here. You know we can't afford to buy meat.'"

Child voice. "'Why not?'"

I lift up my sleeve and flex, my limber arms forming a small muscle. Using my voice as the father's character, I say, pointing to my arm as if there was a tattoo on it. "'Because I spent it here.'"

The audience is in stitches.

"And guess what, gang? You all know what by now. We just..." I pause and hold the microphone out the audience.

"Tolerate it!" the mob clamors in unison, their symphony of cheers thrumming the sweet chords of success inside of me.

There's a part inside the mind of a comedian that has the ability to bisect itself, like a fork in a road. It's this uncanny skill that allows us to perform and, at the same time, stand outside of ourselves, in real time, as if we were a completely different person watching ourselves live on television. It's almost the Ebenezer Scrooge experience when he goes back into time with the Ghost of Christmas Past and observes himself.

I'm doing that right now. It's what I call *satellite* mode.

When I am nearing the end of a gig, sometimes my mind tires and I'm on the verge of losing focus, so I force myself to try to forget there's a crowd in front of me and find my target person. A satellite has two different vertical angles it scans. Up is called the *zenith*, down is called the *nadir*. Since I am usually above the crowd and am looking down at the audience, I call the target person I am trying to focus on my nadir, which roughly means *lowest point*. The nadir reminds me to relax and act like I'm having a casual conversation with one person.

This feeling is what the best comedians create, such as superstar Louis C.K. Before he made it as a director and writer in Hollywood, he broke in his showbiz denim by performing stand-up. His ability to tickle the audience with funny revelations about everyday situations in life made fans latch onto him like honey to a bear's tongue. That's the effect every comedian worth his salt shoots for. That's why I aim to find my nadir. The lowest point takes the edge off and I don't feel like I have to impress anyone. If I flipped the nadir-zenith process, then who knows what would happen? Maybe my jokes would sound forced because of the unnecessary pressure I would be putting on myself by trying to rise to the expectations of the almighty zenith. Or maybe, just maybe, they might improve.

I don't know whom I'll center in on tonight. In fact, I never do. I just peruse the faces until one strikes me. Sometimes it's a guy who reminds me of Cedro. When I pretend to talk to this guy, I spin the jokes a little differently because that's how I have to do it when I try to make him laugh. He's not like a father, willing to chuckle at his child's jokes even when they are otherwise less than humorous. Cedro, simply put, is not an easy one to extract an expression of joy out of. It's like trying to drag a dead elephant out of the Serengeti with a rope and your own body strength.

Other times I try to find someone who resembles my best friend, Yoke. He's like Cedro's alter ego who laughs at just about anything I say, which is exactly why I can't use him to verify how hilarious I truly am or not. Sure, he's good for my psyche, but when I need to test out any new material for my routines, he's terrible. Him laughing at my new material is worth about half a pence to a dollar.

On rare occasions, I hone in on a woman whom I imagine to be my mom, my mom at twenty-seven that is when she was probably still quite the seductress and still with my father i.e. before she bailed on us. Ironically, the two times this has happened, I turned out some pretty solid comedic moments. Instead of conjuring up the hate I harbor for her, on stage it's the opposite way. I imagine how she might be the doting mother who laughs at all my gags while she's cooking dinner in the kitchen, and I am standing there, entertaining her with my wit.

Scanning...scanning...scan—

I found her.

She has straight brunette hair—full, thick, and satiny—that cascades down to about the middle of her back. Her graphic eyes are voluminous and seem to smile without needing her lips to help them. Though she is sitting towards the back of the house, even from the stage I can see her bawdy cheekbones and the hue of her breezy, olive skin. She has an imposing composition of beauty, one like an ocean wave so big no one on the beach could possibly ignore its force even if they tried.

The guy she is perched next to, however, might be a more imposing force. He's poised as a direct and immediate threat to me and anyone who would dare approach his woman. He's in the likeness of Gaston from *Beauty and Beast*. *Strapping* and *gallant* are two words I would use to describe this dark-haired man-child sitting soldier straight in his seat. His shoulders are so broad and firm they could be used as a runway to land fighter jets, and the way his chest pushes out on the threading of his collared shirt, I wonder how the buttons don't shoot out across the room, little projectile missiles clipping people all around. Although I don't want to be an enemy to this hulking beast of a man, the brunette he's next to is not someone I think I can pass on. It may be risky, and I may get killed in the process, but I have to find a way to meet her.

The timer on the back wall points out that I have less than three minutes left. My closing routine includes a set of jokes on voting and politics, perfect to fill out the segment.

Technically I am unable to vote as I am only seventeen-years-old, but no one in the house is going to figure that out. When I was writing my material down, I couldn't resist conjuring up some quick takes on the way people seem to vote during presidential elections. I hope it works.

"So I'm sure everyone is ready to cast their ballots for the next president. As for me I can't wait to vote." The crowd's whistles and cheers signify that they, too, must be active voters.

"Everyone asks me, 'Who are you going to vote for?' I always tell them: Well, I don't know yet, but I do know this: When I vote, I am not going to do it *break-up* style. 'Break-up style?' they say, surprised. I ask them, 'You don't know what *break-up* style is?' 'Nope,' they assure me. I tell them, 'Okay, well, let me ask you this—why did you and your ex break up?'

"'Because she was f-in crazy,' they usually claim.

"'Okay then,' I respond. 'So, if she's so f-in crazy, then you're telling me you're sure as heck not going to cast the same vote as a crazy person, are you?'

A few huffs from the crowd emerge.

"See what I mean, gang. *Break-up style* is not the way to go."

The fans show their respect for my keen analysis by putting their hands together. Then, just when they settle, I blast, "HOW STUPID IS THAT!"

The gallery doesn't outright gush with laughter, but their applause resurges, which communicates to me that they approve of my insight on the topic and my sudden screaming rages. More importantly, the girl, the beautiful brunette I am focusing on is both clapping and smiling.

Yes! I think to myself. *She approves.*

"But isn't it true, everyone? People vote for stupid reasons. Take Obama for instance. How many people do you know voted for him just because he's *black*?" I watch a few arms rise.

"Don't be scared, people, just because I said *black*. You guys are getting all frazzled."

I make a mock audience voice whispering to someone else. "'Did he just say what I think he said? Whoa. That guy's got nerve.'"

I return to myself. "Nerve? Because I said *black*? It's a freaking color! Black. There. Ooh. I said it again. Come on, people. It comes in Crayola boxes little kids color with—are you serious? It's not like his blackness is a secret. It's not like he can hide it or something." I pause since that is a punch line, and the audience laughs.

"By the way, uh, didn't America get the memo? He's *half* black. The other half of him is white. That's right: he's just as white as he is black. Check out the gene pool. It's a fact. Not sure why people are getting all worked up over the color of some guy's half skin color. I mean, come on, isn't it what he does on the job that should matter, right?

"If that's how people reason, then when I need surgery or something I might as well say, 'Uh, sorry, but I want a *Spanish* doctor because, well, I'm Spanish.' If I said that they'd look at me like I was crazy.

"They'd tell me something like, 'Um, sir, you do know that whether or not you're Spanish, black, white, or whatever, your body's still got the same stuff in it, right?'"

The way I act out the voices and the varying tones I add shapes the humor for the listeners. They enjoy the act.

"How ridiculous would that make me? In that case, I'm only going to fear homicidal maniacs who come from a minority ethnic background. If some white guy tries to kill me, I'm going to tell him..." Here I use a faux British accent. "'Sorry, sir, but you're white, and last I checked, the homicide market is cornered by blacks and Hispanics. You just can't kill me as good as a man of ethnic descent can. Therefore, I respectfully refuse your offer to plunge that knife deep into my thorax and eviscerate me.'"

Oohs of instigation resound as does much laughing.

I address the *oohs*. "Don't get all PC with me. The stats are on my side. My people—Hispanics that is—can carve some people up. Have you heard of Richard Ramirez, The Night Stalker? The serial killing of women in Juarez? The Mexican Cartels? They'll roll you up with semi-automatic rifles. *Phrugggggh*," I roll my tongue and make the sounds of automatic gunfire into the mike while using my hands and arms to mimic shooting people with an assault rifle. "If you don't consider the Cartels serial killers then you don't know the definition of *serial* killers."

The crowd claps, accepting my humorous yet true rebuttal.

But I am watching my new reference point, the one girl amidst this entire crowd whom I imagine myself talking to in a one-on-one way. This time, the beautiful brunette is not laughing. Her smile is completely upside down, her face preoccupied and almost distraught, those full-blossomed lips pursed with confusion as if she's seen a ghost floating through the air.

Was it my joke? Did I offend her?

As for Mr. My Muscles Are Too Big For My Shirt, he's smoldering next to his date. I can almost see the fumes rising above his head.

Great. He's going to kill me, all because of some stupid jokes.

"Thank you, ladies and gentlemen. That's my time here tonight," I announce to the audience, then set the microphone back into the clutch.

The Laugh Factory's host scuttles to the microphone stand as I continue to mount off stage. "Let's give an ovation for newcomer Sole Eaby!"

Though I am backstage already, the urging of the applause and cheers ignites me inside. To show my gratitude, I return to the stage and bow, basking before the crowd's standing ovation.

Awesome.

In seconds, however, the house will empty and the patrons will be exiting. If there is to be any hope of meeting the brunette whom I spied during my routine, I have to hurry and pick up my check, then dart through the back door and get to the sidewalk out on Sunset where the fans will be spilling out and trying to get to their cars.

CHAPTER THREE

*I'll bet what motivated the British to colonize so much of
the world is that they were just looking for a decent meal.*

~*Martha Harrison*

It's a little past midnight, but by the fluttering of foot traffic,
the limousines pulling up and swallowing small groups, and all
the chatter flashing through extra-whitened smiles that are
cutting through the dark, it doesn't feel late at all.

"Excuse me. Sorry," I slate as I politely push through the heap
of strangers, most of whom are either so intoxicated from the
alcohol they had during the show or are so jazzed to be out on
the Hollywood strip that they don't recognize me. Is this bad for
my career?

With the crowd thinning out little by little, my chances of
encountering my zenith are shriveling. My heartbeat picks up its
pace and my dilated pupils no doubt are taking over the hazel
color of my eyes surrounding them as I'm thoroughly focused
on the mission.

"So is this about me being a registered democrat?" A deep, male voice threaded with sarcasm looms nearby, louder than the others. "The way I vote?"

A girl laughs, her tone gashing through the babble.

Maybe it's intuition—who knows?—but somehow I think the brunette I noticed inside the club is the female involved in this public disagreement. If I'm right, that means she's arguing with a mutating humanoid monster whose name might be Hulk or Goliath.

"If you think this is because of a few jokes or because of my voting preference, then you really are an irrationally minded donkey. Your Harvard brain's been cooked something good." Yep, that's her. That's the brunette, and, boy, does she have some zip to her. I really either know or don't know how to pick them.

If I'd known my political spoofs were going to cause people to argue right here on the sidewalk in front of everyone, maybe I would have held onto them for another time. I had no idea a comedy stint could cause people to *deeply reflect*. I thought that was what church was for.

In a matter of seconds, the prattling around them softens. The crowd notices the disagreeing couple in their midst, so they listen in, keeping their backs to them so they're not too obvious about their eavesdropping. This is live, curbside entertainment.

For me, I don't feel the need to pretend. I'm all eyes on the humanoid monster that the lean, yet curvy, brunette just called a, quote-unquote, "irrationally minded donkey." Any moment now, he may go green. If he does, well, I suppose I won't be meeting my zenith tonight.

"This really is about that comedian and his political jokes, isn't it? You're judging me on my political preference," the beastly man-child returns. He sounds concerned, hurt, almost...well, human. He may not be a mutating monster after all.

"No. That's not it at all. I've been with you for over a year. I've known your oh-so-precious political beliefs since then."

"Just tell me what's going on," Mr. Monster speaks in a consoling way.

"It's not the jokes that comedian told. It's the fact that I found myself laughing at those people he pretended to be in those jokes, and when I thought about it...I guess the jokes stopped being funny. At least for me."

"Then why were you laughing in the first place?" This time Mr. Monster lets out a dash of anger in his intonation and his dark brown eyes bulge out. That's borderline fury. How many stages of rage does it take before he mutates?

"That's the point. At first they were funny. Then...I don't know...I just realized I don't want to become the person I see myself starting to become."

"So, let me get this straight: You had *'a moment'* in the middle of a comedian's rant?"

"I guess so."

The mutating monster-man thinks, then comes to an epiphany. "Oh, like me. You don't want to be like me. I get it."

Please don't turn big and green. Please don't turn big and green, I beg within.

"It's not about you. This isn't about you. I'm talking about me. But then again, maybe that's our problem, too. You think we're talking about you." My zenith's eyes, her folksy browns, glisten. The reflecting sheen emanating from them is the moisture that precedes tears.

That mutating humanoid's making her cry. How dare he.

By now this pair has enraptured what's left of the pruned assembly of people. Whether the paying customers came for an encore tonight or not, they're getting one as all eyes are on Monster versus Delicate Beautiful Girl.

"I can't believe a comedian's words caused you to have '*a moment.*' Some life changing epiphany." His words are slewed with condescension. "And you want me to be okay with that?"

"You can mock me. That's fine. But like I said, you don't get it. You don't hear my soul speak. I kept hoping you might. But tonight, for whatever reason, I can see that you won't. You never will."

Soul speak. Could it be...no. No way.

"Is this still about...you know," Mr. Monster says.

"Still?" My brunette softens her posture and begins to turn from Mr. Monster. "If it would have been up to you, then I would have been guilty of murder."

Mr. Monster grabs her wrists, not tightly, just to let her know to stay so he can return a comment. She doesn't pull away. "You had a miscarriage. No one murdered anybody. Besides, abortion is legal."

"Legal. Of course that would be the moral line you stand on. Well, not me. For me that line is personal. Internal. And I guess that's what I'm trying to get at."

"You're eighteen," Mr. Monster declares. "I'm twenty-two. We're not ready for a child right now. And it's totally legal—I mean *morally* acceptable—to be able to choose."

My brunette doesn't want to hear anymore. She kisses Mr. Monster on the cheek. "Soul Speak," says my brunette and then paces off a step or two.

Mr. Monster chimes loudly in her direction, "How do you know it was a her?"

She turns to him, her whole being elastic, pulled by emotion. "I just knew. Like I said: Soul Speak."

"Ava, wait," he insists. "At least let me take you home."

Ava. Her name's Ava. Is that short for something? Avana? Avalina? The name Ava resounds throughout every corner inside of me like a screensaver icon when the computer's idle.

Ava doesn't turn around to acknowledge Mr. Monster. He takes a step in her direction, not wanting Ava to find a cab or walk alone even though the boulevard is bustling with a mesh of people.

This is when I do something very stupid.

"Usually when people ignore you, that means they don't want to talk to you." My words are spiked with condescension and sarcasm.

Mr. Monster turns around to see me, now fully emerged from the crowd. "You're that comedian," he remarks, and offers his own snarky comeback. "Usually when something is none of your business, it's safer to stay out of it."

Around us, the crowd inches back in the way the tide falls toward the ocean. Apparently, these people think a brawl might ensue, and they want to both give us space to flail blows at each other and get a front row seat to the blood spill.

I reach into my pockets and yank them inside out, letting the lining flap out to show how broke I am. "As you can see, I'm not too good of a business man."

"You're really funny. Too bad this joke's going to be all over you," says Mr. Monster, who seems to be gliding toward me as each of his steps spans huge chunks of pavement underneath his shoes.

The only thing I can do is brace myself for a full and consummate beating. How exactly to do that, I don't know. They say a heavyweight fighter exerts 750 to 1,200 pounds of pressure per square inch with each punch he throws. What exactly is the best position to absorb that many pounds of pain? Is there even a good position to be in, or are all positions equal?

"Hey," a gruff voice interrupts.

My first impulse is to double-check my own sense of what's real, to see if my alter ego has somehow manufactured some courage in bodily form. Then I realize that if I had an alter ego, he wouldn't be a tough guy at all. My body is just not constructed to house personalities that might tend to get me killed.

"That's not going to happen on my sidewalk."

I know that voice—strong, resonant, snappy. It belongs to the security guard whom I met backstage before my performance.

The security guard plods heavily toward Ava's ex—at least I think he's her ex from what I saw a few moments ago. Standing opposed to this security guard, Mr. Monster doesn't appear so monstrous anymore, but that doesn't stop him from hurling a huge attitude toward the man. "I didn't know this was your very own personal sidewalk. Since when did they start selling this sort of real estate?"

Mr. Monster evaluates the man, a man his same size, his equal, who is poised a mere foot from him. He's forced to ask himself if he wants a fight that is a bit fairer now. With me, Mr. Monster had sure victory, all the odds being in his favor. With Bigfoot dressed up in a security guard's outfit, Mr. Monster's winning handicap shrinks considerably. What will he do?

To me, what Mr. Monster decides doesn't matter. Those two giants can tussle until they both wind up in the hospital for all I care, because I'm not going to watch. I'm going to track Ava down.

"Thank you. You saved my life," I say, passing by the two giants. For good measure, I slap Bigfoot's shoulder a few times.

Though stiff and almost imperceptible, the security guard nods without releasing eye contact on Mr. Monster. I can't tell if this is his way of saying "Thank you" or "I hate you, you tiny and infinitesimal crustacean," but either way, at least he knows I'm thankful. What began as a rocky introduction backstage has turned into a semi-profound bond of brotherly love.

However, I cannot relish in the moment. I have to forge on into the crush of insomniacs blazing The Strip, disappearing from the scene as fast as I can.

It takes almost two blocks before I'm able spot Ava, her pace quick and deliberate. Hollywood's taxi circuit is certainly nothing like New York's where cabs stream down avenues and streets like spawning salmon. If it were, Ava may have flagged one down and been lost for good. Instead, I find myself only a few paces behind her, just past Selma Avenue and adjacent to the Liquor Locker parking lot.

While I'm thinking of what to say to her, I take inventory of her stature and figure which I can clearly see outlined thanks to the way her black sweater clasps against her small waist. Clinging tightly to her hips, thighs and all the way down to her ankles, are her taupe pants. Over those is a pair of quarter-high boots that rise over her calves. She isn't at all tall, not even breaking the five-foot plane, but this is fine with me. I prefer my girls to be mignon and lean yet bearing some athletic tracings in their physique. As far as body and beauty go, Ava seems to be exactly who I've imprinted in my mind as the ideal girl for me. There is more to a girl though, and that's the life inside of her—her heart, her mind, her soul.

Here goes.

"Ava? It's Ava, right?"

Ava turns to me, calculating. Instantly she recognizes me. "Is it customary for the talent to follow the crowd home?"

"Look, I couldn't help but notice the emotional shattering in front of the Factory. Are you all right?"

"I don't need a hero to my rescue, but thank you anyway."

"I'm not trying to rescue you."

"Then what are you doing?" Ava's eyes flint with interest. She genuinely wants to know.

"I noticed you from the stage. After my set I rushed out to the front. That's where I saw you and...um...him..." I elevate myself by standing on the balls of my feet, raising my arms and hands as far up as I can reach.

"His name's Ryan." Ava lets a portion of her edge slip off the features of her face as she grins.

"Ryan," I echo his name, shyness surfacing a bit and catching any witty words that might have otherwise come out. "What a relief. I thought maybe his name could have been Goliath or Hulk."

Ava grins, holding back the laughter that wants to come. "So now that we've identified him, what about you? What's your real name?" Ava hesitates, waiting for me to fill in the blank. "No stage names."

"Sole. My name's Sole Eaby."

"Is there a number after that, Sole Eaby?"

"Number?"

"Yes. A number." Ava hikes up the sarcasm in her words. "As in Bond, James Bond 007. No one actually says their name like you did except for fictional secret agents."

She's quick. I like that.

"How do you know I'm not a secret agent?" I ask.

She scans me up and down. "Too thin. You couldn't intimidate a cereal box."

I surrender to her on this one. "I'm just used to it, I guess. It's my professional introduction."

"Do you mean professional or impersonal?"

"Maybe both. But look, I'm sorry. I didn't mean it that way. I'm just nervous, that's all."

"Nervous?"

"Yes. Nervous."

"You stand on stage in front of hundreds of people and tell jokes. Nervous?"

"I'm just a guy who saw a beautiful girl, and I wanted to meet her. That makes me nervous as it would most guys, I presume."

Ava doesn't seem as if she's heard the honest approach before, but that doesn't mean she's completely going to disarm herself. "Well, we met."

Cars spurn along and passersby continue to wisp about, stirring the flavorful nightlife of the Sunset Strip around us. No one has a jacket on in early October Los Angeles, not even in the wee hours of the morning. To break the silence, I make a suggestion. "Are you hungry?"

Ava allows a large, natural, unrehearsed smile to sprawl out under her cheeks. "I am, actually."

"Great. I know the perfect spot."

Side by side we dawdle deeper into West Hollywood, passing the Gothic cathedral, Chateau Marmont, the storied hotel that was originally an apartment complex but was converted into bungalows that people rented by the night. Bungalow #3 is where famous comedian, actor, and Blues Brother John Belushi died of a drug overdose.

When I recite this factoid to Ava, she doesn't hide her curiosity. "And you know this because you're an architectural zealot or because John Belushi was a comedian?"

"Why do you want to know?"

"It'll tell me something about you."

I shrug. "James Belushi is an icon in the stand-up industry. If you play jazz, it's your duty to know Coltrane, Mingus, and Davis like you know how to breathe. If you write, you have to know Dickens, O'Henry, Milton, and all the classics. Like anything, you have to know where it all began. You have to respect those before you. For me, if you make jokes on stage, you have to know the greats, have to respect the likes of Steve Allen, Milton Berle, and Belushi, just to name a few. Does that tell you something about me?"

We begin our leisurely pace again when Ava notes, "Yes it does. Thank you. But I have to admit, I've never heard of any of those guys. Maybe Belushi, but I couldn't tell you much about him."

"That's okay," I console. "You know me. I'm the only comedian you'll ever need to know."

CHAPTER FOUR

Life expectancy would grow by leaps and bounds
if green vegetable smelled as good as bacon.
~ Doug Larson

Miles of Sunset Boulevard concrete are in our wake. We've hiked past jungles of seedy motels, clubs, bars, closed storefront shops and slews of the most extreme and eclectic confection of people around, including drug dealers and prostitutes. It's been almost an hour since we've met, but it doesn't even seem as if two minutes have elapsed. I hope Ava feels the same. Somehow I think she must because our thoughts have been passing between us as easily as soda through a straw.

Before dropping me off at the Laugh Factory earlier, Cedro told me he was going to park the truck along Horn to try to make some cash off of the hungry all-nighters partying on The Strip. When we're in front of The Coffee Bean which is spang on the corner of Horn and Sunset, Ava and I notice a small uproar nearby. I already know what the bustle and clamor are all about.

"Yep, we're here," I acknowledge the crowd huddled around Cedro's glow-in-the-dark truck.

Ava tries to conceal her disappointment, thinking I've made our destination The Coffee Bean. "Oh...coffee...I thought we were going to eat. I didn't know they served actual food here. I thought it was just pastries and stuff like that." Ava's tone is delicate and not irritable.

It's tough to find girls who don't hiss like snakes and go all fangs right away with their manner of speech when they're annoyed. Ava may be one of the last and few surviving girls who is the way a girl should be: gentle.

"We're not eating here. Our stop's right there." I point to the truck.

Like the sun's radiance over the horizon at dawn, Cedro's neon painted truck emanates sheer brightness as it straddles the curb. Snackers and scavengers of the night are pooled by the service window, shoveling mouthfuls of meat, bread and whatever else they ordered into themselves. The satisfaction printed on their faces tells me that they like Cedro's cooking, or it could just be that they're starving and even salted crowbars would be a treat to them at this hour.

"Eaby Baby's Edible Crazies?" Ava reads the logotype on the side of the truck, her pitch making the words seem more like a question, as if she were translating from Chinese characters into English.

"Catchy? Strange? What do you think?" I ask.

"Yeah, sure. I guess..." Ava politely shrugs, letting me know she's undecided.

Poking out of the serving bay is Cedro's head, his dark hair that is cut short making him appear police officer crisp. He hands a customer an order before turning his sights up and noticing me among the grazers.

"Sole!" Cedro bellows. I wave to him and accompany it with a shrug.

"You must order from this truck a lot," Ava assumes politely.

"Something like that," I stammer uncertainly. "Hold on a moment. Please don't go anywhere, okay? I'll be right back."

It takes a few seconds to weave my way through the sludge of humans and arrive at the door that is on the passenger's side. I track up the three steps that are coated with rubber. When I turn down the aisle that bores through the truck's kitchen, I see that Cedro is not alone. "Hey, Lana."

"Hi, Sole," Lana voices without turning to look at me. She's got her attention and face burrowed into her task of slicing tomatoes and cheese for the melts that they are serving.

Lana is the fabulously fascinating and foxy long-term partner of Cedro's. She's been in the picture since I was about six years old. To this day, Cedro refuses to propose to her, yet Lana, for whatever reason, still sticks around. Personally, I think Cedro's a complete tool shed for not cinching up and locking down such a loyal, attractive, interesting, and loving woman. The lady didn't give birth to me, but she's always been like a surrogate parent. Even though she and Cedro don't live together, she is, just the same, a habitué of our house, and she's no slouch about it. Over the years, she's always been there to pick me up from school and take care of me when I've been sick or when, otherwise, Cedro could not because he was working or spending some *me* time

45

with himself as many do during a MLC[3]. I call her *Lana* out loud, but inside my heart says *mom*... Well, sort of.

"How'd it go tonight?"

"Good," I reply to Lana. "I had them laughing."

"Wow. A comedian who makes people laugh. What a thought," Cedro sparks as he assembles a melt of shredded brisket enclosing it between slices of buttered white bread that's been grilled to perfection.

"You know, some comedians don't actually make people laugh," Lana retorts. "Some are just not funny."

"Then why on earth are they called comedians?" Cedro speculates while handing a customer his brisket melt.

"It's a mystery, dear," Lana muses and hands Cedro another brisket melt so that he can pass it to the next customer.

"It's subjective," I admonish. "Booking managers are just as able to make mistakes on who's funny and who isn't as audiences are."

"I don't know. Seems to me that if someone laughs from someone else's joke then that someone is funny. I don't know though, maybe I'm being too logical," Cedro satirizes.

Instead of explaining that there is sordid and diluted humor prevalent in our culture and that I aim for wit and less of a

---

[3] Cedro is in a full blown Mid Life Crisis. In other words, he's dissatisfied with his life as it currently is, and he's been hard at work giving his life a makeover. It started when I was in fifth grade and, by the time I began middle school, Cedro was all hands on deck for Operation New Life. Since then he stopped being "present," as they say. He's been there physically, to provide for me and all, but he hasn't really been there, if you know what I mean. The cost of his quest has been our relationship. He's just not relatable anymore. Sad part is, he's not completely aware of this. How could he be? He's still looking for his dream life which, obviously, doesn't include me.

slapstick kind of comedy, I put Cedro on the spot. "So, thanks for showing up tonight, dad. Always good to have you there."

Cedro ignores the fully loaded statement. "Did you want something to eat, Sole? Our meats tonight are brisket, ground beef, and turkey." The menu frequently changes, so when he says *tonight*, he means it. Tomorrow's proteins could be buffalo balls and deep-fried insect brains.

"I'll take a brisket with an egg inside, a slice of tomato, and three-cheeses on top." I pause. "I'll also take a turkey the same way."

"You keep eating like that and people are going to think I don't feed you." Cedro sneers.

"You don't feed me. That stopped when I grew past toddler-dom," I counter.

Lana turns and glances at me. She's figured it out. "Who's the turkey for? You or the lucky lady?"

My posture and beaming expression tell Lana all she needs to know. There's no use trying to hide the fact that I'm feeling a bit heady due to a girl named Ava, who is magazine-cover ready and waiting for me right outside the truck.

As for Cedro his brow is raised in an investigative arch, his eyes charged with interrogation, like those of some intense prosecutor. "Oh, so you found a stray," Cedro thumps crudely.

Lana attempts to patch up the gash Cedro created in the kitchen. "I'm sure she's a gem."

"I hope so," I declare.

With little else to say about this situation and since Cedro just maimed any hopes of making this a genial discussion, both Cedro and Lana retreat back to their composing. Within two minutes, a melody of melted cheese, brisket, tomato and rich, grilled toast is served on two paper plates. They say nothing to me, well nothing about Ava, who to them is still just a girl I met.

Cedro extends the results of his compilation to me. "Here you go."

I look down at the finished product and give it a .2 out of 10 for presentation. If this were a song, then I would be holding the recorded-in-the-bathroom demo, the polished version yet to be realized. Nevertheless, the melts are warm in my palms, the heat drilling through the paper plates. This will do me some good since there's a bit of a chill in the air. "Thank you."

The scene outside of the truck is slightly different from just a few moments ago. The flood of people has been cropped, probably a result of natural attrition as we draw deeper into the night. However, this makes it easier to spot Ava. She's checking her phone, the glow from the screen reflecting off of her face. When Ava's done listening to whomever left her a voice message, she slips the phone into her back pocket.

"Melted to perfection," I offer Ava my description of the food when I rejoin her.

"Umm...That. Looks. Lush."

"There's turkey and brisket."

Ava directs me. "Let's each take a half. I want to try both."

"Good idea."

We sink our teeth into our meals, warmth and richness breaking apart in our mouths as we chew.

"So tell me," Ava says, her lips pursed because she still has food inside her mouth. "How do you really know this truck and the owner so well?"

"You mean Cedro? He's my dad."

"Really? That's neat," she beams and contorts her features too, probably wondering why I called Cedro by his name versus the tried and true *dad*.

"*Neat* is one word to describe it, not the word I would have chosen."

"It can't be that bad."

"One would think, at least until it's their dad running a truck."

"He must be a really good cook," presumes Ava.

Cedro is actually not the best or worst cook by any standards. His skills are average; but I don't want to talk about him any more than I have to. "He's not bad."

What I really want to know right now is who called her a few moments ago, but I don't want to directly ask. That would seem too aggressive. If this were a card table, I would double down on the assumption that the caller was Ryan, aka The Monster, aka Goliath/Hulk; but this isn't a card table. I can't use hard, sterile expressions to communicate. I'm forced to use words.

"I noticed you got messaged. You can take a few moments to call him back if you need to. I'll make sure the food stays warm."

"How do you know it was a him?"

"I don't. I was just..."

"I'm just kidding. It was just Ryan," Ava replies.

The fact that she didn't pick up the phone for Ryan encourages me, but I act surprised. "Ryan? As in Ryan from The Laugh Factory? As in Hulk?"

Ava nods and sinks her teeth into the brisket melt. She hums, "Yummy," and covers her mouth with her free hand. "I mean yummy for the sandwich, not Ryan."

"Ryan's going to kill me, isn't he?"

Ava just laughs.

For the next hour we eat slowly and talk endlessly under the canopy of a starless West Hollywood night, snuggled up next to Cedro's trigged-out restaurant on wheels. This, right now, talking to Ava, is how I imagine my romance scenario: I'm offstage and out of character. There's two people, vis-à-vis, the world irrelevant in the immediate space around them, exchanging one-liners and bantering over nothing that has to do with anything—just losing time talking. The hardest part is finding the right person to have these kinds of reclined moments with. But when you do, aren't these the best kind of conversations to have? The best moments to exist in?

"I'm going to get a cab," Ava finally concludes.

"Do you want a ride?" I point to the mobile food unit.

"I'm okay. Thank you though."

This is the first time all night we've found ourselves mired in the swamp of uncomfortable silence since meeting. If I ever want to see her again, I have to take a chance. This means I must be willing to face possible rejection, something I've had my share of experiences with, starting with my good ol' mama. Although it seems a guarantee Ava will give me her cell phone number, I still doubt, mainly because the girl just broke up with her boyfriend, and she may not be ready to distribute such highly sensitive info. Perhaps these past hours were just inconsequential fun for her, and maybe she'll want to leave these moments right here on The Sunset Strip. Forever.

"So, Ava, would you like one last joke? One just for you?"

"Sure," she giggles.

"What did one crow say to other?"

Ava thinks about it. "Can I *caw-caw-call* you?"

"How'd you know?" I ask.

She points to her temples and taps.

"So can I?" I blurt.

Holding out her hand, palm up, Ava says, "Let me see your phone." Before I can reach into my jacket, she hands me her phone instead. "Better yet, here. Put your number in. That way I can caw-caw-call you, but only if I'm feeling completely and summarily bored." Ava winks to let me knows she's kidding and, along with me, laughs at her own hyperbole.

"Of course," I remark. "Only if your two choices are calling me or jabbing yourself to death with toothpicks."

Ava, slowly, takes my phone from my jacket pocket. I'm frozen, caught off guard. She starts to tap on the digital keys. "By the way, do you know where all crows come from?"

I think for a second. "*Cro*-atia?"

Ava hands me my phone back. "How'd you know?"

I take the phone back and, with my other hand, point to my temple and tap.

CHAPTER FIVE

The only time to eat diet food
is while you're waiting for the steak to cook
~ *Julia Child*

For me, school isn't as bad as it could be because my classes are done though the Independent Study (I.S.) program. That means that I don't have to sit through lectures and shuttle through the bell schedule like any other cow in the herd. Mr. Rezen, the I.S. teacher and T-Rez for short, has his classroom on the edge of campus, near the student parking lot. Inside his quarters T-Rez roosts on his leather chair, clicks on his mouse and scans his computer screen. Against the wall, on a folding table, are packets of work that he so graciously bestows upon me during our appointments on Wednesdays. Usually I'm scheduled for about eleven a.m., but T-Rez pushed me back today to almost two o'clock.

"There. Grab that bundle. That's the new week's workload." T-Rez doesn't even bother removing his eyes from the laptop's screen.

Coffee in hand, I amble to the wall and collect the stapled worksheets, then approach him at his desk, dropping my completed work in the bin. "Sure thing, Mr. T-Rez." Like I said, he lets most students call him that as long the *mister* precedes it.

T-Rez gathers the packets from the bin and lifts them up and down on his palm as if he is a post office worker weighing the contents of a package. "Feels like an A," he says proudly.

"Can't argue with that," I say. "See you next week."

The exchange feels like an underground drug deal, but it's all simple economics really: T-Rez gives me a quota, and I have to meet it. I like the structure of it. It also gives me a chance to sleep in and gradually wake up to the morning. While the rest of the world's hair is on fire, I'm in a fog, barely finishing my second cup of mellow-brewed Joe and waking to reality.

The release bell for the entire school has sounded, meaning all the students are pouring out of classrooms and off campus like a herd of wild beasts that have been cooped up all day behind cages and haven't been offered any raw flesh to eat. It's not such a bad thing, running into people I know in the parking lot, except when that person is Gabrielle. Gaby for short. My ex-girlfriend to be specific. The girl who treated me like a Wall Street trader dumps a stock when he realizes it's about to decimate his profit, to paint an emotional portrait.

Following our sophomore summer, Gaby returned for junior year...the term would be *upgraded*. She was Gabrielle 5.0. Her sunny season makeover proved to be a hit. In two months she went from being a ho-hum "really pretty" to movie star gorgeous just by learning and exploiting a few simple tricks:

A) Apply sparkly and glossy makeup to facial features.

B) Get a snazzy hairstyle, complete with bleach white highlights that mingle with natural, sandy-colored hair that canvases the now sparkly facial features

C) Under the head, transform a lithe and slinky body to a toned, magazine-cover, bikini-ready one.

D) Ensure that clothing is trendy and tight, tighter in the way that scales fit over a snake.

Gaby successfully and simultaneously applied all four makeover techniques. No one embraces the idea of a rattlesnake's fangs sunken into their skin, but from day one of junior year, every boy in L.A, including me, wanted to get bitten by the illustrious Gaby. By December of that year, Gaby had already secured an A-list talent agent to represent her outrageous good looks. The rumor going around was that she landed a bit part in a feature film and hooked up with the main star after the scene was shot. Who knows if that's true, but based on how she looks coming toward me now, I can't say I don't believe it.

"Hi, Sole," she says, walking with a couple of her friends. "To what does Marshall High owe this cameo from you?"

"It's nothing like that." I try to dismiss her even though, inside, I'm crumbling like a city experiencing a 9.0 quake. "Just turning in some work."

"Oh yeah," she notes while reading a text. "Mr. Comedian—that's right. Too good for regular old school."

There's not much to say to this, so I just stand there, forcing a confident pose that might collapse any second.

"I heard you're making waves out there. Getting some nice bookings and stuff."

"Something like that."

"Come on, Gab," Amanda, Gaby's friend, insists. "Let's go."

"How about you?" I ask quickly. "How's acting?"

"Oh, you know, auditioning and stuff...a little work here and there. Nothing major. Not yet anyway." Gaby lingers, tantalizing me with her heady, greenish eyes.

"That's good." I hear puberty cinch my vocal chords, making me squeal.

"You're still so sweet," she says, and walks away with her little Victoria's Secret model replicas on either side of her. "Ta-ta."

Now I can effectively granulate right here, on the asphalt, in Marshall High's parking lot. The Wicked Witch of the West melted, but that's because that's what wicked and evil beings do when defeated. After seeing my ex-beautiful-girlfriend-who-broke-my-heart, I pathetically grind into piteous powder, letting the small breeze blow me into the air. Melting seems to be a more dignified way of falling to defeat. The good news is, it means I'm not that evil.

On Wednesday afternoons, for about two hours, I still participate in Comedy Club—*my* Comedy Club. This is my baby. Two years ago, Marshall High didn't have a true stand-up crew, so I launched one. Now we perform against other schools that have their own comedy club. It's like a debate team, except it's strictly for stand-up. Comedy programs are not quite as ingrained in the school system yet, say, as a sport's program or drama department, but at least it's got some legs. Other schools around California and the U.S. are catching on as well. It's safe to say that stand-up clubs and competitions in schools are in the piloting process. Each school also needs a teacher-sponsor to officially sign off on paperwork and otherwise legitimize the team. Mr. Kevin, a spherical, thin-haired man, who is absolutely hilarious, is ours. We all call him Mr. K.

"All right, fellow comics, warm ups. Everybody ready?" Mr. K asks.

By *everyone* he means all six of us.

For warm ups, Mr. K gives us a scenario and he expects us to point out the humor in the situation in five different ways, even if the situation doesn't seem inherently funny.

This is a great exercise because, as a comedian, it forces me to stretch something as far as I can to find the *gelastikos humores*[4]. Like all arms, every scenario has a funny bone and it's a comedian's job to discover it and point it out to others.

Mr. K relays the topic. "A man is driving a car, and his girlfriend is in the passenger's seat next to him. Suddenly, the girl sees another guy pull up beside them. He's alone and looks like he is on his way to a movie shoot as he could be the next Brad Pitt. Instantly, the girlfriend leans over and kisses her boyfriend on the cheek. 'It's over,' she says. Just like that. Gone. Then she gets out of the car and into the car of the guy she just saw. Ready? Set? Go."

My partner, as usual, is my best friend Yoke. He's not at all funny, but at least he's here trying.

"To that I say...umm..." Yoke doesn't have a response. He can't see anything amusing in that. "Man, that girl...she's messed up," is all he can come up with.

"You're supposed to analyze it *and* make it funny. You just did the first part."

"That's all I got," Yoke attests.

---

[4] Soleism #1: *gelastikos humores* is my invented word, what I call a Soleism. Here, I've combined the Greek form of the English word *gelastic*, meaning able to be stretched, with the Latin form of the English word *humor* to get this thing I call the *gelasticity* of humor. It means that everything can be stretched far enough to be funny in some aspect, even my uncertain future, albeit I haven't found anything funny about that quite yet.

I decide to take my turn. "What that girl doesn't know is, I was getting rid of her. Anyone that psychotic—to jump in a car with a perfect stranger—is a little unglued on top. As her boyfriend, I've known this. If you check the guy's wallet, there's a fifty in there...from me. I set the whole thing up to get rid of Ms. Psycho Chick."

Yoke chokes on his hee-hawing. Seeing Yoke laugh is actually quite a risible sight. He literally almost says *hee-haw*. His version sounds like this: *hee-hee-hee-heh-heh*.

"Dude, it wasn't that funny," I tell him.

"To me it was." That's the problem with Yoke and my jokes. Everything I say is the funniest thing he's ever heard, and so it's difficult to tell if what I say is actually that hilarious or if it's just Yoke.

After warm ups, Mr. K winds us through our preparation for The Cashmere Classic, which is an annual competition held at the Dinkelspiel Auditorium on Stanford's campus. All 1,200 seats are already sold out as they have been the last two years. This is the third year in the Cashmere's running, and the second for our school being in it. It's one of the most energized acts of the season. Schools throughout California attend, and the winning school gets to heave their chest out at the all the other schools until the next year. Whoop. Dee. Do. This isn't so much of an incentive for me and neither is the fact that the Cashmere's top comedian gets to go to nationals and rival with other high school comics from around the country. If you ask me, I think they could stand to raise the level of quality of their prizes, say, the winner getting a spot on a radio or Internet comedy show or the chance to meet a talent rep. But no one is asking me. So why do I participate even if the prizes seem like borderline rubbish? It's good practice.

"All right, fellas, Cashmere's coming up. Biggest event of the season. Let's take it *seriously*, okay?" Mr. K winks.

We all guffaw in a synchronized fashion.

"That's pretty good, Mr. K," Yoke discharges. "Taking a *comedy* show s*eriously*." *Keh-keh-keh* is how Yoke's laugh goes this time.

"Good grief," Kyle, a junior and up-and-coming talent voices. "We all got it. Hence the reason we laughed when he said it. But you just killed it by actually giving us a transcript of what happened. Who does that?"

"Apparently, Yoke does," Ruben attests. Ruben, as a comedian, is learning the art of humor, but as a person he's long nailed down the art of compassion, which is why he sort of sticks up for Yoke.

"Hey, guys, just lay off, all right?" I put the final nail in the shed to close up the issue. Sticking up for Yoke is something I've gotten used to doing over the years. Then I drop the bomb on the class. "I've got an announcement to make." I haven't even told Mr. K.

"Okay." Mr. K displays a quixotic look.

I walk up to the front of the classroom. "As you all know, I began this club last year. In that year we've come a long way. Being able to compete in the Cashmere Classic is, of itself, quite an accomplishment." The guys clap and hoot as if they were football players getting amped up for a game. "Well, to condense this whole sad speech down, what I want to say is that this will be my last practice, and," I inhale and brace myself. "The Cashmere will be my last show with you guys."

No one should be that upset. Comedy club is my baby and I can abandon it if I want (bad metaphor using *abandon* and *baby*, I know, but my point still stands).

Yoke looks stunned. I think I forgot to mention my intentions to my best friend. Leaving your supposed *best* friend in the dark of your intentions is the mother of all faux pas. I can assume he's going to grill me about this later.

Before that, each member of the club has their turn at me.

Ruben blares, "Why? You don't like us or something?"

Leo suggests, "Well, thanks for starting all this for us anyway."

Dashawn brazes, "That's cool. We'll be aw-ite."

Kyle joins in. "You think you're too good for us?"

Yoke is honest, which is one of his best qualities. He's not funny, but maybe that's because his honesty switch is set to full tilt. "He *is* too good for us. Hence the reason he's already making money doing stand-up. Well, technically, he doesn't get the checks, I know, because that would technically make him a pro and not an amateur and unable to compete with us. But still, he's the one performing out there, in clubs. That's the real thing."

The silence in the room is evidence that this truth bomb Yoke has dropped is too large for any possible comeback. Mr. K slides up next to me, putting his arm around me. "Well, Sole, I can't say I'm opposed. You have a career in stand-up to get going. We all support you and, as Leo said, thank you for starting this club." Mr. K looks at the five guys slouching in their desks. "Right?"

"Right," Leo, the lone freshman of the clan, speaks. "Thanks to you, Sole, guys like me have found something at school to keep them going."

I feel like a shepherd abandoning his little lost sheep.

Mr. K opens up the class to Q&A. He figures that the other guys can learn more by picking my brain than indulging in comedic exercises. As a result, practice runs longer than usual, which is fine. By the time we leave Mr. K's classroom, it's almost dark. Maybe it's psychological or just plain time to eat, but Yoke and I decide that we are exceptionally hungry.

Within a couple of minutes, Yoke and I have traversed the vacant halls of Marshall High and are in Cedro's tangerine-tinted Jeep Rubicon. Since he's been in the streets all day trying to peddle his greasy deliciousness to curbside customers, he let me have the Jeep.

I don't start the car right away. Instead I decide to control the damage I've done and apologize for committing the best friend faux pas. "Sorry I didn't tell you."

"It's cool, man," Yoke assures me.

I don't believe him. "Really?"

"Not really," he says. "The part about leaving the club that *you* started—cool. The part about telling me at the same time as everyone else—*not* cool."

"I wasn't sure. I've been thinking about it, but I—"

Yoke doesn't let me finish my self-justification. "Don't do that. Just stick with *I'm sorry* next time. If I'm really your best friend, let me in on the thinking process, not after it's all been said and done."

"Deal," I say.

"Now can we get something from your dad's truck?" he asks.

"Let me see where he is. I'll text him."

I turn the key and tell the voice-powered radio to play "Sunburn" by Muse.

"Great tune," Yoke says.

"Song. Jam. Sound. Mood. Melody. Beat. Any of those words will do, dude, but not *tune*. Nobody says tune anymore," I instruct Yoke, and we are officially back to our normal friendship, me as all-knowing Yoda and he as social-Jedi-in-training.

I turn onto the street and head toward the 101 freeway which shouldn't be stamped with bumper-to-bumper traffic right now. L.A. traffic typically starts to ebb after 6:30 pm. When I turn onto the onramp, my phone buzzes, letting me know that I have an incoming text from Cedro.

I'M BY L.A. LIVE. LAKER GAME TONIGHT.

After reading the message aloud, Yoke says, "We are so there!"

"And no one says that anymore either."

CHAPTER SIX

This is what cooking is all about.
Not to be perfect but to make people happy.
~Andrew Friedman

L.A. Live is whirling with fans, and the Laker game is set to begin in thirty minutes inside Staples Center. Right across the street, in the Nokia Theatre, Justin Beiber is getting ready to entertain a phalanx of prepubescent girls, all of who are in middle school and too young to understand what actually constitutes musical quality. These poor lost souls are bristling with excitement, waiting to take their seat to hear an arrogant blonde boy leak lyrics out of his mouth about a subject he knows absolutely nothing about: love. When he sings he sounds like a pinched balloon losing air. Why these girls' parents spent money on this—who knows?

Cedro wasn't the only one with the bright idea that tonight's L.A. Live crowds could yield a hefty profit for food truck operators. He and about four other trucks are trying to cash in on the heavy flow of people who have the option of eating from the trucks or at one of the fine dining establishments the scene has to offer.

When Yoke and I walk up to Eaby Baby's Edible Crazies, there are only three people waiting in line. This is hardly anything unusual.

Cedro hands a customer their order, shoveling a pained look on his face, a look that implies, "I'm giving my best service expression because I have to, although I really feel like screaming in your face, 'EAT AT MY TRUCK, NOT THE OTHER GUYS'!'"

"So, how's it going?" Even though I can infer the obvious, I ask anyway, just to jab him. Sometimes I can be a jerk.

"Look around," Cedro grumbles. "Then ask yourself, 'How can a business survive without paying customers?' If you don't know the answer, then you're clearly not as smart as I thought."

"Wouldn't it have been easier to just say, 'Not so well'? That's three words versus one, two..." I continue to count the number of words he said in his last statement.

Before I can finish, Cedro interrupts, "Wouldn't it have been easier to not ask such a stupid question?"

He's right. It would have been easier because it would have been much more considerate, but I didn't exercise consideration on that turn. The worst part is, I did it on purpose.

I have some ideas that would increase business traffic for Cedro, but I won't exercise that offer of consideration either. I'm no economic genius, but I am fairly versed in modern times, unlike Cedro. To reach the masses of today and not yonder year where Cedro's business sense seem to be, it takes more than a colorful truck and half-decent food to become successful. How do I know this? Because owning a food truck isn't such a subtle and scanty idea. There is such a thing as Food Network, and everyone has satellite or cable which means everyone gets the Food Network. If no one has seen this channel then they've probably landed on the Cooking Channel at some point, which has a show called *Eat St.*, and its sole purpose is to promote the glut of food trucks that patrol the nation at any given time. Has Cedro ever thought of contacting either of these networks to see what he can do to promote his truck on one of their segments? Of course not. And that's why he's slinging his cooking utensils around the truck right now—spatula hits the wall, plastic spice containers crash on the floor, napkins fall like confetti all around. Roll out the yellow tape; it's a kitchen crime scene.

Still, the lingering question is, "Sole, will you help your father out?"

Still, my solid answer remains no.

Yoke and I are standing beneath the service window. "Here you go," I extend my hand up and offer Cedro thirty dollars.

"What's this?"

"It's money."

"Context, smart guy. Context. All of a sudden you're a literalist, like you're some kindergarten baby not yet able to think in abstract thoughts. You know what I mean." Cedro is elevated above street level while in his food truck, so the unpleasant scorn crinkling his face appears even more hostile as it drops down on me.

"It's for the other night's melts and then what I'm ordering right now," I confirm. I knew what he meant, but I was just being an immature crotch-munch.

"I didn't ask for it. If I'd wanted you to pay, I would have told you."

"I know. But I want to help." That's not true. I don't want to help. It's that I don't want *his* help, and by me paying for my food, it's my own little way of maintaining my distance.

"Whatever," Cedro huffs and cocks his head, assaying me with a look of skepticism. He takes the money nevertheless.

I scan the handwritten menu that's scrawled in blue dry-erase marker on a whiteboard posted on the sidewall of the truck. The words OPEN FACE MELTS cite the theme of tonight's offerings. Cedro continues to refuse on developing a motif, a brand to his business. He doesn't put any efforts to advertising on the Internet or even less modern outlets, such as the newspaper or anything of the sort. He thinks that if he makes really good meats and parks somewhere, the business will happen. I guess the whole "If you build it he will come" idea from the movie *Field of Dreams*, circa 1989, has permeated Cedro's processing abilities, causing him to actually think that this is how things work. Thus, tonight Cedro is not serving his customary meat melts smothered in various cheeses between two slices of buttered Texas Toast. His attempt to be innovative has come to simply removing one side of the bread—*ooh, so daring*— so that it's more like a meat pizza.

"I'll take two Ground-N-Pounds." I tell Cedro what I remember from the menu.

Ground-N-Pounds have one slice of buttered and battered Texas Toast on the bottom, grilled so that the texture has a slight *crunch* to it when biting into it, a half a pound of shredded beef on top, various flavors of melted cheeses over that, and mashed beans mixed with onions and cilantro poured on it all.

"Thanks," I indicate as Cedro hands me my order. When I look behind him, in the truck, I finally take note that he is the only one in there tonight. "Where's Lana?"

"On a date."

Considering that Lana is Cedro's long-term fiancé, it's only natural to question this. "A date?"

"With her mother and sister."

"Oh, girls' night out sort of thing. I get it."

"No, actually, you don't. And neither do I. We can't get it. We're guys." Cedro is hedgehog sharp with his spiny comebacks, but he makes sense and even makes me chuckle. "Listen," Cedro says. "I'm getting out of here. I've been here a few hours and haven't made jack for profit. Do you have anything planned?"

I'm not quite sure what Cedro's ulterior motive is for asking about my evening's agenda, so I don't affirm or deny anything yet. "Why?"

"Do you think you could take over and see if there are any trickles of customers after the game and concert? I've got to get rid of this food tonight. It's on its dying bed."

This is another reason why Cedro's food truck enterprise isn't booming. He doesn't care that his ingredients are fresh. He cares only that they aren't spoiled. And, believe me, there is a difference between the two. I've seen the Food Network and due to my *telecation* (television + education) I know that there is a large difference to a customer between a cook who cares to use only the best and one who cares to use what's merely edible. "You mean…"

"I'll give you a fifty-percent cut of the margins."

"You want me to run the truck?" I've worked in the can (that's what experienced food truckers call the kitchen for short) before, so it's not like I wouldn't know how to manage. I've just never operated solo, without him. "I uh…umm…"

Set across Cedro's face is a gloomy horizon of hurt. "Never mind."

Something in me can't seem to allow the sun to completely set on him. Why? I have no idea. Perhaps he'll do something in the future to take me over the edge with him. Until then, I still pity the man. "All right. Sure. I'll do it. But for seventy-five percent." He probably won't go for this, which is all right with me. I don't really want to do it anyway.

Joy creases his cheeks ever so slightly. "Seventy-five percent?"

"Yep."

"Are you sure?"

"No. I'm Sole."

"Ha. Ha. A literalist again when it's convenient."

"And when it annoys you."

"Done. Seventy-five percent." Cedro then goes through a quick series of do's and don'ts, then he and I exchange keys.

Suddenly, I remember the obvious. "What if I get pulled over? I don't have a Class A."

Cedro forgot about that as well. He rubs his chin, pondering the next move. "You're not planning on driving like a psychotic paraplegic are you?"

"Paraplegics don't drive, Dad."

"So then we're good. You drive like a normal, responsible citizen, and we should be fine. See you later." At that, Cedro leaves.

Yoke, as if he's just seen the bones of Jesus, says, "Cool."

"It's not *cool*. It's work. And it's been dumped on us. Come on."

Inside the kitchen it's warm, the grill and the range running making it a sauna. Thankfully, it's a breezy So Cal evening outside. I take off my jacket and lay it on the driver's seat. Before Yoke can start touching things like an infantile child who's been in the world only a year or so, I review a strict set of guidelines in a harsh, militaristic tone.

"Anything else, G.I. Joe?" he asks.

"No, Private Whiny-Pants. I just don't want you to do something stupid. Tonight is not the night I want to know what it feels like to burn to death."

*

For the last two hours, I've made sure to prepare the truck so that it's ready to handle an onslaught of ravenous people looking to hang out and chat with some savory grub in their hands after the game and concert.

On the counter we've laid out the meat, pork, and beef chuck. I shredded it as best as I could. It should be tenderer than it is, considering it was simmered in a crockpot, but my guess is that Cedro didn't put the meat in early enough. Oh well, this is the protein we have to work with, and it will have to do.

I had Yoke prepare slices of bread by smattering butter spread over them. When the orders come, we'll place the thick slices on the flat grill so that a rich crust will form and add a crispy, crunchy texture to the bite in contrast to the soft meat. A melted layer of cheddar between all that will be the knockout punch in the melt.

Since I've actually seen more episodes of *Eat St.* than Cedro, I can confidently gather that the key to street food comes down to a few things: 1) rich and crispy textures combined with 2) soft and tender proteins that are 3) topped with goopy cheese. This trifecta makes street food magic just that: magical. The question about all this remains: Why do I have a more specific approach to what street food should be than Cedro seems to?

I look at my watch and then outside to see how much time has passed. The rustling atmosphere around L.A. Live can only mean that the Lakers game and Bieber concert are just about over.

"Do you think we'll get a big rush?" Yoke asks.

I pull my ear buds out, Cage the Elephant's "Ain't No Rest for the Wicked" no longer filling my head.

At first, the temptation is to respond with a simple *who cares.* Then, for whatever reason, it hits me—this competitive drive and pride. Eaby Baby's is not my business, but I bet I can do it better than its actual owner. I bet I can run this thing better than Cedro. And for no other reason than a perverse sense of pride, I task myself with doing what Cedro can't even do with his own food.

"You know what, Yoke, it doesn't matter. I have an idea that will make people want to come."

"What do I do?" Yoke asks with enthusiasm, setting his book down and rubbing his hands together.

"Just don't ruin it."

"Seriously, man."

"Finish prepping the food like I showed you. They'll be at our window in droves." I smile large and raise my eyebrows up and down quickly in Groucho Marx fashion, the epiphany setting my face aglow. Then I disembark the truck, ready for Operation Entertainment.

"Where are you going?" Yoke yells out through the serving bay window.

"Just be ready," I shout back, not turning around.

I scan the area around L.A. Live, looking for a platform of some sort, maybe a cement pillar or planter. In front of the Nokia, I find that there are multiple rectangular pedestals that are raised about two feet off the ground and serve as the base for the huge, metal sign-stands climbing up from them. When people start flooding out of the arenas, the best place for me to be will be closest to the street. I don't want to just focus on the girls soaking in their deranged afterglow of the Beiber concert. I want the Laker's crowd exiting Staples Center and those potentially going into ESPN Zone or Flemings for a restaurant meal, which means I need to be highly visible.

Posted atop the pedestal, I notice the glass doors from the arenas flash open. Instantly, a torrent of humans piles out. These strangers will be my audience, and they don't even know it. I wait about five minutes for the pack to thicken before I will begin what I call open-air comedy.[5] If I can nail my impromptu comedy sketch, I can hopefully create a buzz around the place and get a lot of people to shuffle over to Eaby Baby's instead of wherever else they were going to eat. It feels a bit strange to be doing this, but I'm motivated and desperate, so I fight through the nerves.

"Well, did everyone hear the good news? There is no such thing as sex addiction. It is not an actual disorder." A controversial topic is a good way to pique the interest of the masses flowing at my feet. It works. A few people are startled and begin to turn toward the voice they hear, my voice.

"Yeah. No kidding!" I revert to my signature scream. "It's called being horny! And as far as I can tell, there is no cure! Every male this side of heaven is born addicted! Yep. Sorry, girls. It's evolutionary biology."

---

[5] Soleism #2: *Open-air comedy*: Open-air preaching was a style of preaching made famous in the 1700's by George Whitfield. He and others like him would rise early, around 4:00AM, study their Bibles, take notes or do whatever else they needed to do to prepare, and would set about on horseback to their planned destination for the day. Then, in the middle of town somewhere, they would stand on a homemade box and shout out, as loudly as they could, the sermon they'd prepared earlier that morning. If crowds formed—great! If no one stopped to listen—oh well. That's the risk they took. Same thing with my open-air comedy.

The collective laugh of a small crowd formed in front of me splices through the din of conversations around us. More heads turn to see what is happening and, out of sheer curiosity, just like little sheep, more flock my way.

"Do we really need *experts* to tell us this stuff?"

I've never actually tried open-air comedy before. Before I went into the I.S. program, I would sometimes draw a crowd around me during lunch, but I realize that was different. I never shouted with the intention of drawing in a mass number of students. It just happened. I would start to tell jokes to make my friends laugh, and more and more kids would come around. Tonight, however, my direct purpose was to unmistakably attract the attention of the group gathered in front of me.

The foot traffic has bottlenecked. Adults of all ages, boys and girls, too, are congealed like Jell-O around me. I don't know how much time has passed, but however long it's been, two minutes or twenty, the initial awkwardness of the whole open-air thing has dissipated. Things are going better than I anticipated, until the unexpected appears in the form a challenger.

A young man, most likely in his early twenties, steps onto the cement pedestal next to me. Uninvited. The thickset lad styled with black skinny jeans and a pair of Converse tips his hand immediately, letting me and everyone else know that he is not here to make friends and that what is happening should not be taken for anything except rude-crude competitiveness. There is no easing into this whatsoever. He pumps his arm like it's a shotgun, literally, and says, again literally, "*Shook. Shook.*" Then he bellows, "I think you could use a little company up here."

"You're not actually supposed to say *shook shook*," I jeer. "The arm motion takes care of that."

The crowd instigates with a choral *ooh*.

"You would know about arm motions, wouldn't you?" he chides, making a masturbatory motion with a closed fist.

Because this statement is loaded, anything I say means I am taking the bait. Against better judgment, I reply, "Hey, pal, you're the one who wants to *keep me company*, right?"

"Yeah, it's not really an opinion. It's a fact. You need some company. You look as tired as your jokes sound."

In a hyperbolic way, I make it a point to scope over his person as if I am looking for something. "I don't see a badge that says you're the Fact-Opinion Police."

"Oh. It's right here." And he gives me his middle finger.

The once laughing crowd is now silent, their pupils fully focused on the standoff before them. Round one is over. *Ding. Ding.* Round two begins.

I pretend to examine his finger. "I'm sorry, you must have me mistaken for a plastic surgeon. There's nothing I can do about the size of your...yeah." I waive my finger toward the crowd and address them directly. "If that's all he's got, then I guess some learn the hard way: Size matters!"

When there's a detonation of hilarity, I don't feel badly. This guy started it. Though he should stop now that I've gotten the audience on my side, he persists.

This guy must be into self-flagellation, my inner ego taunts.

"Oh, wow, the male organ joke," he says. "They say that obsession over male organ size actually reveals serious states of insecurity and feelings of inadequacy held by the one obsessing over them. What's the matter?" my challenger asks as if he were talking to a non-verbal baby. "You missing something in your life?"

His insults make the crowd sound like a laugh track. *Okay. All right. You got me*, I admit to myself, but not aloud.

We exchange a few more verbal blows as prizefighters do punches in a bout, but there is no question who punches harder and who's landed more hits: me, of course.

By the end of the match, in good fashion, the impromptu audience applauds both of us. We bow and, before the crowd can disperse into the night or to their cars, I announce, "By the way, after this *roasting* session, if anyone's looking for some real *roast* to munch on, I'll be at that truck over there." I point. "Eaby Baby's Edible Crazies. You won't find a better slab of greasy grub under blankets of cheese anywhere else!"

When I move forward to step down, the challenger comes over, accepting his loss. "You're legit," he says, extending an open hand to me. "No hard feelings?"

"We're good," I clasp his hand. "Come on and try something. If you tell me your name, it's on the house."

"Jacob," he shares.

Jacob and I hop down to street level and join the flow of people to the truck. I jog ahead of Jacob and the rest, eager to get inside the kitchen and serve up as much food as I can.

"Here they come!" I urge Yoke.

The plan worked to perfection and knowing that it was all designed in my little old brain causes a little circus to train through my body.

"How'd you—?" Yoke begins.

"Never mind. I'll tell you later. Right now, we serve!"

CHAPTER SEVEN

Everything in moderation…including moderation
~ Julia Child

It's into the next morning, or late night, depending on how someone looks at it, when Eaby Baby's Edible Crazies is out of food. Completely. That's how good business was. I can't wait to see Cedro's face when I show him that I ran his operation better than he could.

Yoke is cleaning the can and putting everything away in the cabinets, just like I told him. "How much did we make?"

I finish counting the last of the cash. "Almost two grand."

"Two grand!"

"Easy, Man," I chime. "Don't go yelling it to the world."

"Why?"

"Are you trying to give some unstable schizoid with a gun a reason to target this particular truck?"

Yoke doesn't respond out loud. His silence confirms his understanding of the matter. Like I do, he sets himself back to the task of tidying up the can so that, afterward, we can finally evacuate the area.

By the time I turn on the ignition, the scene around us is as bare as an Olympian swimmer's chest. L.A. Live, a mere hour ago bouncing with festivity, is officially offline for the night. I turn the key, an eerie feeling swarming me in the cocoon of darkness.

One major problem with a food truck is that there aren't too many places to sit. With the passenger's seat covered with our backpacks and Cedro's gym bag, Yoke wonders where to rest his Heinz-Part 57.

"Where do I sit?"

"Just sit on the floor...wherever. But I'm getting us out of here."

The gas gauge is reading empty. *Ugh!* Even when the engine starts to warm up, the needle refuses to move. It stubbornly jiggles next to the E, a tease really, like an exotic dancer who doesn't get very exotic during her stage routine.

"We need gas," I differ in frustration.

"Well, I think we made enough to cover that."

I groan slowly and steadily like a do that is particularly peeved at someone just when he's about to dig into a bone. This should be enough to communicate to Yoke that anytime in the near future would be the perfect time for him to shut up. If I actually used words to tell him to be quiet like I already tried to do, he would find a way to make some remark about the exact thing I want him to shut up about. I learned my lesson the first time.

L.A. in the middle of the night is not the most opportune of moments to be scoping out areas for gas. Any place I go, I'll practically be begging for someone to make a robbery victim out of me. I'd have better odds if I approached the next station and just auctioned my victimization off to the first available assailant. "*Step right up! 60-40 take on my two grand! You get 60 and let us keep our lives! We get 40 and what's left of our pathetic existence! Anyone? Anyone?"*

At the next ARCO on the corner of Rosecrans and Figueroa, just outside of downtown, I pull the truck next to a pump. The only other human being in sight is a male attendant who is inside the store and behind a glass booth. This graveyard crewman is either supremely confident that the sign reading REGISTER HAS NO MORE THAN $25.00. ALL OTHER CASH DROPPED IN SAFE. ATTENDANT HAS NO KEY will deter anyone from attempting a hold-up at gunpoint, or he is so used to seeing masked men girded up with assault artillery pointed at his face that nothing surprises him anymore. Loping toward the glass doors, I am hoping for the prior.

I slip a few bills of cash through the slot under the glass. "A hundred on six."

"What number?" Rick asks, not looking up from his phone screen. I know his name is Rick because the patch sewn onto the royal blue uniform says so.

"Six. Number six. Didn't you hear me the first time?" By the way Rick looks at me as if I am the most insignificant person on the planet, I can tell he's not going to answer me.

"Thanks," I close and walk back to the gas pump.

When I dislodge the nozzle and insert the gas gun into the tank hole, I am ever more conscious of the morbid unearthliness of urban existence squeezing me so tightly that my stomach begins to churn. Maybe I am sensing imminent danger, or it could be that I am merely scaring myself. The dollar counter spins furiously, turning the cents over and over until it indicates that I am one-fourth of the way to completing the transaction. In five minutes, I should be back on the road and on the way home.

"Hey, fool," a voice declares from my left.

I guess *should* is not going to happen the way it *should*, not tonight anyway.

I turn, slowly and scope out the source. In one instance my mind describes to myself the man in the same way a transcript of a police radio call might read as the officer spews the description to dispatch. MALE HISPANIC. APPROXIMATELY TWENTY-FIVE YEARS OF AGE. BLUE JEANS, FIVE SIZES TOO LARGE. BLACK NIKES. WHITE T-SHIRT. L.A. DODGERS HAT. BLACK SUNGLASES. A BLUE BANDANA FOLDED OVER HIS MOUTH AND NOSE, CONCEALING MOST OF HIS FACE. This is undoubtedly bad news for me.

"Uh...hi?" I say it more like a question, not really knowing how to greet my possible executioner.

Out comes the black, steel handgun from the waist and, in one motion, back goes the slide of the semi-automatic, .40 caliber pistol, loading a hallow point bullet that, if discharged, will pierce my forehead and land inside my brain somewhere, either killing me instantly or turning me into a some form of vegetation, maybe a turnip or cauliflower.

"Uhh," I stammer, my hands finding company in the air above my head.

"Give me your money, Ese, or tonight you die."

I'm not sure why, but I notice a running car curbed half a block away. There's the silhouette of a man's head in the driver's seat. This is probably the assailant's getaway vehicle. Maybe this isn't the most organized crime spree of the twenty-first century, and probably a hundred degrees less coordinated than the average military mission, but the little gangster operation carries enough of a threat on my life to elicit my cooperation. "I'm going to reach into my pocket."

"Screw your pocket, Loco," he slights, his voice a combination of a slow-grinding whisper, like he's just churned rocks into sand with his teeth. "I know you got it in the truck."

It can mean a lot of things when talking about a food truck. I have choices. I don't want to just give him almost two thousand dollars without making the guy earn it, so I do what I do best. "Are you hungry? I didn't realize you were homeless. All you had to do was ask and I'd have given you something to eat."

"Oh, funny guy, huh?"

He's pissed. Maybe humor wasn't the best course to take. As soon as the barrel of the Smith and Wesson is pressed hard into my chest, I am firmly convinced that joking with the armed demoniac psychopath was not my best effort, especially considering that he just might move from sidewalk robber to full-on murderer.

I wince from the force of formed metal digging into my sternum. "No. I'm not."

"Then give me what I want so you don't end up painting the pavement red...with your blood, Holmes."

Why won't he just say what he wants? This is no time for him to be poetic and paint word pictures in my mind.

This is a matter of principle now. He's got the advantage, but this lunatic insists on speaking in lyric, tapping into his inner Shakespeare. Do I know what he's talking about? Of course. Does he know that I know what he's talking about? Sure. But the point is why won't he just come out and say it? Why won't he declare, "I want whatever money is in your little truck, Vato-Loco-Holmes," and nothing else? Is this a matter of insufficient brain development due to an inability to read beyond a second grade level? Or do thugs just specialize in being lyrical when demanding what they want? It's like a child, really, and it's frustrating me to no end, but at least *frustration* is better than crap-in-your-pants *fear*.

I could die for this, but I can't resist. "Can you please stop with the poetry, Tupac, and just tell me what you want?"

"The money, Ese!" I could feel his breath with that hiss that would garner the envy of India's most sinister cobra.

"Okay, okay," I brush, feeling the moment slip away through my fingers as something hard thwacks the side of my head, causing a percussive wave of pain to throttle me throughout.

Am I dying? Have I been shot? I try to regroup in my mind, the world slipping from me. I think the trauma of the moment is causing my mental systems to crash. I feel like someone has overridden my hard drive and is force logging me out of existence.

When I come to, I'm aware that I've not been shot, nor have I been asleep. If I had been, then I would have either expected to awake to a friendly face looming over me while I lie in a hospital bed following hours of acute care surgery, or in heaven talking to Jesus about the final verdict on my eternal destination. What I get is me, still disoriented from the smash to the head, standing upright and walking around the truck toward the entrance, like a zombie being controlled by the devil. My hands are reaching up to the sky, making goalposts in the air.

"The cash box," the thief commands as we approach the front steps. "Don't empty it. Just give me the whole thing."

Now the man is turning into a proficient communicator. Finally. Not that this makes me desire to pledge my full allegiance to the Bandana Bandit. It doesn't. The gun is motive enough for that.

We enter the truck. The scent of grease mixed with spices and cooked meats hovers in the air so thick it seems as if there's an invisible fog dampening our skin.

"That crap smells good," the Bandana Bandit says. "You got any leftovers?"

In my entire lifetime, I never thought I'd be serving an armed robber, who is pointing a loaded gun at me, food.

"Seriously?" I ask.

"Do I look like I'm playing?" he snarls. "You're the jokester, fool. Not me." He slithers closer. "Serve me up."

In the canteen, the stainless steel flat griddle, a three compartment sink, one twenty-seven-inch prep table, a refrigerator, and deep fryer surround me. Beneath me is the drainage floor. On top of that is Yoke, sleeping. I don't have time to wake him up.

I open the refrigerator and grab a bowl of pot roast that remains from the night. It's not warm and in no shape to truly function as a menu plate. When we served it up earlier this evening, we jazzed it up by wrapping the tender strips of beef chuck, along with the tender carrots, celery and Spanish rice into a burrito and deep-frying the begeezers out of the thing, then placing that into an open brown box. The sauce on top was the actual gravy that came from the pot the roast was cooked in. It's a Mexo-American flavor that I invented just hours ago out of sheer boredom. The chuck normally takes the better part of eight hours to moisten and cook so that it basically melts when you breathe on it. I had to turn the broth into gravy and add it to the meat since Cedro hadn't given it enough time in the slow cooker. My mouth is watering just thinking about it. The only reason the bowl of pot roast is leftover is because I was saving it for me. Now I'm handing it over to El Bandito Bandit.

"Gracias," he presumes. In one hand he directs the gun, in the other he holds his breakfast. I'm guessing he'll have his little *heina* whip him up a sunny-side-up egg so that he can crack the yoke in the roast.

That sounds so yum right now.

"I'm-a count to five. If I don't have what I need, you die," the outlaw mandates. Cute; he insists on including rhymes with his threats, refusing to let that poet in him die.

I let my fingers swim through a small sliver of space between the stove and the counter. If I were going to make a move for the gun this would be the time. The problem is I don't have any special agent type of moves. The rise in tension is enough to rattle Yoke to the burning nightlife taking place in the immediate cramped space around us. "What happened?"

"Your little friend is wakee-wakee now."

I comment to the menace. "He's harmless. Really. It'd be better if you let him go back to sleep."

"I'll say what we better do. I got the gun, fool," the Menial Menace bites back, striding to me in two massive steps and plugging the hollow end of the gun with my shirt and flesh, again digging it into me. "You feel?"

The shot of neuropathic pain sends pangs of misery to my brain and throat, causing my vocal chords to constrict. "Yep."

The gunman orders me to wake Yoke up, but he turns what should have been a three-word expression, "Wake him up" into a ten-word sentence, most of the words being unnecessary expletives.

I walk up to Yoke, bend down and shake. "Wake up." Cleary gun barrels pointed at my head seem to make me more complicit than I otherwise might be.

"What?"

"Yoke, come on, dude. Get up."

"What...why?"

"Cause *I* said so, Sleeping Beauty," El Scary Bandito rasps.

"I thought you wanted *me* to wake him up," I comment.

The menace seems stunned. "What?"

"I said, I thought you asked me to wake him up. If you wanted to do it yourself, why'd you ask me?"

El Scary Bandito walks up to me and places the gun directly over my mouth. Slowly he forces the metal sphere forward, prying my lips apart until the shaft is partly inside. Then he taunts me. "You do think you're a funny guy, don't you? Go ahead. Tell me a joke now. Kind of hard with a rod of metal in your mouth, no? Might be even harder with a mouth full of hot lead. Would you like that, Little *Boca*? A mouth full of hot lead?[6]"

I point to the cylinder of death stemming from my mouth, insinuating that if he wants me to respond, he's going to have to remove this rather minor obstruction. He pulls the gun out.

"I told you already, I don't think I'm a *funny guy*." How I attempt to mock his Hispanic gangster accent might get me killed; but the good news is, this guy recognizes me as a comedian, or as he puts it, a *funny guy*, so at least there's a silver lining.

"You're going to get both of you killed if you don't shut up and give me the money."

I really should listen to the subtle allusion to my imminent death that was so eloquently pointed out to me by El Scary Bandito, but my sarcasm will not be bridled. It takes control of

---

[6] *Boca* is Spanish for mouth. He's calling me little mouth which I gather is sarcasm. He means I have a big mouth and my new gangsta name, Little Boca aka Little Mouth, represents that. What a night—getting robbed and receiving my own gangsta name. Oh how the stars have aligned for me.

my tongue. "If you want me to shut up and give you the money, you're going to have to help me out with the first part and stop asking me questions. You're also going to have to make up your mind. First you want food, then you want me to wake him up. Come on, man."

The twist in the menace's eyes could mean this is a difficult task for him and he's processing my logic, something he probably doesn't spend much time doing; but most likely it means he's exceptionally enraged. To express his outrage, he gets closer to me than he's been, our eyelashes almost adjoining. "Get. The. Money." His breath, ironically, is minty. For effect, he plunges the gun into my stomach.

Without turning around, I reach over my head to the shiny, metal storage cabinets above us and swing one panel open. I point.

"Get it," he insists.

El Scary Bandito backs away and gives me a small bit of space whereby I can pivot, stretch out my arms, and reign in the cash box. I'm not sure if sociopaths are capable of exuding happiness, but I think I can feel the bliss beaming across the face of Senor Gangster Gone Wild. Money's effects on people never cease to amaze me.

With the cash box secured in my hands, I turn around and hold it out.

"Ahh! Ahh!" Yoke screams like Charlie Brown when he's flying through the air after Lucy has pulled the football prank on him. Apparently, he is now fully awake. "Gun! Scary man with bandana! Ahh!" And apparently Yoke has lost the ability to include articles and verbs in his sentences. This must be the effect intensely traumatic experiences have on Yoke. They degenerate his tongue to a toddler's level.

Realizing Yoke cannot be reasoned with, both Senor Gangster Gone Wild and I turn to look at each other. He is either a) going to shoot both of us b) going to run c) going to grab the cash box from my grasp and then run or d) going to grab the cash box from my grasp, shoot both of us, and then run. My only option, however, is to stand and watch while he decides. I have never received James Bond, superspy extraordinaire training, so I am unable to evade a potential bullet, strip the gun from his grasp, and opt for beating the once-potential-threat silly with my bare hands, all in one motion and in under two seconds.

Senor Gangster Gone Wild determines that he will go with option C.

Phew.

When he is out of the truck and probably in his getaway car, and out of the block as well, Yoke eases up on the girly-girl scream fest.

"You can calm down now," I insist. "He's long gone...probably even deposited the wages into his checking account by now."

This gets Yoke thinking and more subdued. "Dude, I'm not stupid. Banks are closed right now."

"That's right, Yoke, the banks are closed. And the guy probably doesn't even have a checking account either. Either way, he's gone, so you can relax."

Yoke's breaths are patterned, rhythmic, and strained. "Are we going to call the police?"

"No. We're going to go home. To my house."

"Dude, you need to call the police."

"And tell them what? That I, Sole Eaby, don't possess a Class A license and am thus not authorized to operate this fine, food vehicle, and I got robbed."

"You have a food handler's card."

"That's great, Genius, for the serving food part, but it's not a license to drive the vehicle that holds the food. How will I explain who drove us here? Because I am wholly confident you don't have a Class A driver's license either. And how do I know this? Because you don't even possess a regular, run-of-the-mill, Class C."

Yoke thinks about it. "Did he take anything else besides the money?"

"My dignity. Self-confidence. Any faith I had in the innate goodness of mankind. And he took complete control over my life for a few minutes so easily that I am now starting to wonder if we, as people, ever have more than ten-percent control over our own lives at any given moment."

"Ten percent? Really?"

"I don't know. Just take a seat. We're leaving." I walk up to the front and start the truck.

Yoke shovels all the stuff off the passenger's seat and plants himself on it. Under his breath, but loud enough that I hear, Yoke says, "Your dad's going to be pissed."

I forgot about that, and the fact that I stood to make $1,500.00. There is no stock left in the truck and there is no profit to use to replenish the supply. The restocking effort will set Cedro back at least a thousand or so, but of course, he'll have to use whatever's left of his savings for that.

Ahh! The inner girl inside of me screams, but not out loud.

CHAPTER EIGHT

All you need is love,
But a little chocolate now and again doesn't hurt.
~ Charles M. Schulz

I've thought long and hard about the likely eruption that could take place the moment Cedro discovers what happened tonight, so I decided to drop Yoke off at his house. Now would not be the best night for a slumber party.

I am planted in the driveway and have been for the past ten minutes, staring at my own house. Naturally, I'm stalling, going over the events of the past few hours. The facts suggest that none of the evening's exploits were directly my fault.

First off, it was upon Cedro's insistence that I took over the truck. Surely, he can understand this.

Then, afterward, the robbery...this was in no way my fault. The truck needed gas and that's because Cedro left it with us that way. So, actually, this is *his* fault. Yoke and I are the victims.

My reasoning well seasoned, I am ready to enter our three-bedroom house on Ben Lomond Place in the Los Feliz suburb of Los Angeles. It's primed with mature hedges arching the front and an overall picturesque feel about it. If Cedro had not purchased it years ago when I had not even reached the nickel mark in my life, there is no way he could afford it now, but as it stands, we are planked down in one of greater Los Angeles's prime suburban havens.

Around the corner, two blocks from here, is my school, Marshall High, the rather stellar educational plant that I'm proud of, considering it lies in what is otherwise a catastrophic school district: L.A. Unified. Many famous cultural icons have attended Marshall, including Leo D (D as in DiCaprio), resident Hollywood whore Heidi Fleiss, Black Eyed Peas founding member and songwriter Will.i.am, and *Time* magazine's 2006 Man of the Year, David Ho, who, unfortunately, is probably the least famed of the clan. To add insult to this, Cedro was a teacher in Marshall's Highly Gifted Magnet Program before he quit that to create his dream world, a world without bells and brief thirty-minute lunch breaks. Why he left this ideal scholastic setting with full benefits and a well-compensated retirement plan for a chance to run his own business and play roulette with his future economic stature will always remain a riddle to me.

As I pass through the quaint courtyard, I notice the living room lamp on and take a deep breath. Slowly, I punch my key in the lock and turn it, doing the same to the deadbolt over the handle. Inside, I find the house quiet, but more like someone holding their breath quiet. This means there needs to be a release, an exhale, and it will probably come from an irate father. The exhale comes the moment I relock the door from the inside.

"What on earth happened?" The voice is controlled yet strident, the man behind it, Cedro, is as a fisherman trying to reel in the wild desire that wants to be unhooked.

"It wasn't my fault, Dad."

"Wasn't your fault? What are you talking about?"

"Will you let me explain?"

Cedro refrains from speaking, and I spend the next minutes tracing the apex of my night, achieving commercial glory by making two grand in three hours, and the nethermost, getting pistol-whipped by one of L.A.'s lowest, El Bandana Bandito, and then everything in between, but all Cedro hears is being down almost two grand.

"He took all of it?" Cedro is standing, unable to remain seated in his leather recliner.

"I'm fine, Dad, thanks for asking."

"I can see you're fine. You're right here in front of me."

"You could still ask. Maybe I could be traumatized psychologically. Permanently. You have heard of PTSD, right?"

"You, of sound mind and sharp wit? I doubt that. Psychological frailties are beneath you."

"Now I'm suddenly strong and have a sharp wit? You sure have great timing when it comes to dropping compliments."

"You don't want my parental praise? I thought kids needed that to develop healthily."

Ahh! Now I can see where I get my ability to condescend as banefully as any heartless human out there. "Whatever." I default to the standard teenage rebuttal.

A spicy silence aromatizes the room, like a chili that's just been speckled into a pan of heated cooking oil. We've reached the Rubicon and neither one of us is turning back. What is percolating in our minds is about to be dropped into the deep fryer which currently is serving as our living room.

"I got that you didn't call the police. I got that you wanted to make as much as money as possible and didn't want to close up at an earlier hour to be safe. I just...I don't know."

I convince myself to try to be sensitive, to see if Cedro and I can come to terms. I even let go of the fact that Cedro has showed no compassion towards his son, who was almost LAPD's most recent homicide victim. "Dad, I'm sorry. You know I didn't want this. I only wanted to help you out."

"Well, look how that turned out."

"What's that supposed to mean?"

"It means you could have used better judgment...tried getting to a gas station in a better part of town before stopping...maybe called me. Who knows? But something to avoid what happened?"

"I couldn't call you."

"Why   not?"

"Because how you're acting now is exactly how I knew you'd react. It's not exactly something that encourages someone to reach out to them."

"So now you're blaming me?"

I match Cedro's raised tone. "*Now?* Whose truck is it? And whose fault is it that it didn't have gas in the first place?"

"Problems always come our way. It's how you handle them. I *accidentally* left you a problem and you totally mishandled it."

"Well, thank you for the not-so inspirational speech. Now I know for next time then. Only there won't be a next time. From now on, leave me out of your little mobile enterprise venture."

"No problem. And while you're at it, you can contribute to the debt you helped create by paying rent, say two-fifty a month."

"Two-fifty? What?" I cut myself off. "Fine. I'll cover that." I may have spoken too soon. I want to make a verbal U-turn because I don't know if I can truly make good on the rent.

Because I perform and get paid to do so even though I make only a couple of hundred here and there, I am still considered an amateur since I don't technically receive the checks. Cedro gets the checks. They go under his name. This allows me to still be involved in the Comedy Club at school and retain my amateur status. If college is in my future, it will also allow me to receive a possible scholarship for my talents, not that universities have comedy programs or give out scholarships to comedians, but maybe they could give me a general, performing arts scholarship or something. The point is, this is why I agreed to let Cedro take my gig money, cash the check, and give me my dues. Naturally, I agreed to give him twenty-five percent for doing this. What father would actually agree to that and not say, "It's okay, son. I don't need a depositor's fee"? Mine, of course.

It's too late, though. I haven't cut my words off quickly enough. *Shoot!*

"Well, Mr. Big Boy, how about this? I'm keeping every dime you make until you pay me back my two grand plus the full tank of gas that was missing."

"Perfect. I love you, too."

We're in the throes of a cataclysmic stare down. Such glares of revulsion are meant for two archenemies, such as Bane and Batman, Satan and God, et al, but not for a father and son; yet here we are anyway.

"Just one thing," I add. "Didn't you already take out an advance on me when you drained my college fund to fuel your little food company? Wasn't that like, I don't know, almost fifty grand?"

"*Your* fund? That was *my* money. Yes, I'd *planned* on using it for your college fund, but things changed. Sorry."

"Oh, is that how good parenting works? Set your kids up with plans and hopes then pull the rug out from underneath because you feel like changing direction? All because you're in the middle of a midlife crisis? Isn't that the antithesis of sacrifice and all that paternal stuff?"

"That's right. I forgot the part where parents have to accept how-to-be-a-parent advice from their kids. Or that, just because you're a parent, it means your time has passed and now it's all about junior."

The argument between The Hulk and Ava reheats in my mind like leftovers in a microwave. Ava left The Hulk, aka Ryan when she realized that their mindsets were lacking so much harmony that a future together was impossible. What I am hearing from Cedro is similar to that. His complete parenting philosophy in a tiny serving, in appetizer form is that he's not the type of dad to set himself aside for his kid's sake. His definition of life is not to dedicate himself to improving his son's existence. It's to make his own life more ideal. These are his secret ingredients that are no longer *secret*.

Lana pours out of the bedroom like liquid from a spilled glass. "What's going on?"

"Go back to bed, honey," Cedro directs. "This is between Sole and I."

"I have to get ready for work soon. It's almost time to get up anyway." She tries to calm the storm in the living room. "Why don't you come to bed and finish this talk in the morning," she suggests to Cedro, kisses his cheek, then comes up to me. She kisses my cheek, too, and hugs me. "Glad you're home safe. Get some rest."

When Lana is back in the room, I add, "Glad someone is concerned about my safety."

Cedro must be tired as well. He tries to diffuse the situation, heeding Lana's advice. "Sole, of course I'm glad you're safe."

For me, it's too late to diffuse the nuke of disdain about to go off inside of me. "You're really convincing."

"Son, of course I'm concerned."

"Sure, Dad. I believe you."

I don't express my utter abhorrence for Cedro with overdone, dramatic entourage. This isn't a midday soap opera. It's enough that I feel it so intensely inside that it's like I can feel my own soul riveting through every fiber of me, filling me like a gas chamber of sorts. And I think what has died in these chambers is Cedro. Cedro has somehow deceased in me. I've never detested anyone like this before, except for my mother, or the idea of her, who is nothing more than an idyll in my head. Most times she's nothing more than the lady who bailed on us. She is a one-dimensional object of disdain, a plastic toy to throw away, and she will always and only be just that. With Cedro, he had a chance to construct himself before me, to form the person he wanted me to know. But what he built, I abhor. What he formed, I hate because he's a real person choosing to say and do what he does.

"Let's finish this another time," Cedro remarks on his way to his room. His words are a final decision on that matter, no room for refusal.

With that I go to bed, hoping I'll be able to fall asleep before the sun rises, but I doubt it.

CHAPTER NINE

You can forgive practically anyone an a full stomach—
even the devil.

By sunrise, I figure that lying on my back or flouncing from my side to my stomach is not going to put me to sleep. If I look in the mirror, I probably look like a vampire has gotten a hold of me—rings of fatigue orbiting my eyes, pale flesh aglow, and my perpetually nail-thin body that borders on appearing malnourished. I am anything but a phenomenon of good looks at these peak hours of sunrise. Nevertheless, it's time to ditch this place.

It's been almost a week, but I decide to make my first outreach attempt toward Ava. I text:

Hi Ava, it's Sole. We met the other night outside The Laugh Factory. I know it's early, but I was thinking...when you get up, if you're not busy and don't have class or anything, maybe we could get some coffee? Or tea? And a scone? My treat.

Roosted on the edge of my bed, I drop my phone back on the comforter as if it has suddenly burst into flames. I can't deny it. I'm nervous. Begrudging that truth would be, by virtue, acute insanity, and I don't want to be that, so I'll gracefully accept my nervousness. And I don't think there's any shame in this. It's a natural emotion under the circumstances. Ava's responses will either be rejection or reciprocation, both of which are fairly extreme replies in their own right. I wonder, am I more afraid of her not texting me back or her just outright sending me a "*No thanks*"? Is there a better way to get rejected?

There's also another dilemma to face today. I am forced to consider the obvious: I have no car and, even if he offered, I wouldn't borrow Cedro's Rubicon anyway. I'm done with letting him help me.

My other alternatives are to bum rides off of people or use the L.A. transit system; neither sounds too appealing. Lying back in bed, I picture myself riding the bus.

Like anyone else, I get on and put my change into the driver's fee box. Suddenly, out of nowhere, violent images fill the portraits in my mind, all of them snapshots of me lying dead, in my own blood, in the bus's aisle. Strangers peer quizzically at my inert figure but do nothing except strip my lifeless body of its valuables.

That isn't going to work.

I have to find a way to buy a moderately reliable vehicle for under $2,367.22 which is the amount of my entire life savings, the part Cedro hasn't or cannot touch because it's already in my possession and stashed in my personal account.

That's the goal I've resolved to achieve by the end of the day: to be the proud owner of my very own used new car. Buying a car in urgency also means that I'll have to find a private owner who is willing to accept my cash and sign transfer papers to me on the spot. Craigslist is the perfect site to go to for this. If this doesn't work, I'll pick up a *PennySaver* somewhere and look through their ads.

In less than ten minutes, I am showered and changed with a fresh pair of jeans, a comfy, worn-in t-shirt, and my customary, fitted-to-perfection, distressed brown leather jacket[7]. That's when my phone buzzes:

Meet me @ Bourbon St Café. 7th and Vermont in Rampart Vill. One hour. BTW I'm not up for games. Honesty and truth are still virtues to me. As Oscar Wilde said, "Be yourself; everyone else is already taken." If you can't do that, don't come.

Being myself won't be a problem for me, but it could be for her.

One hour seems like I'll be waiting until the next millennium, but that's only because I'm as nervous as a tweeker would be at a drug-free convention. In reality, I'll barely have enough time to make it because, without borrowing Cedro's Jeep, it looks like I'll have to take my chances on the bus. Rampart Village is not far south from Los Feliz, but every trip takes longer via the public transportation system.

"I'm leaving," I can hear Lana tell Cedro, who probably can't hear her because he's still crashed.

From down the hall is a noise that sounds like a rustling of keys against a metal coffee tumbler. The fact that Lana hasn't left yet means a potential opportunity to avoid mugging number two.

---

[7] My jacket is *distressed* because of actual wear and tear, not because I bought it in a *distressed* style. As a consumer, I have a running grievance against the whole *distressed* concept. Though I get the idea that people think worn-in blue jeans, biker boots, and tattered leather looks cool, I don't get the idea that people pay *more* money to buy something that looks tattered and beaten up, but that's just me being logical, I guess.

She passes Rampart on the way to work, so maybe she can drop me off. I scuttle toward the kitchen.

"Morning, Lana."

"Hey, Sole. Good morning."

"Listen, I don't want to keep you, so I'll just ask. Can you drop me off somewhere? It's on your way, I'm pretty sure."

"Where?"

"Bourbon Street Café."

Lana ponders, probably calculating her route and drive time if she agrees to this. "Sure. As long as you're buying."

"I got you," I attest.

"Are you ready? I have to go."

"Yep."

"I don't think I'll be able to pick you up. I have appointments all day. How do you plan on getting back?"

"Umm, horseback?"

"Well, I can see your brain's all revved up, Mr. Smarty Pants," Lana counters playfully. "But really, I need to know how you're getting home."

Unlike Cedro, Lana cares about my welfare and safety, so I confess my plans to her. "By getting the girl to like me enough to give me a ride."

Lana smiles. "Is it that girl you met the other night?"

I nod.

Lana approaches me and puts her hands on my shoulders. "How are things with you and your dad?"

"Just like he left them," I say.

"Like *he* left them?" Lana starts off as if she is going to say exactly what I don't want to hear—that both Cedro and I are equally responsible for the disharmony between us. Then she stops herself. Lana doesn't continue with a three-point lecture on the ethics of being a grateful and respectful child and how it should be me who makes the first attempt at reconciliation. "Come on. Time to go," is all she says.

I'm glad she doesn't lambaste me like a chef does a piece of pork as he's prepping it for the evening's menu. I definitely would not listen to any topic related to how a teenager should be the first to change and not wait for the parent to be the one to do so first. Any comment like that would just turn the dial up on my anger meter.

L.A. morning traffic is no match for Lana. It's been a while s I've been in the leather-lined passenger's seat of Lana's red Mercedes E350 Coupe, but there has clearly been no fall off in her abilities to course through the cluttered streets like the Ghost Rider. In fact, when she pulls along the curb where Bourbon St. Café is, I am surprised she doesn't ask me to roll out while the car is in motion like some Hollywood stuntman.

"You should think about trying to qualify for NASCAR," I suggest.

"A simple thank you would suffice," Lana rebuts. "Or a trophy."

Lana's quick-draw wit makes me chuckle. "Thank you. Did you want me to bring you a cup of coffee or something for your drive?"

"Thanks. Next time maybe. I don't want to be late."

"Lana," I discharge her name the way someone does before saying something heavy, weighing at the edge of their tongue.

She must see the neediness in me. "What is it?"

"I don't think I'll be staying at home for a while."

"Yoke's?" Lana asks. I nod but say nothing. "Don't worry," Lana comforts me. "I'll tell your father about it."

"Thanks."

"No worries. It's probably better I do right now anyway."

The moment I step back and onto the sidewalk and close the door, Lana has pressed the gas and has set her car in motion. If I'd forgotten to snatch my backpack before she took off, there would have been no chance of getting it anytime today. My laptop and life savings are stowed inside of it. Any hope for a productive day is in there.

Walking through the parking lot, I try to guess which kind of car Ava drives. My speculation is that she drives an older, two-door sedan of sorts, maybe a Corolla—except there are no Corollas in the lot. In fact, there aren't a lot of trashy looking cars at all. I've mischaracterized Ava, assuming she drives some rinky-dink car. The fact is I really don't know this girl, save for the one night we spent together sharing a pile of street food. Prejudging someone is normal and doesn't condemn me as some evil faultfinder, right?

Before I open the glass doors to the coffee shop, a sharp pang of timidity rings through me. *Suck it up, Sole. It's man time.*

When I enter, I glance around. Pressed against the wall is a newspaper rack where they have a couple of free magazine stacks, including the *AutoTrader* and *PennySaver*. I take a copy of each then head in the direction where I can see Ava has installed herself. She is not the only girl sitting solo in here, but she is the only one I can spot without needing to look at for more than a split second, and this is from behind.

Her hair is in a loose type of bun, and in the front she lets shadowy wisps dangle loose. If I didn't know better, I would think that she is cranking out a poem on her laptop. She has her legs in a pair of fitted jeans and crossed under the table while she dons a small flannel madras and shields her eyes behind a pair of black, full-frame eyeglasses—the duende of a poetess.

"Hey," I say, setting my magazines down and my backpack in the chair opposite Ava. "Do you need a refill?"

Ava grins, picks up her cardboard coffee cylinder and sips. "One per day, thanks."

"Okay. I'll be right back."

"You know, you're a trusting kind of guy. I could just steal that backpack while you're up there ordering and waiting."

"I suppose."

"You don't really know me. What makes you think you can trust me?"

"Nothing. But now that you say that, you just gave me permission to stare at you the entire time. I could think of worse things to do today."

Ava blushes but buries it behind a brush of her hand. "That's weird."

"According to what you just said, I think it's wise."

I walk up to the counter and order one of my favorite brews that comes from a light, blueberry-flavored bean. The owner, Choi Ok-Rim, tops off my twenty-ounce cup and I hand him two dollars and fifty cents. It's not until now that I make the conscious connection to the geography around me, specifically as it relates to Ava. Bourbon St. is on the hem of Koreatown, and that makes me wonder about Ava's background. It shouldn't matter, and it doesn't really. No fact about her could diminish the impression she's made on me. It's just that I want to know about her. That's just what happens when you like a girl.

I send ten packets of Splenda swimming into the hot Joe, add some vanilla syrup, a little non-dairy, powder creamer, and return to the circular table. I stare at Ava, inspect her actually.

"You're really doing the staring thing? I wasn't sure if you were serious."

Her eyes are not upturned, but they're sharp and risen in the outside corners. She has very little makeup on, so I see their thin outlines. Her hair, now fallen from the unsecured swirl, is thick and wavy, and her morning skin is lightless against sunrays stabbing through the window.

"This is getting strange," Ava says. "Hello," she waves.

"Can I ask you something?" I inquire, sitting down and sipping, untying the knot in the moment.

"Oh, I get it," Ava sparks. She even slaps her knee, feigning an outburst of hard laughter. "You want to know why we're here, near Koreatown, Bourbon St. Café, Asian owned, and all that. You're sort of sketching me out in your head, aren't you? Wondering why I like to hang around these parts of L.A."

"I'm just curious, that's all. It won't change anything in the least."

"If it won't change anything, why ask?"

"To be direct...well, you're amazingly attractive. I want to know the ingredients behind the dish."

"Is that your big game, make a girl out to be cuisine?" She pauses, and I don't say anything, letting the tension waft to her side of the table. "My dad was Spanish-American with a quarter Japanese and a quarter Welsh in him. My mom is Semitic and a quarter European. You do the math."

"Semitic?"

"Hebrew? Israeli?"

"You don't have a family tree. You have a family maze."

Ava smiles. She's the perfect confection of allure and sensuality, but I don't say that. I don't want to come across too intense.

"You said your mom *is* Semitic and European but your dad *was* Spanish-American and Japanese..." It's an implied question of mine.

"My dad died."

"Oh. I'm sorry. I didn't...I..."

"It's fine. Really. He was a good man—loving, funny, very responsible. He took care to ensure that if anything happened to him his family would be, I think the term is, *financially solvent*. He was always a million steps ahead."

Except no one can outstep death. "Sounds nice." Time to change topics. This one hits too close to home. "So what are you working on?"

"My job."

I inquire further. "And your job would be?"

"Web design. I freelance, but it pays well, if you're good."

"Are you good?"

"Take your best guess."

I can't force back the need to laugh at myself out loud. "At first I thought you were writing poetry," I confess.

Ava can't restrain her own amusement either. She and I share a chuckle before she notes, pointing to my backpack, "So I see you brought some of your work with you."

"My work isn't quite as interesting as yours. I'm looking for a car. To buy." I set the *PennySaver* and *AutoTrader* atop the table, then stretch down for my laptop and set it on the table, flip it open, and sit down.

"How'd you get here this morning?" she asks.

"Hitchhiked. It's really an enchanting way to start a day, like I'm some mysterious knight going into a haunted forest on my way to the dragon's castle."

"Except you're the knight covered in metal armor who's standing by a tree with his thumb in the air."

"Sir Hitch a Ride is my Camelot name."

"So really, what are you doing today?" she asks.

"Buying a car."

"The whole day?"

"As long as it takes."

"Have you figured out how you're going to go see these cars?"

"I'll do my research then map out where the cars are. From there, I'll be letting the fine and friendly city transit system chauffer me around."

Ava purses her lips, thinks for a moment before speaking, then leans in. "Tell you what. You do your research and mapping, I'll finish my little piece of virtual architecture, and in a bit we'll go check out these cars."

"You mean together?"

"That's what *we* still means, right? As in *you* and *I*. You did pass second grade grammar class?"

I deserve that remark for letting such a ridiculous question hurl out of my mouth. I'd better not say anything else that might make her change her mind. "Sounds good to me."

Without another word, Ava spills all of her concentration over the keyboard and screen of her laptop, and I get to work hunting down what will be my very first automobile.

CHAPTER TEN

As for butter versus margarine,
I trust cows more than chemists.

~ *Joan Gussow*

After meeting different people at various places around the city, the day has lapsed into late afternoon. It's almost sundown when I finally reach a deal with a twenty-something man who calls himself Chipotle[8]. He's not overly dressed, but by the fit of his slacks and button-downed shirt that he leaves unbuttoned at the top so I can see his tattoo, his pointy dress shoes and Poncherello sunglasses, I gather this guy doesn't make his money by showing up at some very established and very legal job site

---

[8]Anyone who gives themselves a call sign has to be the biggest durge to ever have walked the planet. Nicknames and call signs are to be given *to* someone *by* someone else. If self-assigned, it just shows the person to be about as socially aware as a picket fence. Since there is no way on God's green earth any parent would officially name their child Chipotle, I have a hunch that El Chipotle Grande dubbed himself with the name. However, that is an opinion I'll keep to myself. My survival instinct tells me to do that.

each day. His gigolo/pimp meets urban club hopper style speaks more of a drug dealer to me.

We're standing outside the Lincoln Park DMV on the fringes of East L.A. He told me this is where he wanted to meet and that, if the exchange were agreed upon, we would go inside, sign the car over to me, and then go right back outside where I would give him the money and he would hand me the keys. It sounds like the whole charade will end with Chipotle killing me execution style—a slug to my brains—but, actually, it's pretty smart business for a guy who's trying to get rid of evidence.

Ava's explanation of her father and him leaving his family "financially solvent" explains why she has an onyx-tinted Audi A6 with chocolate leather inside and all the metallic trimmings. The only reason I allowed her to park this fine vehicle outside the DMV office versus just dropping me off was because, considering the *vato-loco* neighborhood we are in, the *homies* will most likely think we're dealers too, and that we're here slanging contraband from her fancy ride, not just another pair of rich victims waiting to happen.

*

After taking care of the paperwork inside the DMV, Chipotle and I are in the parking lot, completing the business transaction, i.e. my life savings into his hands, the keys and some official documents into mine.

"Chipotle...is that like the restaurant?" I finally get the nerve to ask,

"It's like the chili," he scoffs, emphasizing his accent over the "I" so that it sounds more like *chee*-lay. "Because I'm spicy like that."

Like that. Didn't that end tag go out of contemporary lingo at the millennium? I don't say this out loud, naturally. I am sure there's an armed robber inside of Chipotle who is just waiting for some smart mouth, dare-to-be-funny-at-all-costs comedian to let him out. Is that stereotyping? Maybe, but then again, I was victimized by someone who almost fits the exact profile of Chipotle, sans the minor changes mentioned.

"Like the chili," I repeat like he did, emphasizing the accent over the "I" so that it sounds more like *chee*-lay. "Okay."

Chipotle walks off and down Mission Road where, moments later, a car pulls over and he gets in. I feel a bond with Mr. Spicy Like That. All things considered, we did just spend the past two hours waiting in a line that isn't measured in feet or miles, but in orbital rotations around the sun. That's part of the scheme though when the guy selling a 2002, maroon-colored Honda CRV meets his buyer in the DMV parking lot and immediately walks him inside to make the process official. It doesn't take a neurosurgeon to deduce that most likely Chipotle is trying to ditch the car he probably stole from some old couple living in a trailer park in Perris.

I open the door and reevaluate my purchase.

"What are you looking for?" Ava asks.

"Bloodstains," I blurt. "Of someone Mr. Spicy Like That may have killed."

"He didn't kill anyone."

"You don't know that," I say, dismissing Ava's point of view by not averting to it and continuing with my warped theory as I press on the carpeted floor and tug a little. "Or some well-disguised compartments he devised so that he could smuggle his drugs in."

"Not just drugs," Ava larks. "People too."

"Human trafficking. Now you're thinking."

"Do you always stereotype people?" It's a serious question of Ava's.

"I have my reasons," I attest.

"Well, whatever your reasons are, stereotyping has pushed you into a paranoiac state."

"It's not exactly paranoia when some guy who could be Chipotle's brother puts a gun to your head in the middle of the night when all you wanted to do was stop and get some gas so you could get home," I say matter of fact. Ava doesn't quip back with a fistful of sarcasm. "Looks good," I conclude.

"You were robbed? At gunpoint?" Ava doesn't know exactly how to ask about this, and I can't blame her. Not many people get to meet a surviving victim of an armed robbery. It's right up there along the lines of getting the opportunity to meet The Octopus Girl, Lakshmi Tatma, a two-year-old Hindi girl born with four arms and four legs and named after the Hindu Goddess of wealth, Vishnu. "I'm sorry."

"Yep," I respond, trying to sound *positive* about the traumatic experience. "It's quite a rush." Positivity degenerates back to sarcasm. Hey, at least I tried it.

"I'm sorry."

"It's all right. There's no way you could have known."

"I guess I judged too soon." Ava thankfully picks up on the fact that I don't want to exchange psychiatric banter with her. Her apologetic confession reminds me of how I somewhat miscalculated Ava when I assumed she drove a little beater car.

"Well, now we're even." I smile, and Ava absorbs it with one of her very own.

"Even?"

"I sort of assumed different things about you, too."

"Like what?"

"I thought you drove a Corolla and were some artistic city chick or something."

Ava finds my honesty about miscalculating her worth a giggle.

On the brighter side, I have achieved my goal for the day and am the humble owner of a mini, midline, SUV, the kind moms or moms-to-be buy because they're too poor, cheap, or as they say, *practical*, to buy an upper level Jeep, Dodge, or GMC Tahoe. This is my very own nothing-to-be-proud-of car, a now perpetual reminder that I have unambiguously *not* arrived and that I have a long way to go in this life before I reach any level of significant status.

"Thanks," I tell Ava. It just dawns on me that this zenith and I have spent the entire day together. Should I push for more? Survey says yes. "So...would you like to hear the story sometime?"

Ava thinks about it, surveying the surroundings. "Do you mean a real date? Like where you tell me over dinner? Or where you pick me up and tell me in your new car while we get food from a drive-thru and eat in the parking lot?"

"Which would you like? The real date? Or the parking lot?"

"What do you think?"

I pretend to assay Ava as if the choices were difficult. In the background Zapp and Roger's "So Rough So Tuff" grows louder, impeding my thoughts. I check it out. A Chevy Impala blasting the music is getting closer. The driver is a Hispanic male with a shaved head and sunglasses even though there is no trace of sun left hanging in the sky. It's dinner time. He must be looking for a victim.

Whereas my body, out of fear, wants to urinate on itself, Ava sees the humor in the moment. "That's funny."

"I think you mean frightening."

"Not withstanding your personal experience, this whole scenario is a real life stereotype. First Chipotle, now the gangsters rolling down the street."

"I think it's time to go," I conclude, a tremor of worry in my voice.

Ava agrees with my comment by nodding with a sense of caution, as if the wrong move could draw too much attention to ourselves. "You're probably right"

We each get into our cars. I wait until we're pulling out of the parking lot before I call her.

"So, what do you think?" she asks me.

I already know. "Even though I think you are totally the drive-thru, parking lot type of girl, I'll say that you're wanting a full service date because you want to try something different."

"So are you going to ask, or what?"

"Will you go on a real, non drive-thru or parking lot date with me, Ava?"

"Sole Eaby, it would be a pleasure."

CHAPTER ELEVEN

Fish, to taste right, must swim three times—
in water, in butter, and in wine.

French Proverb

My first official date with Ava is a day away. Having just finished my once-or-twice-a-week shift working as a very-part-time barista at Starbucks on The Promenade, I figure I'll waddle about for a while.

"Why don't you just stay here and drink some brew?" Jennifer, a barista asks, winking. "It's free."

"Um, thanks. Maybe next time. See you guys later," I announce to Jennifer and the crew working with her.

"Later, So." In unison, the baristas pronounce the nickname I hold at work.

Even though I have my own room at Yoke's house, I relish a few moments to be alone. That means that sometimes I have to go out and find those places where I don't know anyone, which shouldn't be too hard a task since I'm not famous and am technically homeless. Just because I now sleep in Yoke's spare bedroom, and my clothes and some of other belongings are currently stowed at Yoke's, doesn't mean it's my official residence.

The fall evening in Santa Monica is altogether inspiring right now. The Third Street Promenade is quite the bustle in the afternoons, a place where I can be among people enjoying themselves while I am a mere prop, a figment casually observing them, trying to pick up any clues of how to be happy.

Some of the places I can't exactly go into are the bars and breweries—the whole age thing—which is absolutely okay with me. These watering holes are all about *happy* hour right now, serving the Southland's stressed out cosmopolites who don't quite feel like going home or slugging it out on the bumper-to-bumper freeways. I always wonder: are people *really* happy at happy hour? I think not. If they were so happy, I'm fairly convinced they wouldn't have to lubricate themselves just so that they can forget how miserable their lives are. That's pretty much the opposite of happy...when you're trying to forget about or avoid the life you currently lead.

The weekly farmer's market is tonight, so this is a perfect time for businesses like Cedro's to come and sell. As it stands, if Eaby Baby's shows up, it will not be the only mobile food hub grilling and greasing their select cuts of meat.

Already I spot The Great Crepe, one of L.A.'s newest trucks to hit the streets. The design on their mobile tin can has flowers and a sunset painted on its exterior. If you ask me, it looks like the cover to a tawdry, B-rate, self-published romance novel. For people who can get past the awful exterior and are craving some desert, then, naturally, this is the truck for them. Their claim to fame is Tahitian style crepes, which is strange because crepes originated in Brittany, a region in France. How customers let The

Great Crepe's owner sell French knockoff pancakes is beyond me.

A block down, I spot El Vagón Fusión, or The Fusion Truck. Their mangled, Spanglish name sounds like a gang of third-grade-boy-wannabes who are trying to be hardcore but can't because they're three feet tall and live in Pacific Palisades. The words "Latin Asian Fusion" are stenciled over their fresco of ruby and yellow that assumes images conjured from *Dia de los Muertos*, aka the Day of the Dead. This is somehow supposed to lure in customers with a supposedly-clever phrase that is anything but clever.

What this truck consists of is a band of Hispanic owner-operators who breed traditional Mexican and Asian dishes together (hence "Latin Asian Fusion") and sell its offspring. An example is the age-old taco. To fuse, or rather confuse, the taco with something conventionally Asian, all these people do is roast some pork belly the way a Vietnamese person who lives in Vietnam would, slap some meat into a corn tortilla, then add some cabbage, onion, cilantro, and salsa, and call it Bolsa. I may not be a graduate of any culinary school, but that's not fusion of any sort. If that counts as fusion, then grilling my soiled undies with a dose of Sweet Baby Ray's would count as barbecue. No. That's nothing more than a common, classical taco. Anytime meat goes into a corn tortilla, it's a taco. And tacos then, now, and always, are only Mexican food.

But none of what I say matters. El Vagón Fusión is stealing the show. The line is snaking around Third Street to Arizona Avenue where they must be set up.

And then...

On the corner of Second Street and Santa Monica is where I spot Cedro's truck, little old Eaby Baby's Edible Crazies. He probably paid a pretty penny to reserve this primo spot. Ouch. He, along with one of his friends, Edgar—Lana's fill-in when she can't help out—should be ripping the ocean strip up and setting it on fire; instead they have little more than ten customers, not exactly the haul Cedro was likely expecting. Poor guy is consistently behind the curve with his business savvy. He's clueless.

I still have a couple of hours to kill before I perform tonight in an L.A. club. Should I prance over to Cedro and buy something to eat? *Should?* Probably. *Will I?* Negatory. I think I'll use my meager Starbucks income to purchase a couple of tacos at El Vagón Fusión and then park it at Three Street Coffee and pilfer off the free WiFi while I sip from a café Americano with four add-shots of espresso.

After waiting out the long line, it's my turn to order. "Uh, I'll take a Hawaiian shrimp taco and a coconut curry taco."

To my delight, I see that the attendant is a cute Hispanic girl with all the classic tapestries of Spanish allure. I thought the owner-operators were all male, but I am pleasantly wrong. What I'll try to do is warm up the temperatures of her love waters and, from there, mention to her that I have a friend named Yoke. If she likes me, she's more apt to open up to the idea of being the object of Cupid's love engineering through me.

The girl writes my order down on a pad, rips it from the rest of the stacked receipts, and calls out to the cook. "One Hawaiian and one coco curry!" She turns back to me, hands me the bottom slip of a perforated ticket, and says, "You're number 112."

"Thanks." I take the ticket.

"Your total is $11.85."

"For two tacos?"

"For two tacos," she repeats duteously.

I reach into my back pocket and take out a twenty from my wallet. "These must be some pretty big tacos."

"Big is subjective."

I add a little innuendo to get this conversation rolling in the right direction. "I agree. Do you think you have big tacos?"

"Excuse me?"

"Your tacos. Do you think your tacos are big?"

"That's up to you to decide. On our end, we just concentrate on taste," she defines to me in a literal manner, totally dismissing my overtones.

This is my last chance to lay it on her. The direct approach is my only option now. "So, what do *you* like to concentrate on? When you're not working the truck."

By the way, this is not wrong. Even if I were actually trying to lure this girl for myself, Ava is not my girlfriend and we're not even close to being anything serious, but since my objective is Operation Find Yoke the First Date of His Life, this act of charity with this Hispanic cutie is definitely not criminal behavior.

"Tae Kwon Do," the cutie says to me. "That's what I concentrate on."

"Really? That's neat. What got you into that?" I think I'm making headway with the girl, ready to score her cell number any moment now, my energy increasing before her.

"I don't know. I guess I just really wanted to be able to say *no* and back it up, you know?" She winks, her long lashes fluttering, not in a tempting way, but as if to wave me off. "In case anyone doesn't take me seriously." She hands me my dime, nickel, and rest of the change.

I guess I was wrong about making headway. "Got it," I say, receiving the eight dollars and fifteen cents. There's no use in mentioning Yoke right now, that's for sure. So much for my attempt at humanitarian and civic duty on behalf of Yoke. "I'll just wait for my number to be called since I won't be calling yours."

The Hispanic cutie's face is tight but buoyant just before she winks, smiles, and dismisses me, immediately taking an order from someone else as if I were never there. *Huh? What happened?* Maybe the flirty signaling was her way of saying how much she appreciates the fact that I accepted rejection so well. Wonderful. A pretty stranger is rewarding me for possessing a totally useless social skill: receiving rejection with a good attitude. For the record, I don't recommend anyone be proud to possess such a defaming ability.

I hear one of the male workers in the truck voice his concern. "Are you okay, *mija?*"

"Yes, *Tio*, I'm fine," the cutie responds with confidence. "Just some guy hitting on me."

"I know you can take care of yourself, *mija*," the male voice iterates.

I want to scream to them that I wasn't actually trying to hook up with the girl for me, but for my friend, Yoke, but it's too late for that now. As they say, no good deed goes unpunished. How do girls do that? How did this girl just oust me like that, like she was spraying insect repellant over her skin to ward off an onslaught of gnats and mosquitoes? Am I a mosquito to her?

Speaking of being an insect...

I have no idea what to do with Ava or where to take her on Saturday, the one girl who has not rejected me. The last girlfriend I had, Gabrielle...well, I'll just say those experiences haven't exactly left me feeling robust about my odds in the game of attraction. I can't mess it up with Ava.

"112!" the Hispanic enchantress calls my number.

I amble to her in humility, not willing to dare any attempt at repartee. "Thank you."

"You know," she whispers, looks over her shoulder a quick moment, and then turns back to me and leans in. "You surprised me. You didn't actually keep pushing after I said no, like most guys would. We have a website. You can follow the truck there. Find out where we'll be."

"Why?" I ask.

"Because I just might say yes next time."

I guess I was wrong about her and me and rejection. "Maybe I'll do that," I say to her in a capricious way, as if I expected her to do this all along.

"Good," she says. "By the way, in your order there's an invite to a little soirée on the beach tomorrow night. You seem like a cool guy. You should come."

Calling me "cool" is just another word for "nice" and everyone knows nice guys never get the girl. This is more evidence that, in her eyes, I am a harmless male who has "just a friend" written all over him. *Whatever*, I remind myself, *this girl is for Yoke, not me.* I nod, smile and, with food in tow, take myself over to Three Street Coffee.

Laid out around Three Street Coffee's floors are Moroccan rugs, dim lights, beads, and sitar melodies squeaking like crickets through the beatnik ambience. At a table, I sip my Americano, the hot liquid singing my tongue slightly, and bite into my taco. I spend a few moments outlining my routine for tonight, trying to conjure up some new jokes even though the pending date with Ava is laying siege to most of my brain's hard drive.

Let's see. I went to the DMV. I can play off of this... I start to peck away at the keyboard for a moment, outlining potential jokes.

When I reread the material I've just typed, I recant. *DMV jokes are as stale as a mummy's lips.* Not that I've ever kissed a mummy to know such facts. To eradicate the half page of DMV jokes I've sketched, I hit CTRL + A + DEL.

I wish I could CTRL + A + DEL away parts of my life as easily as that.

After two more sips from my Americano and another bite of my taco, it's evident why the jokes aren't hatching in me. The date with Ava is completely holding my mind hostage. My joke research is now officially on hold.

I Google some key words regarding dating, hit ENTER and scroll down the page until I find a link entitled DATING DOSAGE FROM A REAL PUA. Though I'm not sure precisely what kind of *dosage* I'll be getting from this website, I presume that PUA is short for Pick Up Artist, a guy who is supposed to be some master guru at getting girls. Maybe the PUA behind the electronic curtain could have some suggestions for my Saturday with Ava. It's worth a shot.

There's a free *"InstaChat"* link advertised in the corner of the window. Naturally, I'm skeptical. Who gives *free* dating advice? I mean that's why they have eHarmony and Match.com—because it requires that people actually *pay* for dating privileges. The rest of us have to hope they're connected to an older mentor who can guide them through the tangles of dating. If not a mentor, some guys are lucky to have dads who put their arms around their sons' shoulders and school them on their best tested techniques—ancient as they may be—to get the girl to want more of you by the time the date is over. Not me. Some have therapists. Not me. Others have friends who can teach them the Jedi way of girl-getting. I have none. The closest to any of these is Yoke, and, well, can you imagine him giving me dating advice?

I may as well have the mutant rat Splinter, father of the Ninja Turtles, as my romance consultant.

Me: WHY IS THIS ADVICE FREE? I type.

The site guru responds via the site's InstaChat.

PUA: BECAUSE *WHEN* IT WORKS I'LL KNOW YOU'LL COME BACK AND SIGN UP FOR THE PREMIUM LEVEL MEMBERSHIP.

Me: WHO IS THIS ANYWAY?

PUA: DIDN'T YOU READ THE HEADING ON THE HOMEPAGE?

Me: I JUST WANT TO KNOW I'M NOT TALKING TO THE FREAKING GEIKO LIZARD.

PUA: FIRST, CRAG BRAIN, NO ONE IS TALKING. WE'RE *TYPING*. SECOND, WHO THE FREAK CARES IF I'M A LIZARD? IF THE ADVICE WORKS, DOES IT MATTER IF I'M A REPTILE?

The guy, or reptile rather, on the other end of the chat has a point. TOUCHÉ.

PUA: ALL RIGHT THEN. HERE WE GO. FIRST, WHERE ARE YOU TAKING HER AND WHEN?

Me: THAT'S THE PROBLEM. I DON'T KNOW WHERE TO GO. WE'RE SUPPOSED TO GO OUT ON SATURDAY.

PUA: SATURDAY NIGHT?

Me: YES.

PUA: YAWN. SNORE. ARE YOU BUSY DURING THE DAY?

Me: ARE YOU ASKING ME OUT? THAT'S WHAT I WAS AFRAID OF ON THIS SITE!

PUA: WHAT? NO, YOU KNOB. I'M TALKING ABOUT TAKING *HER* OUT DURING THE DAY. EVERYONE

GOES ON THE SATURDAY NIGHT DATE. THAT'S TIRED. TAKE HER OUT DURING THE DAY, GRAB SOME COFFEE, AND SEE IF LEADS TO AN ENCORE AT NIGHT.

I ponder his strategy. Once again, this guy, or lizard, obviously knows what he's talking about. SOUNDS GOOD. BUT WHERE SHOULD I TAKE HER?

PUA: THINKING...

I wait a few minutes, sipping my Americano and looking at the sunset over the Pacific.

PUA: OKAY. YOU'RE IN L.A. TAKE HER TO A MUSEUM OR SOME PLACE OUTDOORS TO WALK AROUND AND TALK. YOU CAN GAB, RIGHT?

Me: GABBING IS ONE THING I CAN DO.

PUA: GREAT, BECAUSE SILENCE WILL CAUSE IMMEDIATE TERMINATION OF THE DATE. YOU WANT THE DATE TO FEEL ORGANIC—NO PRESSURE. THAT'S WHY YOU GO OUT DURING THE DAY AND IF THE DAY SUCKS, YOU CALL IT. IF IT'S GOOD, YOU XTEND.

Me: HOW WILL I KNOW IF IT'S TIME TO CALL IT?

PUA: BECAUSE YOU'LL BOTH FEEL LIKE ALL THE OXYGEN IN THE ATMOSPHERE'S BEEN SUCKED AWAY AND IF YOU DON'T LEAVE THE AREA PRONTO YOU'LL ASPHYXIATE TO DEATH.

Me: OH.

PUA: SO, IN SUMMARY, REMEMBER THESE THREE C'S: CULTURE, COFFEE, CASUAL. THAT IS, TAKE HER OUTDOORS SOMEWHERE TO WALK AND TALK (CULTURE) THEN FOLLOW UP WITH A JAVA SOMEWHERE (COFFEE) AND KEEP IT ALL CASUAL.

LET IT FLOW. IF YOU GET THESE THINGS RIGHT, YOU'LL GET TO XTEND FOR SURE.

Me: WHAT IF I DO GET TO "XTEND" LIKE YOU SAY? IS THERE A "C" FOR THAT?

PUA: IT'S CALLED CREDIT. AS IN, USE YOUR CREDIT CARD AND SIGN UP FOR PREMIUM. AND TRUST ME, IF YOU GET TO XTEND, YOU'LL BE WISHING YOU SIGNED UP AND KNEW WHAT TO DO.

Me: I THINK I'LL JUST FIGURE IT OUT.

PUA: YOU MEAN LIKE YOU HAD ALL THIS FIGURED OUT ALREADY? OKAY. GOOD LUCK WITH THAT.

Me: SO WHAT'S YOUR NAME?

PUA: THAT COMES PREMIUM TOO. GOOD LUCK. I'M OUT.

Whoever this Jedi of dating is, he's got some solid points, but I'm not signing up for premium yet. If I make it to *Xtend* mode, I'll just figure it out for myself.

After researching some spots in L.A. to impose upon on Saturday, it hits me. I know where I'll take Ava. Cedro used to take me there when I was a boy, before he went on his search for his true self.

*

"A date?" Yoke asks.

"You say it like you're surprised. Are my looks that repellant that you think no beautiful female would accept my invitation?"

"I didn't want to say it, but..."

"Whatever, Yoke. But while I'm out on Saturday, what are your *big* plans?"

"None of your business." Yoke walks out of the guestroom, the room I'm staying in, and returns to his own down the hall.

I remain lying back in the bed, flipping through the television channels. Yoke's parents have HD television in every room, and they get every channel their cable provider offers. Even the nasty channels. They do it for Yoke. They actually want him to *stumble* upon porn one day. It's extreme parenting, yes, but they're willing to try anything to normalize their son. A teenage boy as socially and sexually incongruent as Yoke is quite lucky to have parents who care enough to think outside the box and try whatever might work for their kid. A few scenes of the adult flick on the screen right now both remind me of something and give me the courage to speak of things that can be a bit touchy if the other party doesn't quite approve of the topic at hand. "Yoke!"

There's a minute or so delay before Yoke materializes in the threshold. "What?" He sounds irritated.

"Check this out with me for a moment." Yoke closes the door behind him and sits on the edge of the bed. My eyes are fixated on the images rolling around in the plasma screen and on Yoke's dull expression. "Does this not interest you, Yoke?"

"Not really."

This is worse than I imagined. "I've been meaning to ask you, Yokester, Oh Buddy of Mine, have you ever spent any quality time with a woman who is *not* related to you in any way, shape, or form, and whom you've had some sexual attraction to?"

Yoke's silence indicates that this question is too complex for him, or that he doesn't want to admit it. "That's private."

"I'm going to take that as a clear no."

"That's not what I said."

"It's what you *didn't* say that tells me."

"Tells you what?"

"That...never mind." I sit up. "All this is okay. It's totally acceptable," I try to encourage even though Yoke's sexually inert passion seems to be as abnormal as a mermaid and a grizzly bear mating and reproducing a...a grizbermaid? A mergribear? My point exactly.

Yoke rises from the bed, distancing himself from me, and slumps deep into the armchair next to the bed. "It's not as easy for me to meet girls."

"I know, buddy. That's why I want to know how it's going. I was thinking I could try to help."

"Help?"

"As in hook you up."

"You mean hire a prostitute?"

"I mean set you up with a girl—legally—if the opportunity comes."

"Um, okay. Sure."

I examine the seriousness clouding Yoke's face. "You're supposed to be elated. You don't sound too interested."

"That's because I'm scared you might actually do it and that I might actually have to meet a girl."

"And that's a bad thing?"

"For me? Yeah. It's potentially disastrous."

"Good grief, Yoke. Just go take your meds before you get diagnosed with Girlaphobia."

"That's not a real disease."

"Look, just get your mind ready so that when it's time, you don't make a complete fool of yourself."

"Like I said, that's what I'm afraid of."

CHAPTER TWELVE

Vegetarian: an old Indian word for bad hunter

~ Unknown

Against Yoke's natural inclinations, he finally decided to come with me to Redondo Beach. That's where the party is, the one whom the Hispanic hottie from El Vagón Fusión invited me to.

The house is choking with a mass of enlivened people bedecked in the least amount of clothing the chilly air will allow. It's not summer, so bikinis for girls and going shirtless for guys just won't cut it. In exchange, the girls' attire is tight, their skin spiraling out of their skirts and dresses, usually from high up the thigh on down. Around their torso the clothing is stretched, showing their shapes where the waist meets the hip. Most have the beautiful divide between their teats showing. Even girls with less mountainous hoobies are flaunting. It's an eye-fest all around. Urbanite cool is what the guys opt for—jeans or khakis, well fitted, a button-down dress shirt or t-shirt caked snugly over their upper bodies, and a pair of leather city shoes. Next to me,

Yoke is wearing blue jeans, a loose collared button down, and a pair of Converse Chucks.

I don't mention the fact that he probably won't pass the eyeball test with most of these people. "All right, so are you ready?" My voice is amplified a few decibels so that Yoke can hear me through the music.

Yoke shakes his head and yells back, "She doesn't know you're trying to set me up?"

"Not exactly." I lean into Yoke so that I don't have to holler. "But it should be fine."

"Should be?"

I ignore this statement and keep an eye out for the Hispanic cutie.

"I thought you had a date tonight anyway. With that chick you know. Isn't she going to get mad you're here? Is she, like, your girlfriend or what?" Yoke fills the nervous tension inside him with conversational questions that he blasts out the way bullets are discharged from an automatic assault rifle.

Admittedly, I haven't told him much about Ava. "Calm down, dude. Take a deep breath." I pause, expecting him to obey. "No, she's not my girlfriend, and I'm not married so I can be where I want when I want. And if I were supposed to be going out with her tonight I wouldn't be here. I can keep a calendar. You know that's a skill we learn in, like, first grade, right?"

Yoke doesn't return fire.

A moment later I see the Hispanic cutie creasing through a knot of partiers, a plastic cup in her hand. Her smile is commercial-white, her beauty movie-star-stunning, and her silky, tight dress with vibrant colors is dazzling her petite, but curvy, frame. And the ring on her finger...*what?*

"Hey, Number 112, glad you made it," she greets, her voice level hiked up.

Number 112? She called me by my order number? What is this, a prostitution ring? "Do all your customers get an invite?" I ask, matching her tone so that she can hear me.

"Of course not. I just don't know your name."

"Sole. Sole Eaby. Yours?"

"Angela. Angela Soliz. And who is this?" She's referring to Yoke.

"This is my friend, Yoke Regan."

"Hi, Yoke." Angela holds out her hand for him to shake.

Yoke is frozen and doesn't return the friendly gesture.

"He's really shy," I attest.

"That's okay," Angela says, moving in close to me. "I was looking for *you* anyway."

Whoa. There's a clear diamond rock mounted atop this girl's left ring finger and a warm lyric of flirtatiousness from her lips dancing around my ears. And there's also Ava and the fact that Angela is supposed to be for Yoke. Oh boy. My plan clearly had a lot of holes in it.

"You were?" I ask nervously. "Why?"

Instead of telling me that she wants to get to know me more deeply or plant her billowy lips over mine, she solidifies, once and for all, the fact that coming here may have been a mistake. "Well," she begins, backing away from the side of my face. "There's someone I want you to meet."

That Titanic-just-sunk-look that covered the face of the young, business girl who rejected me when I tried to pick her up while working Cedro's food truck is unquestionably masking mine right now. I remain speechless.

127

Another girl, who could be Angela's clone, breaks through the throng of people and slides up next to her. Accompanying this girl is a guy, slickly garbed. His stylish, wavy hair and rock hewn face make me wonder if this guy just came back from talking to Steven Spielberg about the next movie he is going to shoot. He puts his arm around Angela's small waist and kisses her cheek.

Oh. I see.

"Hi," the girl says. There is no ring on her finger.

"Christie, this is Sole, the guy I was telling you about."

"It's nice to meet you, Sole," Christie salaams.

It takes a moment for my mouth to catch up with my mind. When it does, and I break out of my stupefied trance, I adjoin her with a greeting. "Nice to meet you, Christie."

"Sole, this is Eddie, my fiancé," Angela notes.

Eddie offers me his hand and I clasp it. "Good to meet you."

"Likewise," Eddie returns.

"Guys, this is Yoke," I say, not caring at all how smooth the conversation is.

Yoke waves as if he is a mobile mannequin on Hollywood Boulevard pantomiming mechanically to passersby.

"Yeah, well," I say, not covering up for Yoke this time. "This is fun."

"Christie is my younger sister," Angela begins to vocalize her sibling's resume. "When I met you, Sole, you seemed like such a great guy. So sweet. I wanted you and Christie to have a chance to meet each other."

Now the chips are on the table. "Oh," I acknowledge as if to say "I get it now." Except I don't say the words.

Regardless, Angela and everyone pick up on my thoughts.

"Yeah, sorry about that, dude," Eddie chimes. "I told Angie that she should have straightened all this out earlier. I mean, hey, I would have thought Angie was hitting on me, too, the way she made it sound and all. When she told me the story I was like, 'That dude totally thinks you're digging on him, Ang.'"

"Huh, huh. Yeah," I fake a laugh.

"No hard feelings, Sole?" Angela, or Angie, or Ang—whatever her name is—asks.

"No worries," I say. Inside I am mounting the strength to impose my comeback, which is really just me being honest about my motives, the same way they've been honest with me. This is the only opening to squeeze in my little confession, otherwise it won't make sense and will be completely ectopic. "Truth is as much as Angela is totally beautiful—Eddie, you're a lucky guy..." I add a little flattery to the mix to ensure that I make friends and not enemies out of these people.

"Aw," Angela and Christie purr in unison.

I continue. "Well, in all honesty, I was actually trying to set my buddy Yoke up with Angela. I'm sort of into another girl right now and, well...yeah."

Everyone laughs. I turn to Yoke, and even he has the slight wrinkle of a grin on the corner of his mouth. In seconds, all of us are enjoying the irony of it all.

"Cool," Eddie breaks in after we're all done laughing. "Well, guys, enjoy." Eddie escorts Angela toward the deck at the rear of the house.

Christie begins to follow. She stops briefly and turns to me, walking back. "What's your number?"

I tell her and she dials it. My phone buzzes and I repeat what's on the screen. "Yep, that's mine," Christie affirms.

"Thanks," is all I can think to say.

Christie plants a kiss on my cheek. "If you find you're not supremely into that girl you mentioned, find me. Okay?"

Christie is just as beautiful as Angela. "Okay," I say. "I'll do that."

"I hope so." Christie walks off and I follow the switch and sway of her figure until it is engirded by the crowd.

"Sorry about that, Yoke." I reach to a table next to me and grab a bottle of Dos Equis.

"Dude," Yoke is excited. "You just totally blew that ultra hottie off. What the hell is wrong with you?"

I take a sip from the bottle. "Now you're suddenly master pimp of the year? And no, I didn't blow her off. I got her number, didn't I?"

"How do you know it's not a fake?"

"Dangledink, she called me right in front of us."

"Oh, yeah."

"Clearly she's only a phone call away." I scanned the party, wondering what our next play would be. "So, what do you want to do?"

"Can we just go home now?" he asks.

CHAPTER THIRTEEN

There is no love sincerer than the love of food.

~ George Bernard Shaw

It's ten o'clock on Saturday morning and The Nethercutt Collection museum in Sylmar has been opened for an hour by the time we arrive. Not being able to take food or drinks inside, our 7-Eleven coffee is getting cold in the plastic cup holders aboard The Curse of the Maroon (the official name for my car) while we're perusing the exhibits.

"Wow. These are like what Al Capone would have driven." Ava is describing the collection of vintage cars from early twentieth century eras—antique, classic, and post-war.

Parked on Persian rugs, the cars, numbering over one hundred and thirty, are flaunting their sheen as Hollywood stars do on the red carpet.

"Pretty shrill, huh?" I add.

"Absolutely fierce. One guy owns all this?"

"J.B. Nethercutt bought his first two cars for $5,500, a Duesenberg Convertible Roadster and a DuPont Townie. It took him over $60,000 to restore the first, but it won a lot of prizes."

"Any money?"

"Sure. Prizes included cash, but for all the money he put into his cars, it wasn't the winnings that allowed him to refurbish them." To me the cars all around us are stories, not just sophisticated heaps of metal. "It was his business."

"What kind of business?"

"Get this," I declare, like a professor who's lectured this fact a thousand times and, instead of it becoming tedious each time he tells the story, it gets more riveting. "The guy dropped out of CIT and went into selling cosmetic beauty products with his aunt. After years of collecting and restoring, J.B. and his wife decided to open this museum in 1971 to show off their cars, and never once did they charge a dime."

"That's, um, very historic."

"Do you know the name of the beauty company?"

"No, but I bet you want me to guess."

I make a fist at Ava, pretending to threaten her. "Or you can deal with this."

"Since you put it that way. Um, let me see...uh...L'Oréal? Clinique? Lancôme? Pantene?" Ava watches me shake my head. "Any French company that sells beauty products—I don't know."

I laugh. "Merle Norman."

"Never heard of it."

"Isn't that amazing? Something you've never heard of was so big it bought all of this and sold millions of dollars' worth of products—right under our noses."

Ava studies me. "Why do you know about some craggily old dead guy anyway? Do you secretly *use* his product? You do, don't you? At night when you're all alone..."

"You found my secret."

"I thought so."

"Really though, the best comedians must be well-read. I read anything and everything I can get my eyes on. Would you like one more little fact?"

"If I say no, you're going to kill me, right?" She shows me her fist. "Just be ready for my combat-grade defense."

"You know for about thirty thousand you can open up your very own Merle Norman beauty supply store?"

"Interesting. Maybe we could go into business together."

After walking the grounds for over an hour, we're strolling the Grand Salon, which is a showroom laced with marble pillars, crystal chandeliers, and painted ceilings. Plump and shiny Cadillacs, Renaults, and Miverna's glaze the exhibition, but as ornate as the room is, my stomach is a lot less inspired by the scenery. It's time for lunch. I know the PUA online said to take her for coffee, but I'm hungry. "You want to grab a bite?"

"You know with my line of work," Ava says, "when I hear someone say that my mind hears something different."

I remember Ava constructs websites. "I can understand why."

"Sorry. Bad joke. That just came to me. I'm not sure why I shared that."

"It's fine, and the joke wasn't bad. I like that you feel free to share."

"You do? I'm not ruining your perception of me? The mystique isn't ebbing?" She makes circles in front of her with her hands.

"Ebbing? No." I make circles back. "It's more like you're evolving with me."

"Evolving. I like that."

"People have to evolve around each other. They can't stay the same way they started. No one should stay the same as when they first meet someone. Conversations and character should become more developed and natural. You know? Evolve."

"So are we still in the primordial stage? Or have we at least *evolved* to caveman status?"

I crouch down and pounce around, tickling my armpits like a delirious gorilla. "Me don't know."

Around a host of vibrant, but otherwise lifeless automobiles, my antics brush Ava with pleasure. I can't say the same for the strangers around the exhibit room, however. Irritation soils the faces of a sophisticated-looking couple. They are not quite contented with my ape impressions. Clearly, they've mis-recollected their youth and early stages of romance. Their pleated noses make it seem as if they have just smelled a diaper smothered with diarrhea. Maybe if they weren't so busy over-exaggerating their pompous speculation about the early 1900 era's cars they might remember how they once were.

Fortunately, it's not the strangers I am trying to make laugh. "Evidently they haven't evolved," I whisper to Ava while we are standing in front of a red Cadillac.

Being within arm's reach, I catch Ava's hand and turn her to me lightly. Ava's gaze into me is flirty and shy, but most importantly, it's focused. Whatever I've said and done so far has passed her approval checkpoints. This is the perfect time to get the kiss over with. *Casual* is what the online dating guru said, but I can't resist trying to make a thicker connection with this girl, one not diluted by superficiality.

"I remember the conversation outside of The Factory that night." Ava keeps eye contact, waiting to hear me out. "The miscarriage and all. Are you okay?"

Surprisingly, Ava is not rattled out of the moment. She doesn't shift from my nearness, and her eyes become even more attentive, peering into me, or through me, rather. "I made a choice. Well, a mistake really. And I know how to make better choices now."

Me? A better choice? If only she knew. I'm not the best translator of looks or passion as they pertain to making moves, but I'm going to go out on a limb on this one. I think this means that now is the time for a kiss, and I would be smart to go with it.

"So," I say, moving in closer to Ava, "let's get out of the Stone Age. Would you like to evolve with me?"

She nods, a modest mime of pliability.

"Are you sure? Is this okay? I mean your last relationship and what happened and all." I know, I know, I am almost trying to talk her out of this, but I can't help it.

"Unless something's changed since Biology 101, I don't think a kiss is linked to procreation, not directly anyway. And trust me," Ava gives me a stern expression. "There will be no indirect link either."

It's clear I am making more out of her past than she is. I put my hands up the same way an assailant does when he indicates to the police he's not planning on resisting. I look at the dilly of a car next to us. "You mean we aren't going to end up in the back seat there?"

Ava shakes her head, a simper holding place now. The invitation to kiss her remains printed on her.

Lord, her dark, bubbly eyes and indulgent beauty look like that of a Disney princess.

I don't dare let my eyelids fall until I can almost feel Ava's skin tickle mine. That's when I know that Ava won't move back. Lightly I lay my mouth over hers. She receives me, moving her lips to let me know we're on the same wavelength. Maintaining the *casual* theme, I make sure that the length of this affectionate connection isn't the equivalent of an intense love scene that leaves two people exhausted and wondering what to do afterward. I get the taste of her mouth—something like if chocolate cake a la mode were ever made into breath flavor; although, that could be the coffee. Every other thing is washed away. I feel like someone just hit the reset button in my entire body. I'm completely chill. This is when I know it's time to break away and save some for later.

"Not that I really don't want to ride off into the sunset with you in one of these cars here, but I'm ready to grab some lunch."

"Let's do that," Ava concedes.

*

Mulholland Drive slices through the Santa Monica Mountains and offers pristine views of L.A., all the way to Ventura County and the entire valley behind it. I park along one of the rest spots, grab our bag of food purchased from Korean Kuts, a food truck that sells sausage and kimchi, and guide Ava on a hike down Los Liones Trail. It's a gentle incline that winds for about a mile before coming to a stop near the south end of East Topanga Fireroad. I'm actually not much of a hiker, but from what I researched, this trail is lush and popular, with pristine views and mostly smooth paths designed for amateur trekkers.

Ava follows behind me. I purposely don't say much, letting both of us learn to become comfortable in common silence, and, of course, some self-selected music playing through my portable wireless speaker.

"You don't mind, do you?" I refer to the song I started off with, "Under Cover of Darkness" by The Strokes.

"Perfect." Ava confirms. "The Strokes are shrill."

For about twenty minutes Ava and I listen to nature, The Strokes, and other songs in my, what I have labeled, *whimsical* mix. We pick at leaves and flowers, spot squirrels, and sigh at the view of all the city mayhem just down the hill. The structures spiking up from downtown look as tiny as little Lego pieces, the horizon and the stretch of boulevards veining from the city's architecture at a safe distance. We're not far from that, the place we live, but even this mild separation helps with gaining perspective. I find our spot near the end of the hike, under the mild fall sun, lay a blanket down over the ground and pitch our picnic.

"The famous Mulholland Highway," I say, circling my arms around like a salesman showcasing a room of furniture. "You know these mountains inspired a movie called *Mulholland*."

Ava scans the dirt and rocks around. "Does anyone die of snake venom in that movie?"

I snicker. "Not that I know of."

Ava and I take in the scenery all around us, sneaking bites of our foreign delicacies.

"So, is this nature or what?" I ask in a facetious way.

Ava shakes her head, and I begin to as well. "Nah, not really," we say simultaneously and take another bite of our sausage and kimchi.

"It's just so forced," she critiques after swallowing. "I mean, I appreciate it, but it's sort-of nature—not really nature-nature. Know what I mean? It's faux nature. It's people wanting to think they have a serene side to them, but it doesn't quite work with the urban all around it."

"*Faux* nature. I couldn't have said it better," I agree,while chewing the rest of my food. "Um...I have a confession," I declare.

"I'm not a priest, but go ahead. I'll do my best."

"I'm not really into hiking. I just thought we could try something like this because I thought it'd be kind of fun...different." Honesty is something the PUA would be warning me against if he could speak to me right now.

Ava can't hide her chortle. "Look at us." She's referring to our city style clothing. "You think I couldn't tell?"

I join her in guffawing at our being out of place, reiterating what she said a moment ago. "But I do agree with you. This isn't really *getting away*."

The fated silence that the PUA warned me about is present. That means I've created an atmosphere that isn't casual. This might be where Ava terminates the date.

"I don't mean to pry, but, is *getting away* something you dream of doing?"

"Dream of? No. Plan on? Yes." I sigh, waiting for Ava to comment, but she doesn't. I add, "Sorry to get all profound on you. I guess this whole faux-nature thing inspires a different side of me."

"It does that to people."

"Is that good or bad?"

"It's cute. I like it."

"Is *cute* the equivalent of an A, B or C? I'm kind of feeling like it's a C."

"C? No way. I meant it like a B-plus."

"But not an A?"

"A's are for something totally extraordinary and unique...reserved for experiences that could only happen if you know that person."

"How can I boost this B-plus to an A? I'm no slacker, you know."

Ava thinks for a moment, then a grin buds across her face. "Stand up."

"I already am."

"I mean do your stand-up thing."

"My *stand-up thing*? You mean one of my comic routines?"

Ava sits on the blanket, Indian style, and looks up at me. "Yep. Just for me."

I take the challenge. "Okay."

Performing for one person with the same verve as being onstage is difficult, and so is trying new material on the spot, but I am going to attempt both.

I peer down on the blanket, Ava's leftovers and the packaging strewn on the wooly thread. "Hi, my audience of one, I'm Sole Eaby."

"Hi, Sole Eaby."

"You know the audience isn't really supposed to talk back to the comedian."

"Why not?"

"Because when you do, it just means you're asking for the comedian to roast all over you."

"Oh, I can handle that," Ava says.

"Okay," I say. "Here goes."

"So I was thinking about food. And, I have to say, these days everyone loves food. Food has grown into an obsession. It's no longer just fuel for your body. It's a freaking lifestyle. It's the equivalent of what gas is to a car, yet we talk about it like it's a

Picasso on a plate. Imagine going to ARCO and fueling up a car with the same mentality as eating food."

I change my voice to mimic a lady. "'Oh my stars, you have to go try that new 87 octane. It's so savory and rich. My car loves it. It's got this nice cinnamon flavor to it.'"

Ava laughs.

"It's true. We are totally obsessed with food. Yes, food is wonderful, but it's just food. Or is it? Now we have what is known as the *psychology of food* apparently. They now say what you eat reveals truth about somebody's character and personality. And I guess there's some truth to that.

"I was in line ordering some food the other day, and the line was long. While waiting, I heard this heavy breathing. You know how *large* people sound just standing there, taking in air." I inhale and exhale loudly and slowly. "It sounds like...like Darth Vader."

To exaggerate the effect, I put my hand over my mouth to create a haunting echo and then I breathe slowly and deliberately like the evil villain does in the movies. Ava shifts on the blanket, mirth blooming all over her and spasms of laughter coming from her.

"When I turned around, the psychology of food was confirmed. The guy, Darth I'll call him, turned and said to me, 'Luke, I am your father. And as your grossly obese and overweight father, I tell you to obey me and...'" I scream, my Sam Kinnison signature. "Get out of my freaking way so I can order first!'"

Ava combusts before me, turning to ashes any doubt of my comedic skills. "That's so hilarious. You just made this stuff up?"

Inside, my ego dilates to the size of a giant Cyclops, and I feel invincible, especially because the jokes I told have not been refined. They've not been crafted for the stage just yet. I've been thinking about them, but have yet to really hew them out. "I just turn what I read into jokes."

"Well, keep turning then. Encore! Encore!"

Just as I am ready to go off on another joke, my mind goes back to the past.

It used to be that Cedro would at least try to show support, if only absent-mindedly. I remember Cedro and I as he would perch himself on our living room sofa or, in the summertime, on our backyard patio furniture and listen to me work out my jokes. Even then, I knew his mind was somewhere else, probably exploring the potential for life (namely his own) on some imagined planet. I knew because even when something was not funny at all, he would still fake a laugh. One time I said, "I just killed someone today. Sliced him up pretty good." He went into his fake laughter while keeping his head buried in some how-to book. He's one hundred percent gung-ho on that search-for-life exploration. Will he ever find the life he is looking for? Will he ever notice the life that's right in front of him?

"Sole, are you all right?" Ava notices me having drifted off.

I shake my head. "Fine...fine. Sorry."

"Old ghosts?"

"If the still-living can be considered ghosts..."

"Sorry. I didn't mean to conjure them up."

"*Him*. Not *them*. It's just one ghost."

I spend a few moments retailing the events of my somewhat tragic life, mainly involving how my mom left and how Cedro's been checked out since I got old enough to recognize the difference between a dad who's physically present and mentally engaged, and a dad who's just a warm body but completely disconnected from me. I remind her of the culminating event of Cedro's midlife crisis, at least as far as it concerns me: how I came home after being robbed at gunpoint, and all Cedro cared about were his business margins.

"How are you doing with that anyway? That psychopath had a gun to you and you seem fine. I know I don't know you that intensely, but most people would turn a little wacky over something like that."

"I guess the way I see it, the guy was pretty straight up about everything. That was our only connection. He wanted money and that was that. It's worse with people like Cedro...people you have to keep dealing with and who are just all over the map...totally disjointed from what's important—putting money before family."

"Sorry. I really hope you guys can make amends."

It's time to change the subject, time to do what I always do, and that's laugh off everything and make serious matters into jokes. "How about your encore?"

"Please do," Ava nods once with a chirpy smile.

"Well, I'm young, and that means I'm, you know, looking around. Not necessarily a *soul* mate or anything—just looking."

Ava raises one brow to note the corny Sole-soul pun and to pose a look of skepticism. She doesn't quite realize that when comedians include jokes about themselves, most of the time they are fictionalizing their lives and the stuff just isn't true.

"It's nothing personal," I play along. "It's part of the routine. You have to learn to separate my jokes from me."

"Still learning," she winks.

"So, in this whole dating ecosystem, I have a real problem with the animalistic concept of the trial and error method of looking for a mate. I mean it's so time consuming. Meet a girl, impress her, gab, strategize, and then try to get lucky. It's freaking exhausting, especially if you have anything else to do. If you're a freaking tiger—great! All you do is paw around all day in the jungle. Not me. I don't have the kind of time. Or those big freaking paws.

"So, like any smart young man in the modern culture, I've learned to do what all wise entrepreneurs do: outsource. And by outsource I mean I've hired someone to find me my future mate. Someone who knows what all men want: Mattel!"

Ava's shocked into hilarity, taken by the frankness of the joke and the humor all at once.

"You might be thinking I'm a chauvinist, but I can assure you I am not. I simply say the truth. Mattel made Barbie and did a fine job—let's get that straight right now. The movie industry is a billion dollar industry, and, last time I checked, the girls the guys want and the ones girls want to look like do resemble Barbie. There's a reason they're on the A-list, and it's not because they're great actresses. *A* is not for *actress*. *A* is for...well...you get me."

Ava plays the dissenter. "That's not true. That's just too much now."

I address her as if I am holding a mike. "Oh, we have someone who disagrees. I don't even have to know you to say this, but I'm going to go out on a limb here and bet you're the girl who says, 'You know, Barbie's measurements aren't real. No woman can actually be that way and walk.'" My whiny girl voice solidifies my point.

Ava can't help but break down into fits of joy. "You got me. Guilty. I'm that girl."

I sit down next to Ava. "Shouldn't girls just accept that Barbie looks dang good and that they're just spiteful because all their men want them to look that way?"

"Uh, no."

"Uh, yes."

"So if all guys want girls to look that way, why do they settle for girls that don't?"

"Desperation. Guilt. Insecurity. Guys are like fisherman. Some stick to what's available close to shore and what will bring a small, steady income when they sell their catch in the market. Others go deep out to sea, gamble and think they have what it takes to bring in the catch they really want, the one that will bring them the big bank."

"Did you just use a George Clooney metaphor?"

"*The Perfect Storm.* Can't deny its truths."

"No I can't. And you can't deny that girls are always going to hate on Barbie until you guys stop wanting us to look like her."

I rub my hands together the way a thief would in front of his treasure. "This will be the one war that will never experience armistice."

After a breath of the Hollywood Hills air, Ava suggests, "So are we at war?"

"War?" Here I pause. I want Ava to know that as much as we banter, this small part is a bit romantic. "You look way better than Barbie. In fact, Barbie is the one hating on you. If it were up to me I'd make you the standard."

"You're pretty straight forward. Did they teach you that in guy school?"

"Is it too much?"

Ava thinks, letting me hang on her pursed lips until they open. "No. It's refreshing to know exactly where you stand."

"Evolving, remember? Like I said, I don't like misdirection."

Again, keeping with the casual theme, I take my cue and drift into Ava. This time I let the kiss linger, letting casual melt away into something more chemical.

Maybe I won't need to register for the PUA's premium subscription.

CHAPTER FOURTEEN

You can tell a lot about a fellow's character
by his way of eating jellybeans.

~ Ronald Reagan

When I called Ava to see if she wanted to catch one of my shows that had just booked me two hours before the opening act, she said she was with a girlfriend of hers. *Bingo*, I thought. She and her friend could meet up with Yoke and I. I started by asking Ava a few questions about her friend. When she asked why I was co curious, I told her about my eccentric friend Yoke and my quasi-diagnosis of him having Asperger Syndrome[9].

---

[9] Yoke doesn't really have Asperger Syndrome, at least I don't think he has an official diagnosis, but he does display some catastrophic social practices that I'll call Awkwardness. I know that's probably not going to be a legitimate clinical term found in *The Diagnostic and Statistical Manual of Mental Disorders* (DSM), but it doesn't mean Yoke isn't capable of turning a perfectly good situation like we have right now—two willing girls talking with two willing guys—into a total catastrophe. For the record, Awkwardness, in my non-professional opinion, should be in the DSM.

That's my way of saying that he is completely and utterly weird and awkward in social scenarios.

"He's not going to scare her, is he?" Ava was referring to her friend, Katherine.

"I hope not." I had to be honest, thus no guaranteeing that he wouldn't.

Ava agreed and said that we could all meet at L.A. Café. She said it might work out since her friend is understanding and open-minded. Does that mean she's ugly?

The rush from being on stage doesn't dissipate immediately. It's like a very slow leak that takes a while to lose all that's inside. As a result, I'm pretty jacked right now, sitting in my car and driving to meet Ava and her friend at L.A. Café and making sure that Yoke isn't going to back out on this part of the evening.

"There's someone I want you to meet," I say to him. "So don't even think of not showing up and ruining the evening. Remember our talk?"

"No *'how've you been?'* or anything? I haven't talked to you much this week and that's how you greet me."

"Just shut up and be there. Okay? I told you I was going to set you up." To seal the deal, I play the best friend/sentimental card, i.e. that it's important to me for my best friend to meet a girl I am fast into. "Come on. You're my best friend. I don't want to double with anyone else other than you."

"Let me ask my parents."

"Don't give me that. You know they're going to chauffer you anywhere you want."

Yoke doesn't drive or even have his license, but he doesn't need to. His parents are always willing to tote him around anywhere, especially if he tells them he's going to be with me— not that I am the paragon of absolute virtue or anything like that.

I am not, and I'm certain Yoke's mom and dad are very well aware of this; but what Yoke's parents are also very well aware of is that their boy doesn't make too many friends, and, since I am his one and only good friend, they figure that they might as well encourage this. They're smart for doing this. The alternative is letting Yoke spend countless moments alone, in his room, painting his nails black, and becoming a follower of some serial killer sadist on the Internet and thereby becoming his protégé, copycatting all his previous crimes and enjoying his new name as *The Yokamaniac* or whatever the media will title his murderous identity. Maybe that's a bit much, but my point is, Yoke needs me, and his parents know that.

*

L.A. Café is one of my favorite late-night haunts—open 24-hours and infused with a vibe that is ultra-renaissance. If you're any type of artist, musician, or actor then most likely you've found your way here sometime after midnight and before dawn.

"Hey, what's up?" I greet the girls and sit opposite of them in the booth across the table.

"So, are you sure about this?" I hear Ava's friend, Katherine, whisper from across the table.

Ava assures Katherine in the same incognito tone. "It'll be fine."

Katherine has a lake of lush hair pouring down to just below her shoulders, the contrast of grayish green eyes against the brown quite an exhibition. The features of her face lay symmetrically, so she is definitely attractive. She does have one setback, however. She's probably pushing a size 7, meaning she isn't what you would call bikini-model ready like Ava. This is probably good for Yoke because if Katherine were a perfect ten from head to toe, a) he may not be able to get a word out and b) she probably would have about five hundred other options for the evening that don't include meeting some guy named Yoke.

We exchange useless small talk for a few minutes, then Yoke arrives.

"Hey, guys," Yoke plops himself next to me since Ava and Katherine are planted together across the rectangular wooden slab. For once, he's got perfect timing.

"Hey," I say nonchalantly.

"Hi, Yoke," Ava says. "It's really good to meet you. Sole's said a lot about you."

"You too." Yoke, standing over me, is slashing me with the hard cruelty in his eyes.

Truth is I haven't been saying too much about anything to Yoke. After he figures that the only way to truly kill me is to actually pick up one of the knives on the table and stab with me it, Yoke decides to sit down, not offering his hand for a standard shake to anyone.

Yoke has never been in this position before. He's never been close to having a conversation with a dishy girl.

"Yoke, this is Katherine. Katherine, Yoke."

"Hi, Yoke," Katherine smiles.

"Hi," Yoke raps another curt response, the awkward greeting now officially part of the transcript.

I take this as my prod. "So..."

This doesn't work either. There's another ungraceful silence at our table.

"So how did it go tonight?" Ava asks me. To include Katherine in the conversation Ava says, "He's a comedian, remember?"

"I think it worked out," I respond.

"Are you funny?" Katherine jams me up.

I don't know how to answer. Not wanting to unleash a nuclear assault of sarcasm toward Ava's good friend, I decide on being genial. "I hope so."

"He's hilarious," Yoke boasts, sounding irritated that he has to defend my sense of humor.

"I try to be," I suggest.

"What makes him so funny?" Katherine challenges.

"It's not *what*. It's *that*," Yoke banters. "His reputation is unquestionable. Because of him Marshall has a comedy club, and we compete against other schools."

"Sorry. I didn't know," Katherine concedes, flying a white paper napkin in the air. "I surrender."

"He just gets a little intense with the subject." Smiling, I apologize for Yoke, who doesn't even try to soothe the situation.

Yoke is actually 99% nice guy, but, as stated, he has what I call a 1% autistic side, those inadvertent quirks that are about as timely as a suicidal terrorist attack on a placid, street side café. When someone conjures Yoke's internal guerrilla-gone-wild, like Katherine just did, and unintentionally brings it out, the 1% beast in him roars. Well, it's not really a roar. It's non-threatening and mostly just a bother, like a chipmunk's rant because someone took his nuts; but still, it's extremely annoying.

"Marshall High?" Katherine asks.

By the slight discomposure about Katherine, I know that Ava didn't quite explain to her that we are a few months younger than they are. Not wanting to be guilty of the same social crime Yoke is—awkwardness—Katherine recovers with a playful smile. "So, what's comedy club?" she submits.

"It's like improv, right?" Ava submits.

"Nothing like it," I begin. "Improv is unplanned and takes a different kind of training. Stand up is labor intensive...a bit smarter. You have to create your script and then bring it to life before a live crowd. It's closer to theater or film in that respect."

"He's really good," Ava brandishes.

"As I already mentioned," Yoke insists.

Katherine speaks before Yoke's insistence can taint the energy around the table. "So, Sole, you sort of pioneered the whole program at Marshall?"

"That's what I said earlier," Yoke responds with disgust.

I elbow Yoke under the table, the bony point right into his side. "Like I said, he's just really intense...really into the whole thing." My subtle rescue attempts of trying to apologize and cover for his abrasiveness are not enough in this situation. I needed to use a little force.

"Right," Katherine notes with wide eyes, unable to hide her shock at Yoke's pushy demeanor.

To break up the stale malaise that has crusted over the table due in part to Mr. Rude and Obtrusive Himself, aka Yoke, Ava asks, "Well, I'm going to refill. Would you like something?"

"Sure," I say. "Surprise me, please. Thank you."

"Anyone else?" Ava requests.

Katherine rises from her chair. "I need a refill, too." She says that, but what she really needs is relief from the tension Yoke created. "I'll come with."

Now it's Yoke and me sitting next to each other.

"Dude, sit on the other side," I instruct.

"It's not a big deal. Besides," Yoke suggests and scoots closer to me. "I like sitting close to you."

"What the—dude, get over there."

Yoke laughs and moves over to where Ava and Katherine were sitting. "Got you," he says.

Before shooting back a comment, I realize that this is the first time Yoke actually has spun something and turned it on its funny side. I start to laugh along with Yoke. "That's pretty good."

"I've been saving that one," he says. "Comedy Club's been helping me out."

"Hey, man, that's great. Pretty soon you'll be doing real stand-up," I return.

Yoke returns to honest and serious phrases. "Trying to get there. But this is good for starters."

"Yes it is," I encourage him. I know I should correct his misbehavior from a moment ago, but like I said, that's like trying to scold or correct an autistic kid. They won't get it any more than Yoke would.

"So, uh, is she, like, officially your girlfriend now?" Yoke interrogates.

This is when I realize that I haven't mentioned to my supposed best friend much about Ava. "I don't know."

"You don't know?"

"Look, dude, when you start to get into the girl scene, you have to realize things are sensitive and complicated. You could ruin it by trying to put labels on your love."

"Wanting clarity is a label? Maybe this whole thing isn't for me then."

"Don't tap out yet, man. At least try it. You'll figure it out pretty quick. I know it."

"Just like I had to figure out for myself that you're pretty heavy into this Ava girl?"

"Come on, Yoke."

"You are supposed to be my *best* friend, right?" I wait for Yoke to even out the discomfort between us. He makes no such attempt, except to say, "That's two things you've held back from me. I might have wanted to hear how you felt about her."

"Dude, loosen your bra strap. Besides, I don't know how I feel about her."

"Yes you do. And I don't sound like a whiny girl; I sound like a victim. You're the one who said, 'I promise I won't leave you in the dark anymore.' Remember?" Yoke's banjo twang impersonation of me reveals his irritation.

"I didn't say it like that."

"There you go, focusing on the non-issue and totally ignoring the point."

Yoke's right, and if I am going to show any signs that somewhere inside of me is a compassionate human being, I should retract. I sip my coffee then declare, "You're right. I'm sorry. I just got busy and...well..."

"I get it. I just wanted *you* to acknowledge it." Yoke looks at his watch. "So, is this the time when you tell me that you're going to back out of the Cashmere, too?"

Shoot. The Cashmere Classic. It's coming up.

I should be more into it than I am, but I'm not, at least not until the hosts up the ante on the prizes for the winner, like maybe some cold, hard mazuma or a prime time spot on a comedy network.

That's when an idea hits me, and I think I regain my interest in what will be my last high school competition. "No, I haven't forgotten," I say.

"Whatever."

I try to recover, needing to play this next hand right. I have a wild idea brewing in my head, and I have to throw Yoke a bone if I want to better my chances of getting something back in return. "Look, I'll pick you up Friday night. We'll ride up there together and have some fun."

"A road trip?"

"Yep."

"Mr. Kevin won't let us."

"Mr. Kevin won't let *you* guys."

"That's right. You get special privileges."

"Something like that," I say, and sip proudly from my blueberry brew loaded with Splenda and non-dairy creamer.

Yoke continues. "He says the van is leaving at five in the evening on Friday. No exceptions."

I wink. "Don't you stress about such trivialities, my good friend. Mr. Kevin will let you. Trust me."

Yoke smiles, wanting to believe I won't let him down this time. "All right then."

"Hey, Yoke," I add. Yoke knows I'm going to ask him for a favor, but at least he doesn't lose that smile. "Don't tell your parents that I'm not planning to go back home. I'm sure they know everything's not well, but...well..."

"Got it." This is where Yoke's friendship and understanding reminds me of who he really is to me despite how badly he stumbles in front of girls.

"Thanks."

"You know my parents love you. In fact, they'd probably rather have you than me there anyway."

"That's also most likely true."

Yoke enjoys the farce and joins me in the playful mood for a moment, then turns back to the topic of me staying with him. "But seriously, how long do you think?"

Yoke knows me too well. I don't deny it. "I don't know."

Yoke winks. "Well, you can stay as long as you'd like, just as long as we can share a mattress."

"You're a disgusting man, Yokester. Do you know that?"

When I look up, I see Ava and Katherine, who plops down next to Yoke. Ava is holding a plate in her hand. She sits down next to me, sliding closer until our hips almost meet in the booth-style bench, and sets the plate down in the middle of all us. Four forks spike out like spokes in a wheel from the circular dish.

"It's the fish-of-the-day plate," Ava attests. "Dive in."

"*Dive* in? That's a joke, right?" Yoke surmises.

"Ooh, you're quick," Ava fends. "They were actually getting rid of it."

"Of course they were," Yoke squeezes his rudeness in again. "It's almost midnight. Who wants to eat that?"

Ava explains. "They said there was nothing wrong with it except that they cooked a wrong order and all they can do with it is throw it out or give it away. I told them I'd take it."

"You can try it first," Yoke challenges. "Who knows what they did to it?"

Ava bravely slips her fork into the soft fillet and cradles some in the prongs. She brings it to her mouth, inserts, chews, and gulps. "Mmm. Pretty good."

"See, Yoke, you worry for nothing," I say.

"What's the Cashmere?" Ava asks.

"You heard us from over there?" I wonder. "Wow."

"Actually I heard you from right there." Ava points to a spot.

I turn and look to see where her finger is guiding me. It's a tile square about ten feet away from us. How much did she hear? When I accept the fact that I probably talk louder than most people, due to my stage persona that has clearly seeped into my normal personality, I turn back to the table and go on as if she heard nothing other than the current topic. "The Cashmere is short for The Cashmere Classic. It's an annual high school stand-up competition."

"Isn't stand-up something covered in physical education?" Ava's bad puns are an attempt to shrink herself in hopes that everyone, namely Katherine and Yoke, can relax.

"That's funny," Yoke blurts and follows it up with belly-busting laughter. He thinks small chops of wit are the apex of humor. Poor him.

Katherine rolls her eyes, utterly sorry that she came. As awkward as Yoke is, I don't want him not to get the girl. Once again, I am in rescue-recovery mode.

"Yoke didn't mention he's actually performing with the club at the Cashmere."

Katherine's mouth rolls, her pursed lips forming a curious expression of disbelief. She says to Yoke, "You? You are?"

"Does that surprise you?"

"Actually, yes." Katherine has no problem dispelling the truth. "You're just so...I don't know...serious?"

"The way you say *serious*," Yoke mocks Katherine's girly accent of the word. "Is that a question or a description?"

I look at Ava. We're enjoying our friends poke at one another. However, before this night detonates and there's nothing left of us but limbs and parts all over the place, I widen my eyes, implying to Ava that I need to intervene. "You know, Katherine, Yoke is actually pretty funny."

"Actually?" Yoke jabs at me now. "That's kind of backhanded."

"Kind of? No. It is. Nevertheless, I meant what I said. You're a pretty funny guy, all things considered."

"You're serious?" he asks.

Ava, Katherine, and I begin to laugh.

"What?" Yoke asks, not getting anything in return but our continuous snubbing. I'm expecting Yoke to rise up and call his parents to pick him up. Instead, he does what I've never seen him do. He begins to deride himself, chuckling at his own irony.

"I just asked if you were serious about saying I was funny. I'll fall on that one."

We're all loose now, conjoined through humor. More importantly, Yoke has grown before my eyes. He not only grasped the comedy that irony brings, he was able, for the first time as far as I'm concerned, to laugh at himself. Normally he would have turned completely irascible. This is refreshing.

"So I was thinking..." This might be the time to seal the deal with Ava and Katherine. I haven't even mentioned it to Ava because, like I said, I'm not overly excited about it since high school trophies seem a bit insignificant as far as prizes go for me at this stage in my life. However, I do see a personal gain surfacing before me. "Maybe you girls would like to come to the Cashmere."

"Sure. Where?" Ava inquiries.

"Palo Alto."

"As in up north Palo Alto?" asks Katherine.

"That's the one," I tag.

Ava and Katherine look at each other. I turn to look at Yoke. His face is painted with uncertainty. To assure him that I know what I am doing, I wink with my left eye, the one that the girls can't see from their profile view of me.

The girls have not spoken, and I am not sure how silent negotiations can be such an intense interaction, but apparently Ava and Katherine exchanged some serious ideas between each other without saying a word.

"Sure. Just give me the place and time and I'll drive Katherine and I," Ava notes.

Again I turn to Yoke and smile at him in reassurance before looking back across the table. "I was thinking more like a road trip."

Katherine is almost in disbelief. "All of us? Together? In one car?"

"Yep. Six hours in a car with highway and Yokester here," I say to Katherine.

Yoke is coyly looking down, making me take full responsibility for this fiasco. Ava and I aren't quite a full blown couple yet, but we've had enough time for her to feel more comfortable about the decision. Ava and Katherine look at each other. They say nothing out loud, but there is more serious communication going on in their eyes. Without a word ever coming out of their mouths, they've reached a verdict. "Okay," Ava voices. "But we'll definitely get our own room."

Yoke finally enters the talks, wanting to reinforce his good guy persona in this discussion. "Oh yeah, sure. Of course. I mean we wouldn't have it any other way."

"I don't know," Katherine objects.

"It might be fun," Ava counters.

"Might be?" I respond with light drollery. "If you want, Yoke and I will sign an affidavit that declares we are not masked murderers or part-time serial killers. We can even get it notarized if it'll make you feel better."

"And turn in a copy to L.A.P.D.?" Katherine chuckles.

I think she's convinced.

"Okay then. It's settled. Road trip and comedy," Ava confirms.

"To road trip and comedy," I say, holding up my cup of java.

Ava, Katherine, and Yoke adjoin their cups with mine over the middle of the table. We toast and sip.

CHAPTER FIFTEEN

Cookies are the sweetest little bit of comfort food.
They are very...personal.
~ Sandra Lee

The blue haze aglow from the television in the master bedroom is evidence that Cedro has most likely drifted off to sleep while lying on his bed. He parked his food truck in the corner of the driveway, leaving room for me to park my car, The Curse of the Maroon. This must be coincidence. Among other things, I haven't told him that I purchased a car.

I really don't want to go inside and, just as I'm thinking of backing out of the driveway, my phone buzzes. It's an incoming text from Ava.

PLEAES DON'T BACK OUT! LEAVE THE DOOR OPEN. IF ANYTHING JUST DO IT FOR YOURSELF :)

Ava has made it clear that the worst thing I could do to myself is not try to do what I can to *leave the door open* between Cedro and me. That's what she keeps saying about the issue. *Leave the door open.* Why? Because if I fail to even try to reach out to Cedro and include him in my life, I'll accumulate a heap of guilt inside

161

of me, like dirty laundry that never gets washed. That heap will then be something I'll have to carry with me for the rest of my life. When putting it that way, the stakes are quite high. What's a decent guy to do?[10]

If I want to absolve myself of any and all future guilt, I have to try to get Cedro to come see me perform for my last high school competition, my last stand as an amateur, in Palo Alto. I'm at the edge of adolescence, and when I go into the next stages of my life, I don't want the regret of a sour parent relationship weighing me down. If I do everything I can do, then I can always know that it wasn't my fault, and knowing that is quite a powerful bit of knowledge for my psychological state. If Cedro chooses to not do his part and come see me perform, then that's all on him.

Armed with the right disposition, in one fell swoop, I cross the threshold of the front door and scud for Cedro's room, like a phantom floating across the floor. Unlike a phantom, however, I am present and in full form, right at the foot of Cedro's bed, wearing my Jack Purcell's, jeans, and customary leather jacket. I wish I were an invisible being right now.

Though I expected to see Cedro crashed out, what I find is an unoccupied mattress, the bedding tossed and wrinkled. The blue haze from the television illuminates the darkened space around me. I turn to see what Cedro was watching. It's Jeremy Renner in *The Bourne Legacy*, the scene where he is in the Philippines, in the chemistry lab, and three armed, Filipino security guards are trying to subdue him. Renner's character, Aaron Cross, is manhandling them as if they were children. The fact that Cedro was, once again, watching this recording through

---

[10] For the record: I do consider myself a *decent* guy.

his DVR means he must have become inspired by watching Renner's tactical ploys.

It's not real, Cedro.

Figuring as much, I walk outside to the backyard patio where Cedro trains. Even though it is late into the night, I know he is probably shadow punching and kicking three invisible Filipino guards. Yep. As I open the French doors, I see him under the rope of lights that surrounds the covered veranda wailing away at the not-really-there assailants. From what I can tell, he's taken out two invisible guys and is in the midst of obliterating a third—all with his bare hands. Wait...he added one last kick to the third guy. Now three not-really-there Filipinos are writhing in pain on the backyard patio. For emphasis, Cedro acts as if he is standing over one of the men and holding a gun to him, the gun that Cedro supposedly stripped from him. In his tank top, Cedro's flexed arms are taut, showing all the ink crawling down his toned skin.

His moves were quick and looked extraordinary, but all I could think is, Why wasn't it him who was robbed that night? Maybe he could have had a chance to put his badass persona to work.

What a crank.

"So, are they dead?" I ask about the invisible Filipino men.

Cedro goes along with the act. "The two on the ground are unconscious. This guy, though, if he doesn't shut his mouth, is going to get a bullet in the head."

"So your fingers are gun barrels. I see. What caliber?"

".45 calibers of pure lethal, thank you."

"That's great, Dad. Really. But we need to talk," I pronounce in my best raspy whisper, just like the spies do in movies.

"All right," Cedro agrees gruffly. "Give me a minute."

"If you shoot him, make sure you clean up the blood," I say, heading back inside. "I'll be in the living room."

Since one minute might turn into a few, maybe ten, I sink into the sofa and decide to bide my time by surfing the Internet on my phone. I search MSN for some yellow journalistic headlines which always gives me Hail Mary material for my routines. Hail Mary jokes are just like last second, length-of-the-field touchdown passes in football. When a comic needs a last second score with the audience, he's got to have some random, trendy, quick-draw stuff that he can shoot out from the hip. As I read the headlines, I practice commenting on each one in my mind, entwining the information like a seamstress until it becomes a joke I might use on stage.

MSN is good for stuff like this because they always post the results from otherwise useless polls that people read to make themselves feel smart. For example, some people will quote a statistic that goes, "Research says that the Millennial generation (that's mine) is 37% more narcissistic than the Baby Boomers." Uh, yeah, that's because we're smart enough to realize that instead of living for the *next* generation that will *not* in the least be grateful or care at all about our grandparents' sacrifices, we're just going to cut out the middle man and live for ourselves. What's wrong with that?

Another useless headline I click on is "Top Ten Things That Men Love about a Woman." That's just a preposterous poll and, no matter what the articles says, anyone knows this is based on lies, even if a man wrote it. Reason: There's no way a man is going to admit the truth in an article meant for the world to see. Either a woman wrote the article or a wannabe man who's had his spine surgically removed by a domineering woman did.

The article suggests that what men really want in a woman are cute and fluffy things, such as, number one, "Her Ability to Detect Our Crap." That may sound good on the Internet and bring out the warm-fuzzies, but in real life—*ehh*. Not true. I'm not a full-fledged man yet, but I know that I have a general idea of what I do and don't want in a girl, and one of them is that I don't want any girl of mine detecting when I'm trying to pitch her a heap of garbage. Would I want Ava to know when I do? Of course not! Otherwise, why on earth would I have pitched a piece of trash to her in the first place?

Here's another one men supposedly love: "Her Sweet Tooth." Wrong again. Men don't think it's at all *sweet* when their girl stuffs balls of chocolate in their mouth. Why? For one reason and one reason only: if a girl indulges her sweet tooth, she'll! Get! Fat! And no man wants a fat woman. I sure don't. How do I know? The television. Hollywood. The porn industry. The cultural standard. My hormones. My eyes. Etcetera, etcetera. The expectation for a girl is sheer hotness and glossy beauty, whether people (or I should say *women*) like it or not. If a few noble souls out there want to demonize the ideal woman—news flash! It doesn't change the ideal or my desires.

On and on the list goes until the top ten things men supposedly love about women is complete. When I finish reading, I let my phone drop to my chest and slouch down deeper into the sunken sofa cushions. I ponder, continuing to rewrite the article in my head from the point of view of a man who actually has the moxie to say what guys really want and feel. I imagine all guys' top ten would go something like this:

What Men Love about a Woman.

1. Her Utter Dedication to Maintaining Her Miss Universe Hotness at All Costs, Including After Childbirth. That means

that if my woman doesn't want to do this anymore, I'm moving on to the next one who does.

2. Her Willingness to Always Vie for Her Man's Attention through Priming and Style, Never Taking Her Appearance and Performance for Granted Because Other Women Are Out There Appearing Their Best and Performing to Get Your Man's Attention. See number one.

3. Her Attitude: Or Should We Say, 'Lose the Tude, Girlies!' It's Not Cute and, By The Way, If A Little Woman Thinks She Can Roar At A Man, Then Ladies, Don't Cry Abuse When a Man Roars Back. Or Did You Not Know a Man's Attitude is Bigger Than Yours? I guess I have a lot to say on that issue, too. It probably has something to do with the fact that the main female figurehead in my life deserted me before I knew how to spell my own name. Does that sound like psychobabble? Maybe. But it doesn't mean it's not true.

4. Her—

"So how's it going?" Cedro asks.

It's been eleven minutes since I left Cedro in the backyard with his invisible Filipino guards, but at least I spent my time wisely, creating and lodging backup material in my head. "Going," I answer.

"Good," he says, wiping off his perspiration with a towel. The conversation starts off stilted, flowing about as smoothly as someone trying to ride a unicycle for the first time. "So I noticed your car."

"Yeah?" I rebut dismissively.

"Yeah. Neat color."

Now I know he's lying and hasn't noticed much. Why was I expecting more than this? No understanding male would ever think that The Curse of the Maroon is neat. It's a sad excuse for an SUV and is typically owned by average, middle class families who want a real SUV but can't afford one in the likeness of, say, a Land Rover or even an Expedition. Its entire existence is an insult to a teenage boy. "You think?"

"Yeah, sure. Why not?"

I don't even answer that. "Look, Dad, I know we haven't talked in a couple of weeks..."

Cedro crashes my introduction. "I know, son, and I'm sorry about that. It's my fault. I feel terrible. I was just frustrated and I expressed myself wrongly." As an ex-teacher at a sophisticated high school, he still retains his proper use of grammar when he's trying to be sincere. Most people would say *wrong*. He says *wrongly*, the correct adverb form.

I want to believe Cedro. I do. It's just difficult. Like an attorney, I dissect his semantics to see what truth holds once I'm done shredding up his thoughts.

I feel terrible. If he felt so terrible why hasn't he gone out of his way to address this with me? Why didn't he try to make it to my last gig? Why hasn't he tried talking to me or calling my cell?

I was just frustrated. No way. He's not *just* frustrated. He's in the throes of a midlife crisis and doesn't even recognize the damage he's causing. By trying so hard to cure himself he's cursing me as a by-product. That's the irony. When someone in his shoes tries to gain the life they really want for themselves, they end up losing the one they have.

I expressed myself wrongly. Of course he did. Admitting he cares more about money or a business than the life of his own son is constitutionally barbaric, right along the lines of treason, which is punishable by death. So then why hasn't Mr. I Expressed Myself Wrongly tried to right his wrong? When I poke holes in his apology, my guard is on Def-Con 4 Red Alert.

"Okay," I start on, discarding his apology like moldy cheese. "Well, if you're sincere, here's your chance to, I don't know, make it up to me." I watch Cedro's face, his disheveled hair and grimy shadow building up like moss not able to hide the way his muscles tighten to a cringe. "You're not *that* sorry, are you?"

"I haven't even said anything, Sole."

"Neither have I, yet your face is saying everything."

"Okay, look, I'm sorry for that, too. Tell me how I can make it up to you."

"I have a road trip this weekend. It's the Cashmere Classic in Palo Alto."

"The Cashmere?" he asks.

I've already told him about how legendary the Cashmere Classic is. I told him last year even, and he still couldn't make the time to go. He missed seeing me take third place. I won't bother now with specifics. "It's the Super Bowl of high school stand-up. I took third place last year. Remember?" I point to the trophy roosting on top of the mantle.

"Of course," he blurbs.

But I know he doesn't.

"You want me to go up north?" Cedro asks. "To drive you?"

It's impossible to refrain from withholding all disgust. I try, but some bleeds into my tone. "I have a car. Remember? The maroon thing?"

"You're going to drive it all the way up there? Are you sure it's fine?"

"No, I'm not sure it's fine, but it's the only car I have."

"You can borrow mine."

"I don't want to borrow yours. That's why I bought mine. I don't want to borrow anything from you anymore. And, anyway, none of this is the point."

"Right," he utters. "You want me to go."

"Yes. To go. Just to go—I don't know, for me. Just to go for me. I don't need or want a ride. I don't need anything from you. It's just for you to go watch your son perform. Is that too much to ask?" I pour on the drama. Some part of me wants to believe this myself, but I know that I am completely going Machiavellian on him, using him to appease any destined guilt or regret that could soil my soul forever. I'm trusting Ava on this one. She is the one, after all, who lost a father. Right now, doing what I can to not give Cedro an out, is quite a lot of corridors to pass through in attempt to live a life free of the rueful pangs of remorse, but I suppose that's how the world works. Nothing is a straight shot. If it were, there would be no need for manipulation.

I decide to play the wild card to acquire a loud and sound *yes* from Cedro. "You can even take your food brood up there. There's probably some game going on up there. Maybe you can try to score a nice profit there."

Cedro begins to think out loud. I can see him plotting his agenda as he speaks. "I'll check the Warriors and Kings schedules. Oakland and Sacramento are within reach. I can try to sell at their games. Maybe on the way I'll stop and try to get those Google geeks on their lunch break in Mountain View."

Already I am not Cedro's priority, but I have to remain focused. I am on a completely selfish mission of self-absolution, and I must stay the course if I am to clear myself of any potential guilt that might creep up on me later in life due to this moment. "Yeah. You could do that as long as you make the Cashmere because that's the point."

"Right. *The point.*" He makes air quotes for this. "Of course. What time?"

"It's all day Saturday. All. Day. That means you might not get to sell on Saturday, unless people at the Cashmere let you."

"What about at night? After the Cashmere?"

"The finals are at six and should end by eight. Like I said, Saturday might have to be on off day for you."

"You know for sure you'll be in the finals?"

My eyes touch the ceilings of my lids and the I-can't-believe-you-just-said-that look is pouring out a tumult of condescension on him "Yes. I know for sure I'll be in the finals."

Cedro attests. "That's pretty arrogant of you."

"Yes," I quip. "My arrogance is pretty, isn't it?"

"Whatever." Cedro scrolls through the apps on his phone, thinking aloud. "I could secure some city permits in the next two days for those cities and...yeah, sounds good."

"So you're in?" I confirm.

"I'm in."

This is deplorably tragic, but I am the only one of us two who recognizes the utter tragedy of it all. A father and son will both be convening up north, in the same city, supposedly united by the single event of my performance: the performance of Cedro's son. All the while neither the father nor the son actually cares about the other being there. Neither of us is truly going for the other. Neither of us will be in the same city for the same reasons, and that's just plain crushing. We should be in Palo Alto because a father and son want to be there together, to support one another, but that won't be the case.

I am selfish to have manipulated Cedro. I admit it. The truth is, I don't actually care if he goes for me anymore. I've already shut that part of me off as easy as a faucet bars the flow of water. That's what happens when a father chases an alternative existence at the expense of his current one.

I chuckle out loud because the irony of it all has just hit me. Like father like son, I guess. We are both equally selfish sitting across from one another.

"What?" Cedro asks.

"Nothing," I lie. "I'm glad you're going." Boy, I'm pretty good at this manipulation stuff.

"Thanks," he says. "Sounds fun."

"One more thing," I say.

"Sure."

Now the second part, the part where I declare my independence. "I'm going to be staying at Yoke's until further notice. I know I haven't officially told you, so I'm doing it now."

"You're moving out?"

"I've already moved out. But I bet you didn't notice that either."

"So you're officially gone then?"

"Officially? Sure. I guess." I don't ever want to come back, but I am trying to be *the bigger man* about this, so I refrain from saying *Yes, of course officially, douchebag*.

I watch Cedro's face tighten. He's trying to control the fibers under his features so that no emotion is given away. Even this tells me he doesn't want me completely gone. I expected this. He and I are in the same place with one another. We both will not surrender our rights to the other, but we each won't summarily banish the other from our sphere of existence. Which hand will he play? The caring father who's suddenly resurrected from the dead? Or the one-tracked father who's all hands on deck for creating the life he's always wanted for himself?

He plays his I'm-a-member-of-the-mafia hand. "I suppose you'll want to stop paying rent."

"Do you mean, 'I suppose you'll want to stop stealing my earnings just because you're acting as my finance manager until I'm of age?'"

"I suppose it just works out nice and fancy," he declares.

"Great."

But of course, Cedro has to have the last word. "If you come back to crash—even once—then you get charged for a full month. Even if you crash here just one night, in thirty days, you owe the two-fifty."

"I'd rather sleep on a park bench."

"I guess everyone's gotta try it once."

"What about the short month? February. It only has twenty-eight days."

"I know how many days February has, Smart Guy," he declares.

"And on leap year?"

"That's three years away." Cedro's teeth are grinding rocks.

After a quiet moment, I jest. "So, if I crash here and don't pay the going rate, are you going to take me to small claims court? Or just hire Guido to put a slug to the back of my head?"

"Only one way to find out."

"Spoken like a true negotiator," I add, my I'm-unfazed-by-you act on display.

But I am fazed. I'm still expecting him to speak like a true father, one of these days...

CHAPTER SIXTEEN

A good cook is like a sorceress who dispenses happiness.

~ Elsa Schiaparelli

Lana and Cedro headed up to Silicon Valley Thursday night. Cedro wanted to be there so he could pick up his permits by Friday morning and then try his hand at selling his menu around some of the tech businesses, like Google, during their lunch hour. In the evening, he plans on riding over to a Golden State Warriors game and selling to their fans.

As for me, I am riding up I-5 with Ava, Katherine, and Yoke. Katherine's ears are wrapped in headphones and plugged into her iPod. Yoke is linked to his phone. Ava and I, however, are sharing space, wrested by the bawdy, impulsive feel of rock monsters, Kings of Leon, who are taking us through Lost City (and it's no wonder why they named this Podunk splotch of nothing out in the middle of nowhere just that). This is the perfect band to drive to for hours at a time, from point A, Los Angeles, to point B, Palo Alto.

Save for the lush melodies creaking from Anthony Followill's haunting vocals, the car has been void of conversation for the past hour or so. The song right now, "Radioactive," is like a morsel of crème brûlée cultivating my soul softly through the speakers. The purple sky from a sinking sun goes perfectly with the ambience. I check to my right to see if the music is doing the same for Ava. She's tapping away on her laptop, probably hammering out her latest website. But I notice something else. Her glossy, billowy lips are ever-so-slightly mouthing the lyrics.

"Louder, please," I softly exhort.

She doesn't even realize she was doing this. "What do you mean?"

"You're lip-syncing, but I can't hear you."

"You don't need to hear me. That's why Followill recorded his own voice."

I turn down the volume, letting the lyrics nimbly pour through the speakers. "There. Now we can hear you sing Followill's lyrics."

Ava doesn't hesitate. She goes right along with the chorus. *"It's in the water/It's in the story/It's where you came from/The sons and daughters/In all their glory."* Her voice, leafy and dewy with a vibrant little falsetto, disarms me.

"Your voice...it's nice. Do you make music, too?"

"I sing because I enjoy it. My father taught me how to hold a tune."

Her father *taught* her something? Profound. I'm jealous. Cedro taught me one thing: how to resent life with visceral passion.

"I couldn't hold a note even if you stapled it to me," I confess.

"Sure you could," Ava disagrees. "Everyone can. It's just learning to control your own voice and using what you got. But rest assured, everyone can sing. Try it."

174

The worst thing I can do is make a big deal about it. So when the chorus returns, I take a go. *"It's in the water/It's in the story/It's where you came from/The sons and daughters/In all their glory."* My tone is more of an ambulance's siren mingled with the sound of a police helicopter raging overhead.

Ava doesn't mock me. She ponders, trying to fix my musical deficit. "Too much, that's all."

"Too much?"

"It's the most common mistake people make when trying to sing. They try to sing too much. Too loud. Not everyone has the Mariah Carey, Jennifer Hudson *boom* voice."

"Aw. The boom voice. I see." I'm exaggerating the fact that I don't understand.

"Just sing the melody softly. That's the key. When you hear most songs, the melodies just flow. The song just sounds bigger in the recording, but most songs are really nothing but little ditties. The worse thing to do is force it."

"It's kind of like me. I play out bigger in life than I actually am," Yoke blurts from the back.

"Exactly like you, Mr. Worldwide," I crow as we careen through the Grapevine Peak just outside of the sparsely populated city of Lebec. "I had no idea you were listening. I thought you were buried in your headphones, being Mr. Culture back there, completely ignoring the awesome sunset and watching your little movie screen."

"What can I say?" Yoke says. "The perks of being larger than life mean I'm more majestic than awesome sunsets. I don't need to admire things lesser than myself."

Katherine takes out her earphones. "You're joking, right?" she asks in disgust.

"On a serious note, do you guys want to stop for food or, in your case, Yoke, to take a wee-wee?" I ask.

Ava and Katherine laugh at Yoke's expense.

"Ha. Ha." Yoke responds. "Well, we wouldn't be out in the middle of nowhere and I wouldn't be holding in my urine if you had taken the 101."

"Your mom's out in the middle of nowhere, dude," I jeer. "The 101 is the longer route."

"Whatever. Just stop when you get a chance, dude," Yoke grunts.

I look to Ava to see what she's thinking about a pit stop. She shrugs. "Either way's fine with me."

"Let's just eat," Yoke and Katherine inadvertently say together.

When they do, their reflection in the rearview has them expressively searching each other, wondering how they could be thinking and feeling the same thing at the same time. It's an eerie romantic interlude between the two, and it's peculiar to see. They're just as struck by the unexpected moment as I am.

*

Kettleman City, California, population 1439, surprisingly has an In-N-Out. Inside, Yoke is content in his own little world that is populated with three In-N-Out cheeseburgers, a sloppy-goopy order of animal fries, a large Sprite, and his smart phone that is streaming a comedy film. He's so self-contained it's a wonder he can function in the socio-cultural world around him at all.

Yoke removes his headphones. "I should have just gone in the van with the team," he grouses.

"Are we not entertaining you enough?" I attack Yoke, expanding my eyes to hint at him that he is ruining it with

Katherine and potentially for me. Holding my tongue one time is my limit, and I already reached it.

"What's up, Yoke," Ava asks gently, sipping her Diet Sprite.

"Nothing. Never mind," says Yoke, raising the volume on his phone so he can't hear us ask him any more questions.

Any rapport Yoke built with Katherine has been decimated. Katherine offers Yoke a second look of disgust. Ava pleads with Katherine to make the best of it, not using words, but only the features on her face. Katherine holds her position—utter displeasure.

"Don't pay any attention to him," I mention to Ava. "He hasn't been visited by his fairy godmother yet. She'll come soon, and he'll feel better."

"Maybe that's why he's like that...because no one pays any attention to him."

I can't help but cackle out loud, and then that turns into deep shotgun laughter. "Between his parents, his grandparents, and me, we spend a good dose of our time trying to pay attention to him. We're the only ones."

"Maybe that's it. Maybe he wants others to do so, too."

"That's the catch. We try to show him love so he won't be so insecure and weird so that he'll then act normal enough for others to want to pay attention to him."

Ava's face contorts into a cute curl, her mouth reeling in one corner of her mouth. "Yeah, it is a savage cycle of emotion."

"The savage cycle of emotion," I repeat. *I like her mind.* "If I'm honest, I guess I consider Yoke like a project of sorts."

"Maybe The Human Socialization Project? Which would make you...Professor I Can Make You Normal."

"At your service," I bow. "Now, young lady, is there anything I can help *you* with in the area of human socialization? Perhaps you need to learn how to engage in a romantic partnership with the highest form the human species has to offer."

"And who might that species be?"

I clear my throat, hike out my chest and pretend I'm straightening a suit coat on me that I am not wearing. "Yours truly."

"Your modesty is almost undetectable," Ava ruefully says.

I smile and stare at her, taking her in. The playful challenge allows me to ingest the sheen of her eyes, the presumptuous beauty of her presence.

Ava winces from the cat and mouse stare off, retreating shyly toward her shoulder. I let my eyes chase her until she turns back to me and whisks away a strand of hair her from her face, setting it behind her ears.

Katherine and Yoke, plugged into their headphones, look at each other. Yoke inserts his finger into his mouth, mocking a gagging motion. Katherine nudges her head and Yoke nods with a smile. Simultaneously they rise from the table, grab their food trays and find a different table to sit at.

"Well, at least they agree on something," I say.

"And when they trace the origins of their weird romance, they'll have to say that we are responsible for bringing them together."

"I've always wanted to play cupid. But I'm not sure I want those two on my portfolio."

Ava laughs. "So why comedy? What made you choose that?"

I decide to be honest. "Just your average, cynical teenager who decided to turn all that misanthropy into an honest vocation."

"Okay. I get that. I got my reasons to be *misanthropic* too," she's flashing two bunny ears with her fingers on either side of her. "But why?"

"Why I chose comedy or why I'm so spiteful about things?"

"Both."

"Well, why not?"

Ava laughs. "You're not making sense. But let me show you what I mean." She clears her throat. "First, why I'm not a misanthrope. Well, for obvious reasons, I could be. I could be the world's biggest Scrooge. The whole my-dad's-gone thing sort of qualifies me.

"True."

"But that's useless. Pathetic actually. So I'm going to hate the world because of my loss and pain? How is that even reasonable? It's pitiable, at best. Like I said, I loved my dad, and I know he loved me. I miss him. I miss him a lot. But nothing's going to bring him back. And, I don't know...I just hope to see him on the other side of eternity."

"*Hope.*" I mouth the word as if I am learning how to pronounce it.

"Hope." Ava repeats like a teacher of a foreign language, modeling the word's simplicity.

"It's a short word, but there's nothing really simple about it."

Ava smiles. "Small word, big impact."

"Like the tip of knife. It's tiny. But when it nicks the edge of your skin, the pain is huge."

"Something like that."

"So how'd you get it?"

"It's not a disease. You don't catch *hope* like you do the flu. It sounds corny, but I believe it's something you choose to have. People have this misconception about things like hope and love.

179

Cupid ruined it for everyone. I mean, now we think we have to be struck randomly with the ability to love. If you're five, okay, you can think that. But if you're able to generate any kind of rational thought—no way. You either choose to or you choose not to."

She has me thinking, but I'm not ready to come to Jesus at this desolate In-N-Out establishment. "I don't know. I kind of like being jaded. It gives me license to hate the world."

"At least you admit it."

"At least?"

Ava sidesteps a possible and useless argument and attempts a U-turn back to our topic. "So, anyway, that's why I'm not a misanthrope."

"And why I should not be."

"I didn't say that."

"You don't have to. Anyone who has hope instinctually wants others to have it as well."

"So that means anyone who's a misanthrope wants everyone else to hop aboard the Train of Shame with them?"

"It's the way it works."

"You're in a flat spin there, Maverick. I think it's time to press eject."

"*Top Gun* metaphors."

"You're a guy. You do know what I'm talking about, right?"

"Of course."

Ava scopes me out as a doctor would someone who claims an illness with no visible symptoms. "A real life misanthrope undercover, hiding behind comedy. Interesting." She sips more of her Diet Sprite. "You know, I never finished my answer."

"Please, finish."

"As I was saying, I have my reasons to be misanthropic, just like anyone else. I have my tragic dead dad episode. And my one and only serious relationship had its casualties as well."

Ryan. Mr. Monster/Pro Choice champion. The miscarriage. That's right. "So you're over that?"

"I realized that when I told him the night we met, I had already been over it. I just didn't have the nerve to say it until then, I suppose."

"And my comedy skit gave you the perfect out."

"Gotta roll with the punches when you can, right?"

"Have you ever heard of Hypercas Morphological Syndrome? HMS for short. No relation to PMS, by the way." My unusual habit of creating words and diseases by using etymology, in this case the word *cas* carrying its origins in Germanic roots and meaning *to fall*, comes out of me like bark from a dog.

"HMS, huh? Is that a real term? Or is that some sort of *Sole* Speak?"

Sole Speak. Unbelievable. Ava gets me.

I hear Ferdinand from *The Tempest*, in my head. He says to his admired Miranda, *Hear my soul speak: The very instant that I saw you, did/My heart fly to your service.* My heart has fallen for Ava, in this random In-N-Out burger in Kettleman City, population 1439, of all places. Oh well. I guess this is as good a place as any to fall in love.

Out loud, of course, I play this whole thing down. "Sole Speak...are you accusing me of inventing my own, new language?"

"No way. Maybe a dialect at best, and a very primitive one like, say, that of the Khoisan people of southern Africa." Ava makes herself giddy with her own humor.

"Thank you for your insulting words. I feel much more retarded now," I play back. Then the serious sets in like a shoreline fog, and I can't help but express the truth. "It's funny that you say *Sole Speak*. There's this thing I have in my head where I always make up words, like HMS and stuff. And if a person gets me—I mean really gets who I am—then they'll understand me and actually like to listen to me speak my *soul*. You know, *soul* as in *Sole* Speak. And they won't think I'm deranged or anything."

"I get it," Ava chimes. "So what does HMS stand for?"

"Well, you know what *hyper* means. *Cas*, etymologically, means *to fall*. And *morph* you know, means *to change*. So Hypercas Morphological Syndrome means to fall in love so quickly that it changes your life just like that." I snap for effect.

"So do you have HMS?"

"Wouldn't you like to know."

"You know, Sole, it's hard to find people who talk about anything the way you do. Everything is so superficial. It's like people are afraid to uncover anything real in their conversation. They get scared of real words and real thoughts. But not you."

"I couldn't agree more."

"So you're sort of on this search for all those long, lost Sole Speakers out there?"

"I guess so," I blurb. "Have you read *The Tempest* by Shakespeare?"

Ava's eyes tell me she gets everything I am saying. "I love that play."

"Well, that's where Sole Speak comes from. It's a *play* on my name," I jest.

"Ha. Ha," Ava bites back. "But really, I know that part. It's my favorite part of the play. Act 3 scene 1—God, I love that part. It's so romantic. Ferdinand meets Miranda, Prospero's daughter, and he tells her to hear his—"

"*Soul* speak." Ava says this at the same time with me.

We look at each other and pause, surprised at what happened. I let the invisible, heady reality passing between us continue for a few seconds. Would it be insane if, right here, in a fairly trafficked burger joint, I dropped to a knee, grabbed a French fry, twisted it into a deep fried potato ring and proposed? *Easy, Sole. Love is not on the agenda. Think how mama bailed. Love leads to messes.*

Ava responds. "I get you, Sole. I really do."

"Then may I indulge you in another Soleism?"

"Please do."

"Having conversations like this is what I would call poetifound," I say.[11]

"Poetifound?" Ava says, considering the invented word. "As in *poetic* and *profound* married into one word?"

Good Lord...this girl really does get me.

"I know. I do that a lot. Like I said, it's my Sole Speak. You really don't think it's weird? That I'm weird?"

"I said I get you. I meant it," Ava confirms. "You know, you should make a dictionary out of your Soleisms. Call it The Sole-tionary."

"I like that," I add. *But I love you.*

Before we rise, Ava takes a pen from her handbag, the one that houses her laptop, and clicks the back so that the purple ink is ready to scrawl. I watch her as she takes a napkin and draws on it. I suppose being a digital architect, which is a sophisticated

---

[11] Soleism #3: *Poetifound* is something so rich with meaning that the heart floods with intensity.

skill, means she can also draw freehand. Until now, I would have never assumed such things for web designers.

Ava has drawn a reproduction of an In-N-Out menu. On the menu's left side Ava has sketched three burgers that have faces on them. Two burgers have the face of a boy, with hair like mine that falls to my neck and my overall features. I can clearly see it's me. The one burger that's a girl has a cataract of dark hair falling over the bun and a pair of the cutest eyes, like those Disney eyes, roomy enough for a car to drive through. On the right of the menu are dollar signs. TWO OF YOU FOR ONE OF ME.

"Art history is not my best subject," I suggest.

"I still want to know two things about you. Remember? You tell me two things and I tell you one."

"I'm not saying economics is my strongpoint either, but I can clearly see I'm getting the short end on this deal."

"You can always renege. That's fine." Ava is blithely pretending to scowl at me.

"Two for one. You want to know why I'm a misanthrope and why comedy is my venture. And," I scan the napkin art, "in return you have offered to tell me why you are *not* a misanthrope—"

"Which I've already answered."

We break into small chortling together. "And then some," I concur.

"Are you suggesting I talk too much?"

"You said it. I'm not suggesting anything," I spiel. "But I have a new wrinkle to add to our deal."

"Shoot."

"I get a second question. No two for one. Two for two or all bets are off."

"Okay. Deal."

"I would like to know why you are a *not* a comedian."

"Because I'm not funny."

"Now that," I laugh, "is funny."

CHAPTER SEVENTEEN

Lunch kills half of Paris,
supper the other half.
~ Montesquieu, 1755

For the last hours, the ride up the I-5 has been relatively restless for me. Ava and I have talked sporadically, but mostly I let some music daintily play through the car speakers while she completed designing her website. We still have yet to finish our conversation.

Yoke studied his routine a bit, the one he's going to use at the Cashmere, then turned on another movie, this time using his iPad because it had the larger screen. He's like a stowaway brat mommy and daddy take on the family vacation, always needing some form of stimulation so that he doesn't rack the two in the front seat with unending questions of irrelevancy. Of course, all this around me has left me to making up jokes in my mind, contorting thoughts and ideas in my head as music scrolls through my iPod, this time Imagine Dragons and their *Continued Silence* EP, softening the coarse night surrounding the car as it carves through the canyons along the shadowed path.

"Done. Finally," Ava celebrates, closing her laptop.

"So who's the lucky customer?"

"I wouldn't say lucky. They paid for it."

"What'd they get?"

"Exactly what they paid for," Ava chuckles. "Are you sure you're asking what you really want? I'm answering you, but I think you're wanting answers to different questions."

"You're right. What I want to know is what kind of business it is."

"That's the best part. It's a local L.A. business duet. These two guys—partners—have decided to begin what they call the Crossroads of Clothes. It's an online thrift store. People donate clothes and these guys market them like any major brand would, like, say, American Eagle or something similar to that. It's pretty neat to see used clothes at thrift prices advertised like higher end, name brand clothing."

"That a great business idea," I submit. "Never heard of anything like that."

Any sign of city life evaporates as I merge onto Route 152, the Pacheco Pass. This is thirty miles of sheer and utter blackness. Hills and canyons stretch out for miles, but, from this highway, I can't see anything farther than three feet outside of my windows. The DEER CROSSING sign adds more tension to my already frayed nerves. If Rudolph or Bambi's cousin comes barging onto this highway, it's going to be him or us who lives, but one of the parties is dying, that's for certain.

Ava lifts her knees to her chest, her mignon figure curled cutely in the passenger's seat, the cardigan she's wearing and leggings stretched down her athletic legs, a cozy look about her. "Ooh, this is kind of eerie."

"Not kind of eerie. It is." I check the gas tank. It's at half a tank, which should be enough to get us through a string of hick towns and to Highway 101. "This is the kind of road sociopathic sadists dream about when someone asks them, 'Hey, Billy, where would you like to travel when you grow up?' 'Highway 152.' 'The Pacheco Pass?' 'Yes, ma'am.' 'Why, Billy?' 'So they can't find the bodies.'"

Ava is humored. "Always joking." She rolls down the window slightly, the cool evening jetting through the slit between the glass and doorframe.

"So...why I'm not a comedian," she begins the conversation we left at In-N-Out a few hours ago. "Because I suppose I'm the type of person who has no problem with it when someone else makes me laugh. I am one hundred percent, absolutely content in that position—never feeling the need to have to make others laugh."

"But you do. You make people laugh. You're witty."

"I didn't say I don't talk to people and make jokes. I said I am not the type of person who feels the need to make others laugh. I like that others have that burden and I just get to enjoy it."

"Would you say I have that burden?" I sip a Starbucks brew from my cardboard cup.

"Absolutely."

"And you'd be right."

"Of course I am. Now it's your turn."

My turn. It's my turn to get deeply human with Ava. "I'm a misanthrope because I'm like all misanthropes: things have gone south on me, so this is how I respond."

"Okay," Ava snips. "We all get that. But you're evading the topic. You have to be specific, as in saying what actual things have gone south on you. Kind of like I was honest about my father."

I pause. I've never expressed the whys to anyone. For miles and minutes I say nothing, and Ava doesn't insist. She realizes that we are not wading in the shallow end of conversation but that we are submerging ourselves into the abyss of ourselves. Because she's never tried to hide herself from me, I have assumed that her whys were somehow more inconsequential than mine, but that's not true. That's not true at all.

I merge north again, this time the highway tightening to one lane as we pass through the garlic fields of Gilroy, the odor smacking about inside my nostrils. "You know how your dad died?" I begin. "My mom didn't. She left us. I was young...I was five, so I've pretty much been used to it. But the point is that my mom wasn't taken from me. She took herself away, and I guess that sort of pisses me off."

"Understandable," Ava softly adds.

"But that's not all. The parent I'm left with, for the past few years, has gone from having a quasi identity crisis to a full out, Def Con 4, Code Red Emergency Midlife Crisis, and he's so self-consumed he doesn't really know or care that I exist."

"Know or care?"

"I haven't decided which one. The jury's still pending. It's probably both, and knowing that is just too much to take in, so I'm pretending it's only one or the other."

"What has he done? Or not done?"

"The kicker was not him quitting his job. That's his business. His prerogative. He's a big boy. But the problem was he promised me I had a college fund that would pay for any University of California or state education. 'Cool' I thought. 'What a great dad. Saving for me all these years.' Ehh! I was

190

wrong. Then he goes and uses all of that—*my* college savings that he swore were mine!—plus his savings, to start his food truck business that's going this side of nowhere faster than a cheetah on 'roids."

"I'm sorry."

"So am I."

"So college isn't an option?" Ava asks. "And don't think I'm judging." She waves as if I am ten feet away. "Hello, I'm Miss Not a Single College Credit to Her Name Save for a Few AP Credits She Earned in High School."

I gaff. "It could be an option. Loans and stuff. But I don't know...I don't know about that."

"Have you applied?"

"To a few places."

"He's going to Grand Loser University," Yoke blurts, aroused from his slumber.

"Perfect timing, Yoke-a-Doodle-Do."

"Are we almost there?" he fusses.

"Gladly, yes."

"Why?" Yoke attests. "Because then you'll be rid of me."

"Ding, ding, ding," I return. "Correct again."

While Yoke is mumbling something to himself, Ava kisses me on the cheek. "Sole Speak. Who knew you had to drive six hours away to find some real conversation?"

I wait for Yoke to taint this precious advance of affection. To my astonishment, he doesn't bash. "I like her," is all he says.

"So do I," but I'm glancing at Ava when I say it.

*

By ten o'clock the formal test is over. The Curse of the Maroon has passed. It has successfully traversed almost four hundred miles upstate.

The Marshall High Standup Team is staying at La Quinta Inn & Suites. It's a peculiar feeling to think of shacking up for the night with this group of comics. In fact, the closer I get to the reality of this situation, the more frightened I become. It's not that I see myself above the guys in the Marshall High Comedy Club, but reality says that my traditional high school days are past. Ava, one year graduated, solidifies these feelings, and more than before, I'm almost completed with my independent studies and will thereby be done with the sinkhole of life known as secondary schooling. So, am I better than them? No. I'm just ready to leave them behind.

But first, I have to not only survive this weekend, I have to seize it. This weekend is the vertex of my high school comedy career. I still have my fledgling stand-up career outside of school, but that could take a while before any fruits come from it. I have to win.

The school budget has allowed for two rooms, and Mr. K has one of those. That leaves five guys for another room. There are no girls on the squad, so feasibly one of us could stay with Mr. K, but that's just strange and not going to happen. Mr. K is a grown man and a teacher. Keeping staff members at a safe distance is where most students want to keep them, unless, of course, they're engaging in illicit affairs with one. As far as I know, not one of our guys is gay, and there's a gold ring stapled tightly around Mr. K's podgy ring finger which, I assume, means he's married. To a girl. By the way he has often been known to cite anecdotes about his second-grade child and wife, Mr. K appears to be a straight-up family guy.

"Sole, Yoke, what's up?" the boys from the team spatter their greetings in the hallway after answering our knocks.

Yoke continues to show progress both comedically and socially. "Oh, thank God. I never thought I'd be so glad to see you guys," he cries as he mock hugs Leo. If Yoke had hugged Kyle, a senior, he most likely would have been lying on his back right now, but since Leo is all of five feet and three inches tall, and a freshman, he goes along with the embrace. "Spare me from Sole, please."

"He's a homeless pet," I say. "He'll be fine. Just give him a snack, some milk, and rub under his chin." This chiding of Yoke is not a customary habit for me. When we're around others, I usually coddle his fragile psyche, but since he's socially progressing before my very eyes, I push a little, just to see how he responds.

"Bow wow," is Yoke's rebuttal. It's not the best, but it's definitely a solid display of a more fortified character, and that, in the end, is what I want to see. He's my best friend and, though I know outwardly people might think I detest him, I am really after his best interest.

Mr. K appears in the hallway, his room right next door to the one the guys are in. "Ah, glad to see you guys made it."

"It's not a drive I want to make again, at least not in the dark."

"Did you take the route that took you through Highway 152?"

"Yep."

"Yeah, it can be pretty intimidating the first time through, especially at night."

"So, we're in one room, you're in the other?" I ask.

Mr. K denotes, "Yep. Your room has two beds. Two to a bed and one on the floor. Or one can stay on my floor."

Ruben adds, "No. No way. No one's sharing. We flipped for the beds. I got one, and Kyle's got the other. Yoke, Sole, Shawn and Leo are on the floor. We already got some extra blankies for them."

There's no way I'm going to stay in Cedro's room, but I won't tell the guys that. Even though this isn't the Hilton or anything close to that kind of establishment, I do have enough money to rent a room at a dinky Motel 6 where they probably have regular specials if I sign a waiver that says I won't call the police and rat out the drug deals going on next door. That sounds better than my two options at the moment. "My dad's room is just a couple of blocks away. I think I'll just stay there."

"Oh, come on," Ruben resounds. "It'll be fun—all of us together!"

The hallway goes deafly silent, and everyone offers Ruben sarcastic stares.

"I'm not sure *fun* is the word you want to use to describe a room full of guys," I suggest. "Which is why I'm—"

Leo implores, too. "Come on, Sole, I want to glean from the master."

"This isn't Shinobi Training School, and we are not ninjas. Please don't call me master."

No one I've ever seen can lift one brow higher than the other, to the top of his scalp, like Mr. K. The peak at Mt. Eyebrow is telling me to show some leadership and compassion toward these misfits.

Against better judgment I say, "Fine. I'll suffer the night here."

The four comedic hopefuls pat me on the back and maul me like a horny dog in heat does the nearest leg. I laugh because they don't realize—or don't care—I just walloped them with a huge, backhanded compliment.

"Okay. All right, you hounds," I add playfully. "I'll be back in a bit."

"Where're you going?" asks Mr. K.

"I brought friends to check out the show. I need to take them to their room."

"By *them* you mean *her*," Yoke declares.

"Ooh," Kyle jeers.

I feel it's my duty to humble Kyle. "Does a live, flesh and blood girl impress you that much, Kyle? I guess it would since you're accustomed to having to pull a string to get a girl to talk to you."

Even Mr. K laughs at that one. "Just one more thing."

Leo rubs his hands together. "This is going to be great."

"Leo, that rubbing thing you're doing with hands and the excitement in your voice...it's scaring me," I say.

"Do you want to feel how warm they are?" Leo gests.

"That's it. I'm getting my own room."

"Come on, So. I'm just playing."

"Fine." I turn to Mr. K and prompt him to finish his earlier statement. "What were you saying?"

"There's a new prize for the Cashmere's winner: a potential scholarship offer and air time."

"No way!" I say.

"Yep," Mr. K assures. "If you win—"

"*When* I win," I clarify.

"Well then *when* you win, a few universities are looking into offering a Performing Arts scholarship."

Though that sounds pretty good, I'm more interested in the other prize. "And the other prize?"

"A weekly spot on a local Internet radio comedy station. It's done by region because many of the stations were open to it. They were all clamoring to sync up with the Cashmere."

"It's real legit this year," Ruben totes.

"Can't wait," I say nonchalantly, downplaying it while pedaling to the elevator. Without turning around to face them, I sling a thumbs-up over my shoulder.

The team goes back to their room and does Lord knows what. One thing the hotel doesn't have to worry about is these guys acting out their fantasy rock star dreams in room 217. They won't be boozing it up or trashing the room anytime soon. What they might do, though, is use their laptops to get their fill of hyper-graphic cinematic art, also known as pornography. With no parents or filters, the Internet is a wide open plane of opportunity. To me, it sounds disgusting and I am more than pained to think that I will soon be sharing the same room with a group of guys who will be eye-groping other people doing what they want to be doing. I can see it now: there will be a rotation for the bathroom and you'll need skis to walk over the floor covered in…well, like I said, that's just an utterly detestable mental picture.

Downstairs, in the lobby, Ava is waiting for me. Katherine is poised in a germ-infested lobby chair on the other side. "All squared away?" Ava asks me.

"Yep. Now to your castle," I say.

She holds out her hand, and I take hers in mine as we walk to the car, prattling on in useless non-versation. Driving to the hotel where she and Katherine are staying, Katherine plugs into her phone and fades away in the back seat. I spend most of the short drive telling Ava how desperately I don't want to return and share a room with four other guys who are probably, as I speak, getting their hands pregnant.

"That's outright disgusting," she agrees.

"You're telling me." I have an incoming text from Lana.

"Everything okay?" Ava inquires as she and I walk inside the lobby, Katherine already at the front desk handling the check-in.

I paraphrase aloud as I read. "She says they haven't gotten back yet from Oakland. They were trying to sell after the Golden State Warriors game."

"Do you think they did well?" Ava asks.

"Who? The Warriors or my dad?" I make myself snicker with this one. "Maybe if he was the only truck there—sure. But since he probably wasn't—no. I'm telling you, it's only a matter of time before his little mobile enterprise goes under. He's definitely no gastronomist[12]."

"You're happy about that, aren't you?"

"To be honest, yeah, a little...but not completely. And for the life of me I can't figure out why. It's sort of bothering me. I should be elated that he's going to fail after how it all began. Any truly spiteful person like me would be overjoyed to hear that your nemesis failed."

"But you're not, like you said."

"Nope. And it's killing me that I don't know why."

"Maybe that's a good thing."

"A good thing?"

---

[12] *Gastronomy* is the art and science of good eating, and *good* is a subjective, relative term. Cedro's definition of good is obviously bad, hence the reason his truck always underperforms and loses him more money than anything else.

"Sure. That is, if your goal is to be a normal, decent, compassionate human being...if your actual desire is to mend your relationship with him. That is what you want, right?"

It's quiet for a moment, the only sound coming through the speakers overhead in the lobby, playing some terrible version of a classical favorite by Joseph Haydn. The management could at least spring for Beethoven or Haydn on CD instead of playing a symphony knockoff remade by some company that sounds like it should be named Bob's Philharmonic from Planet Chuni.

I'm not summarily convinced that my ultimate desire is for the restoration of my relationship with Cedro. My spite runs that deep. Should I admit this aloud? "Of course," I say, not confessing.

Katherine doesn't wait for us. "I'll be in the room."

"See you there," Ava bids Katherine then turns to me. "Well, did you want to come up to the room for a while?"

Katherine, still within hearing range, comments, "Should I get my own room?"

Ava's invitation doesn't inherently imply that our G-rated love affair thus far will instantly morph into a non-rated, hot and heavy, lust affair, but the thought crosses my mind anyway. Along with the thought, images begin to assemble in my mind, and I see me in a room with Ava, and Ava wearing only her underclothes, the rest of her hued skin snaking out from her lacy undies, an Ava I haven't seen, but would most definitely like to see. It's one of those bucket list things: *have to see Ava in a matching lingerie set before I die.* However, with the possibly of talent managers in attendance tomorrow, I need to be at my best. Getting fatigued halfway through the day is a risk I am not willing to take, even if it means the possible chance of seeing Ava denuded. Unfortunately, it will be easier to fall asleep in a room full of Marshall High's quasi-comedians buffing the banana than to spend the night with Ava. Even if nothing happens, just being alone with her in a room with a bed would do more for my energy level than Viagra for a lethargic, elderly guy. And, in all honesty, something would probably happen.

I shake my head so that Katherine can see that she won't need to vacate the room to give Ava and I some alone time. Katherine pushes the wall button, and the elevator opens. She walks into the box and the doors seal her in. To Ava I respond, "Want to? Yes, but I have to get back."

"Okay." She lifts her small suitcase and begins to walk away. "Goodnight. See you mañana."

I'll definitely see you before that...in my dreams.

CHAPTER EIGHTEEN

I am a great eater of beef,
And I believe that does no harm to my wit.
~ *Shakespeare, Twelfth Night, I, iii*

"Welcome to Dinkelspiel Auditorium on the campus of Stanford University," the host pronounces into the mike at exactly 10:00am.

A thrust of music blares through the auditorium's speakers and a boom of applause channels through the acoustically tempered room. An immediate surge of human voltage charges the place, and I, along with the rest of the performers feel like *this* is the place everyone on the planet wants to be.

With twenty-six schools being represented, time and order are a must, which is why the rules are quite stringent. Through the first three rounds, each performer is limited to one minute and a half of stage time. That means that some kids have traveled hundreds of miles for ninety seconds of shame.[13]

After each round, one of the five participants from each school is axed, leaving one less for the next round. Then there's a brief twenty-minute intermission between rounds. Add the process up over four rounds, and it will take us until six in the evening when the finalists will get three minutes of glory time which starts at eight o'clock. By this time, the judges are burned out while the finalists are completely amped. In other words, the top performers have to be at their funniest. Mediocrity will go unnoticed.

Last year I took the bronze, which isn't bad when considering the winner now has an agent and is booking some nice venues on the circuit. This year I expect to win. If I can't beat a bunch of amateurs then how can I expect to make it in the cutthroat entertainment business?

The judging panel is comprised of two performing arts professors, one from Berkeley and one from Pepperdine, a high school principal chosen from an out of state school, three teachers from nearby surrounding states, a student from Stanford's engineering school, a parent from Oregon, and superstar guest, Dennis Miller. This panel's comedy scale is sure to be so comprehensively unbalanced that if you asked anyone what it means to be *funny*, it would be hard to find a common interpretation among the group. This randomness is supposed to create an objective approach to the selection process.

---

[13] I say *shame* because *glory* is only for those who are actually funny enough to make it to the finals.

Fine. Whatever. Funny is funny, and that's all I have to concern myself with.

I'm excited that Dennis Miller's here. Now, I know it's going to take some serious needle-pointed wit to cause him to come up to me after today, introduce himself, then dub me Mr. Comedy Extraordinaire, but that's what I'm going for. As I've mentioned, I'm quite ambitious.

Each judge has three categories by which they value the participants. The first is completely subjective and worth ten points. It's the OVERALL IMPRESSION column. It basically allows the judge to assign the comedian a number, ten being extremely funny, one being dull as an eraser.

The other two categories are worth five points. One category is called WIT. Essentially, this means that the humor is based on content, meaning, word use, punning, and anything related to semantics and thought.

The third category is labeled EXPRESSION. This slot is left for the way the material is presented—tone, voice, inflexion, etc. It also means that all five points are lost if more than three swear words are used in a routine. I can't say I disagree with this. I'm old school and believe true humor uses profanity selectively, if at all. Modern comedians use it at every bend, and people think this is the absolute limit, but to me anyone paying for a comedian who swears constantly is like paying to have a heap of garbage poured onto them. You can go to any thuggish malcontent on the street for that, or hit up any random garage, i.e. man cave, during evening hours. There, you'll find a bunch of guys, strung out men playing pool and drinking beers, trying to be as funny as possible by roasting on each other. These are what I call Garage Heroes.[14]

After tallying the totals through two rounds, remaining from Marshall High are Kyle, Yoke, and I. Yoke gets the nod first for us. Whether or not he goes on past this third round, Yoke is already a smash by doing well enough to convince a judging panel to not eliminate him after the first fifteen seconds. Kyle and I listen from backstage, watching through one of the multiple plasmas they have set up for us.

"So, uh, kids are, like, on all kinds of meds these days. We have every acronym in the book. ADD, ADHD, NDP, OPD, AOTAD. By the way, AOTAD stands for All of the Above Disorder." A small roar from the crowd is encouraging for Yoke.

"So my mom had me checked out for, uh, SPD, slow processing disorder because, well..." Yoke uses his mildly mentally disabled act, and the audience is on to it. With the pause, the laughter grows as they realize that no explanation is coming. The pause *is* the explanation. In the past, Yoke would panic and go on, thinking he'd messed up the punch line and thereby not allowing the audience time to let the joke seep in. It took a lot of explaining from me to get to him to realize that this is a great technique and, if he got it down, could be useful for him, like it is now.

---

[14] By the way, Garage Heroes are absolutely free. And pathetic. All they do is consume cheap beer, watch sports, talk about how badly they want to go back to the high school years, and spew out a heavy dose of burned out "momma jokes." Sound fun? I don't think so. So why anyone wants to give a comedian credit for slewing out a bunch of curse words without actually saying anything truly funny is beyond me.

"Yeah, and the doctor wanted to give me medication. I said, 'So, you're saying I have a problem.' The doctor lied. 'No, Stan—my real name by the way—you don't have a problem. It's just to, *uh*, speed things up a bit inside.' I smiled because he said *uh*."

I laugh. I've never heard this routine before. It's going great. The audience isn't as into it as it should be. His best joke might be behind him, and that's not good this late into the competition. I hope the judges find it in their hearts to give him a good score.

"It's true. I thought he and I were, *uh*, like brothers or something. Because he said *uh* like me I thought, 'Hey, maybe he has SPD too. Maybe SPD isn't such a bad thing.' So I asked him, 'Do you, *uh*, take this stuff, too?' 'Well, we're not really here to, *uh*, discuss, me.'

"And then I got it. His *uh* wasn't because of SPD. He was doing that I-don't-know-how-to-say-this-but-I'm-trying-to-be-polite thing. After that I had to go on Prozac for the Big D—" Yoke pauses, letting the crowd figure it out. When they start to chuckle, he says, "Ladies, don't get worked up. I'm not talking *Dirty* here. D is for depression." The audience sounds like a laugh track. It's a short, polite offering. It means Yoke hasn't absolutely crushed them with his humor, but he still has them going in the right direction.

"Thank you. That's my time." Yoke departs the stage.

Backstage, I celebrate with Yoke. "All right, man, that was great."

He's a thousand smiles in front of me. He nailed it as best as he could possibly hope to, and he knows it, and the best part was I got to witness, live, for the first time—ever!—that he's put it together like this.

"Feels good, doesn't it?"

"Better than good," Yoke attests, giving Kyle a high five.

"When did you come up with that routine?" I wonder.

"I've been working on it for the last couple of weeks."

"What about the next round? Are you going with tried and true stuff, or you coming out with some more new material?" I don't really think Yoke will make it that far, but I'm trying to be positive.

"You'll have to see," Yoke boasts.

"Well, I'm pretty sure you're clearing this round for sure. That routine was killer," I state.

"So you're already counting me out?" Kyle counters after listening on for the past moments.

Yoke and I both cock our heads to the side and stare at him with our lips pursed. The three of us know that, of the remaining participants from Marshall, I'm the sure thing. That's not arrogance. That's fact.

"It's either you *or* Yoke...and *me*," I confirm. "That's what I'm saying. And you know I'm right."

"Or left. As in *left* out." Kyle guffaws at his own joke. I mean literally puts the *guff* in guffaw, throwing his shoulders into it, making them bounce up and down. One of his legs lifts up to the cadence of his gyrations, making him seem utterly strange. I've never seen this before, and, by the way Yoke's chin is on the floor and his mouth could fit a whale in it, I can tell he hasn't either. Kyle is really feeling the humor in the air, I guess.

"Don't ever let anyone see you laugh like that," Yoke says. "It looks like some ritualistic dance they teach at the Penn Foundation."

"Holy Yokes," as in *holy smokes*. "That was hilarious." I turn to Kyle, instigating a little backstage cut-down session. "Do you know what the Penn Foundation is?"

Kyle looks confused. "It's probably where your mom goes for weekly therapy."

Yoke is now in fits. I can't help it, but I was cut down at the knees and am laughing right along with them. We're all making the best of a tense, nervous time.

"Kyle, you locked and loaded?" Mr. K says. "Come on. You're on next."

Kyle goes to the on-deck circle where the next comedian waits before he's ushered into the limelight. He looks loose and comfortable after our raillery, which is a good place for him, or any performer, to be before they stand in the midst of a crowd's scrutiny.

Within the first twenty seconds, it's clear that Kyle won't be advancing to the next round. He's up there, holding the microphone, speaking as if he has literally run out of material.

"What's up with reality television? There's nothing real about it. I mean, *The Bachelor*, all those cooking shows, VH1 and those gossip programs—none of them have anything *real* to them. Especially the girls on there. They're, like, plastic everywhere. No girl *really* looks like that."

Three or four people expel what sound like forced huffs of humor. The rest of the crowd is silent. I'm so embarrassed for Kyle right now. I can't bear to watch, so much so that I walk away from the monitors until it's my turn.

*

Yoke—to my surprise—and I stand as the lone Marshall High reps going into round four. This time, I'm slated to go first in our school's time slot. I walk to the stage, well aware that my competition is not Yoke. I will be the lone Marshall High comic after this round, and when I am, Grunge Snieds seems to be the one I'm going to have to best. He's the one who's in the way of my airtime which means more exposure, which means a larger fan base, all of which brings me that much closer to a full-fledged showbiz career. No way can Snied, a kid from hole-in-the-earth Fresno in the Land Time Forgot, i.e. Central California, beat me.

No way.

"Well, I'm going to talk about relationships. You might be asking, 'What qualifies you?' Let me tell you what qualifies me. A broken heart, friends," I start my spiel.

The crowd sympathizes in unison. "Aw."

"Yep. Get your heart broken, and you're automatically propelled to guru status in the realm of relationships. For example, in attachment theory, it's suggested that we seek love in our relationships the same way our parents did or didn't love us. Well, my parents swatted the life out of me, so I guess that means I'm looking for some kinky love. Can we say S and M?"

The audience is with me. They chuckle. However, I'm peeking at Dennis Miller. He has a glint in his eye. *Yes.*

"They also say that, during our primal years of humanity, in the geological ages of the past, it wasn't evolutionarily feasible to stick around the family after the kids were four. Why? They say that if a child makes it to four years, then survival is almost a sure bet, so it's time for the man to then seek more mates and spread his DNA around to ensure the continuation of his genes." I raise my eyebrow as if I am evaluating the absurdity of the claim. The auditorium roars with approval. "I think I'm suddenly a strong advocate for evolutionary theory! All you conservatives out there, I guess sex addiction and womanizing shouldn't get such a bad rap after all. It's got a rational explanation, people. It all goes back to survival of the fittest. I bet Darwin had quite the concubine.

"Well, I have the best fix for this relationship stuff. Why not, instead of marriage as the official institution of the land...why don't we design relationships around the perfect model: The sport's contract!"

Dennis Miller appreciates social commentary and humor in the same package. It's his specialty, his style, and I can tell he likes my sketch right now. His bushy hair and stern looks are peaked with pleasure. He doesn't seem to be analyzing for a contest. He seems to be enjoying himself, as if being a paid audience member were his only task.

"Sure it would work. The four-year mark would be the max term allowed. After that, you can opt for an extension or enter free agency." That's a punch line, so I pause to hear the applause.

"In free agency, other people are free to make offers to you. They can entice you away from your current mate by offering you a better personal profile: better personality, more money, a hotter body, and the usual stuff humans use to attract potential mates. Then, from here, the original partner has an option to renew and match the offer, *if* they want you to stay. Let's face it: they may want you out as much as you want to get out, like the managers and owners. If your original partner still wants you and chooses to match your highest new offer by, say, promising to look hotter than ever or being kinder than ever before, or whatever else you're demanding as a free agent, then you can resign with them. But again, this is for another four years. The whole lifetime thing should no longer exist."

The smart angle to this gag doesn't cause outright eruptions of laughter, but it's a steady pleasure through clapping that the patrons in the auditorium give off. This is what Dennis Miller gets when he performs, and he's considered a contemporary icon in comedy. I own all of his DVD's and listen to his radio show consistently. I'm a self-proclaimed expert on his comedic style.

"As for the trade clause, partners are free to trade anytime, no penalty. It's called divorce. And the buyout clause, well that's already in place. It's called alimony. Thanks, all. My time's up."

Backstage, I'm not anxious, but Yoke is. He's grown this forest of optimism in him in a matter of minutes, thinking that he actually might have outdone me in this round, thinking he may be the one to reach the finals.

However, when the official list is cast, there are twenty-six participants left, and Yoke is not Marshall High's last-standing hero.

"It's all right, man," I exhort. "You did great."

"Go ahead and say it."

"Say what?" I ask, trying to keep my voice down. Backstage is quite the bustle right now, bodies ambling about in every direction.

"That I did great and, if it weren't for you, I might have had a chance."

"Well, I mean, I didn't think I had to say it. That would be like saying, 'the sun brings light' every morning." I'm kidding, but Yoke has gone back into his Asperger's mode.

"Whatever. Just go ahead and win the darn thing." Yoke walks off.

"Thank you for your permission, dearest friend. At least I think so," I bellow, watching Yoke ooze into the mire of figures trolling around the premises.

When the announcement is made that after an hour of intermission the finals will commence, Yoke's little attitude is long out of my head.

CHAPTER NINETEEN

Training is everything. The peach was once a bitter almond;
cauliflower is nothing but cabbage with a college education.
~ *Mark Twain*

The main mistake I have to avoid is thinking too hard about the prize and the airtime that comes with it. *Ooh, I need that.* If I think too hard about what I want, I'm sure to choke. My focus should be narrowed to the single unit of nailing one punch line at a time.

Many performers choke because their focus is on the reward or goal and not singularly on the performance itself. It's like this: if an actor is on an audition and his mind is on getting the role, then he probably won't get the role because he's going to think too much about what comes after the audition and thereby miss his mark during the performance. Likewise for me: if I go on stage and try to get the airtime, I won't; but if I traipse confidently before the audience, grab the mike, and center all of my attention in that moment, which would be to nail my routine with precision, then lo and behold, I will probably obtain the prize. This is my strategy.

Standing off to the side of the stage, behind the curtain, I watch George Snied. He's made it with me this far, the finals where each of the final five candidates has three minutes of stage time.

"Being young," George says to the audience, his voice heavy and bottomless, quite an irony for a gaunt kid with fluffy hair, "you get the question a lot, 'So, what do you want to do?' I know what the question means, but, really, it's an awful question to ask a kid. Think about it, you're asking someone who's at the very bottom of life, who's looking up at life from the base of the freaking mountain, how life looks from that point of view." George acts enraged.

"At my age, I'm at the bottom of the food chain. I've got no money, a skill set that comes with a public education from Fresno of all places... It's like asking plankton when a whole bunch of whales are swimming nearby, 'So, what do you want to do with your life little fishy?'"

The crowd loves it. I have to admit, it's making me giggle.

George continues. "Or like asking a surfer paddling out in the Red Triangle here while a host of great whites is circling the area, 'Hey, what do you want for dinner?'

"I'm telling you guys, teenagers don't want to be asked that question. There's a reason we all seem cynical to adults: because we are! This is how teenagers turn deadly. It's not our fault. We're practically provoked. Example: a peppy guy who's been successful enough to put life in a headlock and come out on the winning end asks with his happy little successful look, 'So, young guy, what do you want to do with life?'

"That makes me want to say, 'Well, I didn't know it until now, but I think I'm aiming to be America's most wanted killer, right after I take my hands and tear your little, happy, successful face apart.' I think I'll go by the moniker Facelift."

The interaction between an audience and a comedian is like a dance, a waltz. The comedian must always be the one leading the dance. As far as George is going right now, he's maintaining his waltz with the audience just fine. I know because, even though I'm holding it in, I truly do want to laugh. This guy is hilarious right now.

Damn! Mess up already, Snied.

Time for some perspective: Confessedly, I am jealous, but I can't let jealousy take over me. George's success with the crowd is to be expected. I am not the only funny guy in the room. George and others are rehearsed humorticians as well as I am. [15]

"What about the people who crashed and burned in life and think how wonderful it must be to be a teenager, with their whole lives ahead of them. These people don't understand either. For one, the first thing I'm thinking is, 'I sure as hell don't want to end up like you.' So they ask all excitedly anyway, 'Wow, what are you going to do with yourself?'

"'Um, after I strangle you with the strings on my backpack, I guess I'll have to take to fulltime crime.' Thanks, everyone. Time's up." George bows before an explosion of applause and finger whistling.

---

[15] Soleism #4: *Humorticians* Humorticians are all around us, and they work round the clock at being funny—when lying in their beds, lying in the dark, driving from point A to point B, walking around, or even when they're busy doing something. They never rest and will look at any situation and try to make it funny, even situations that are dead to humor. Hence the word, hu-mortician. Like morticians work on dead bodies, humorticians work on dead, humorless situations until they become funny. They are always making up jokes in their minds for the sole purpose of being able to use those jokes in their next social scenario.

George is a tough act to follow. I'm really going to have to nail this one.

Before I am introduced as the last act for the night, George passes me. It's the first time our paths have crossed this closely. We aren't officially mortal enemies or anything, but he and I have silently embraced a competitive hatred for one another that never existed before today. Things like that just happen because people compare the skills of two people they find similar, and they decide to make enemies out of the two-of-equal-talent. In sports it was Larry Bird versus Magic Johnson, Kobe Bryant versus LeBron James, and Tom Brady versus Peyton Manning. Since the day began, it's been apparent that George and I, the two-of-equal-talent, would be standing off in the championship round, one of us destined to take the prize.

George's clownish bowl of curls atop his freckled face stops next to me. "I don't know what it is, but I just don't like you," George says, sniffing once.

He actually sniffed. Once.

"That's heartbreaking. Really," I say. "I'm scarred for life now." I step away from him, knowing that George is trying to get me off track before I'm set to go on. I won't fall for it.

And he won't quit. He strides to me, imposing his gaunt frame beyond the invisible sphere of safety that surrounds me and all humans. "The whole anorexic look you got going on would be in fashion if you were a bee-yotch. I thought you were out of style, but now that I take a good look, you're right in line with the times."

"Threatening a fellow competitor? What kind of educational program do they have going on in hole-in-the-earth Fresno? How to Be an Inept Criminal? You'll probably end up getting caught and star in your own reality show: *Most Retarded Wannabe Felons.*"

Right when George is going to counterblast with either a threat to my life or a scathing joke, the host says through the P.A. system, "Please welcome for the last time tonight, Sole Eaby."

I trod to the stage, greeted with handclapping and smiles. This is it. After these minutes, the score will be tallied and the winner will get his weekly spot on a well-trafficked Internet radio comedy show. Oh yeah, and maybe the scholarship. I have to forget that Dennis Miller or anyone else is listening. I have to do what I do when I'm in the clubs, that is, I have to find my zenith since, with Ava, I no longer look for a nadir.

I scan for a moment and find Ava, and the rest of the time I pretend it's she and I somewhere, anywhere, like back in L.A. in the hills, and these jokes are all for her.

"As you can see, I am Spanish, which makes me sensitive to cultures. I appreciate people of all cultures. Don't you? I mean, don't people think up some crazy stuff? You have to love it. Take primitive people for example, such as the Naskapis. They think that having a bad diet might cause the spirit of Wendigo to enter a person and turn them into a cannibal. Okay...I'm not sure about that, but hey, if Jenny Craig were smart, she'd figure out how to put Wendigo on her payroll. Shoot...every American would look thin and fit within a month."

My first swing knocks it out of the park, so I continue with the cultural course.

"Personally, I have to say, my culture is quacky. In the Spanish culture, people don't use facts. They, um, embellish. Tell stories. For example, I have a grandma who doesn't remember people like normal people do. Most people say, 'Remember the girl with the pretty eyes and long hair?' Or, 'What about the short girl with

215

the cute body and soft voice?' Things like that are normal. But my grandma, she would remember the things that no one even saw."

I use a faux, Spanish accent for my grandma's voice. "'Mijo,' she would say when asking about a girl. 'What ever happened to the niñita? The one who never wore stockings?'

"'Uh...what? Lots of girls don't wear stockings, grandma. For many reasons. The main reason being they don't sell *stockings* anymore! Leggings and tights, yes, even pantyhose, but stockings? Not since Ronald Reagan was president, Grandma.'"

Shots of amusement are discharged, one right after the other, until the room is laughing all together.

"At least she never figured out why the niñita didn't have her *stockings* on, though. I don't know if that's a cultural thing or a crazy-grandma thing, but...

"And how about the cultural war over food in Britain and France. Apparently, the French like their occasional taste of pan-seared horse brain, but the Brits were repelled when they discovered some of their supermarkets were selling Sea-biscuits."

Punning is a risk. Any comedian has to carefully evaluate the audience's responses to his first pun. If his crowd receives it, then they'll like more. If not, then no more puns. The Palo Alto fans appreciate a good pun apparently, and that means I should keep on word playing.

"When I think about it, horsemeat is kind of...it's pretty *hei*nous if you ask me."

It's important to pause for a pun. What I get is the usual gust worthy of such innuendo.

"Yeah, horsemeat ranks right up there with eating dog. But I mean, we're not arguing with Mexico over their dog tacos as long as they don't try to export here. Britain and France shouldn't be dissenting over issues like horsemeat. It's not *neigh*borly."

After some minor applause, I turn to cultural jokes. "Well, another part of culture is feminism. I know people think, 'Wow, pretty brave to talk about such touchy-feely topics.' Yeah. Whatever."

The audience laughs at my prosaic tone.

"You think traditional feminism is dead? Yeah right? Let me say one word: *Twilight*. That little old story that generated billions in the box office? Yeah, that one. How about Bella, ladies?" I turn my pitch to a whine. "Bella, Ms. I Live for Only Edward; Ms. My Life is Only Worth Whatever My Boyfriend Thinks it's Worth. Teenage girls are taking this stuff in like it's crack. For those ladies who hate women who find any definition of themselves in a man...sorry."

The crowd simultaneously claps and breaks into hysterics.

"How about classroom culture in schools? One teacher back East doesn't approve of her girls wearing mini-skirts to school because girls should be, quote-unquote, 'noted for their brains and character.' Let me guess: this teacher was created with a brains-only option. Looks and mini-skirts aren't available in her version—ugly!

"Yeah, I think any girl who's smart enough to realize that she's pretty hot and that mini-skirts look pretty darn good on her has displayed some fairly solid brainpower. Isn't that called *logic*? Let show you: Mini-skirts go with hot girls the same as suits go with businessmen. These girls have figured it out early."

I respond to the mixture of laughter and instigative *oohs* that come from sexist comments. "This is a cultural spoof, people. Don't give me your 'I can't believe he said that,' response. We all know sexism is alive and well in our culture. Women's lib worked. It didn't fail in our culture. This is just how some girls want to liberate themselves. Don't hate because you can't pull it off. If some girls can and want to, why hate? The only women who don't want girls to be known for the bodies and beauty are ones who don't look good in mini-skirts."

Applause and cheers combust to let me know that my wit is connecting with them.

"That's all I got for now. Goodnight. Thanks for your support." I set the cordless mike in the clutch atop the stand and walk away, stage left.

The host is already on the raised platform and reaching for the microphone before I can disappear behind the curtain. "Let's give all our performers a well-deserved round of applause, ladies and gentlemen. And give yourselves one, too. And thank you, judges and Stanford University, for helping us make this year's Cashmere a great success!"

Hoots and hollers and a thunderous standing ovation collide in Dinkelspiel Auditorium.

"Will our top five finalists please come out onto the stage one last time?" says the host.

In no particular order, the five of us bound onto the stage, standing next to another, shoulder to shoulder. We all smile. Two are clapping. George Sneid is bowing. One girl is doing a little twisty, three-sixty dance, her arms waving in the air. *Oh, brother.* I put one thumb up from my right hand. *Yay.*

"Well, it's come to this," the host relays the beginning of the end. The resounding cheers abate into the walls and ceiling all around. Not until the last voice is still does the host continue.

"Our judges have spoken and tallied the final results. In fifth place, from Glendora, we have Thomas Mitchell."

Thomas walks forward, bows, and seeps back into the line, a loser.

"In fourth place, Samantha Fausto, from nearby San Jose." Samantha clasps her hands over her head. Another loser.

"And taking bronze for this year's Cashmere Classic is Jeffery Steel, from way down in San Diego." Jeffery doesn't even feign any form of resolve. He's bitter, and shows it with a curt step forward, a mechanical bow, and a stiff posture as he returns to the line.

Now it's between George Sneid and me, just like I thought.

"And after pulling it off by one point, ladies and gentlemen, this year's Cashmere's Classic winner is..." The host pauses, letting the tension marinate. He figures that by announcing the champion, it goes without mentioning who will take second. One name will be called, and it had better be mine.

"George Sneid!"

What? George Sneid? There has to be some mistake.

If George Sneid is the winner, that makes me the runner-up, otherwise known as the first loser.

CHAPTER TWENTY

It's been said that eating is as much as a matter
of the mind as it is the body.
~ *Leon Rappoport*

The scrum following the daylong event is like a release of refugees from an internment camp. Family and friends scramble to find one another in desperation as if they're wading through the wreckage of what a tornado left behind, not a mere comedy competition.

I'm in no mood to mingle. In fact, I find myself a statue, frozen in the same place, smoldering like a pile of sticks and leaves near a campsite, any minute now ready to burst into flames. It feels like I've been whipsawed by one of those intergalactic creatures from *Cowboys and Aliens*, his long, tusk-like nails dug into me and ripping me apart, and I'm still alive enough to enjoy the burn and sting of my own tendons and organs exposed to the atmosphere.

It's not just that I lost. I can recover from that. I have more jokes and more audiences awaiting me. It's the fact that I lost a glut of potential exposure that would have come with being on air. A weekly feature on a congested Internet comedy station is primo. Hundreds of listeners tune into these stations. I need to expand my name, my brand, and the radio segment would have done that. The sooner this happens, the sooner real money will start coming in, and the faster I can be out on my own, Cedro and my juvenile life a mere memory.

There is also the little bit about the scholarship. Though the fully paid tuition to a not-yet-listed university was a potential prize and not my favorite of the two, it would still have been useful to me had I won. But we know how that turned out. Strike two.

"Hey, Sole," a voice, like a blade, jags through the din.

I turn around to see who it is. It's Dennis Miller.

"Hi," I stammer as I greet the iconic comedian. "I mean hi, Mr. Miller."

"Please, that's my father. Call me Dennis."

"Okay." My acute, fawning tone is awkward. I'm star-struck. I think the fact that Dennis Miller has caught me in a moment of vulnerability, specifically one that highlights me as the grand loser in a standoff against a central California jerkoid named George Sneid, makes me particularly more servile.

"So," he starts off, trying to make this moment more comfortable for both of us. "Great show."

"Thank you." The way I say it lets him know I don't really believe his compliment.

Clearly, Dennis Miller is a man who has little time for useless banter or groveling. "Look, Sole, I just wanted to come over to say that you had my vote. I think you've got some real talent."

I start to light up before him as if the ceiling were splitting open and angels were descending from the skies.

Miller continues, noticing that his words are reaching me to my very core. "I'm serious. You got some showbiz potential. Just be willing to pay your dues, all right." He holds out his hand.

I clasp his firmly with mine. "Sure."

"I'll be in the Inland Empire in a couple of weeks—San Manuel Casino. It's probably about an hour east of Los Angeles. I'll leave two tickets for you at will call, okay?"

"I'll be there!"

"Great. Okay, Sole. See you there at San Manuel, if I don't see you in showbiz first!" At that, Miller walks away.

I watch him long enough to see the flurry of people swaddle him like a blanket does an infant. In this observation I notice that he doesn't directly approach anyone else. People are stopping him, naturally, wanting their five second gibe with a famous personality, but he's certainly not aiming to talk to anyone else in particular the way he did with me. This means that he, Dennis Miller, Humor Man Extraordinaire, went out of his way to find *me*, just to give *me* a personal message of encouragement, his own Hallmark quip—from Dennis to Sole. It means he believes in *me*. My mind frames the memory like this: *To Sole: Hey, man, keep it up. You got real talent. See you in the big time one day. Your True Fan, Dennis.*

While I'm basking in Miller's afterglow, some strange sense is trying its best to impose itself and intrude upon my little moment of pure rapture. I don't want to turn to see who or what it is, but I must. When I do, the spell cast by Miller is broken, and I see...I see *her* coming toward me.

It's Gaby, and she keeps getting closer, and even more stunning. Looks may not be *everything*, but according to my still-a-boy-but-almost-a-man body, there isn't *anything* about her looks that doesn't make me activate inside. Maybe it's safe to say looks are *almost* everything.

I notice that Gaby—surprise, surprise—is not alone. She's gallantly striding toward me next to a sophisticated guy, a man actually, who's all swanked out in his city attire, his Hush Puppy shoes, perfectly tailored pants, a bit-too-tight sport coat, and a t-shirt with the band name Pearl Jam scrawled over it. I can't tell if the guy's black-rimmed glasses are prescription or not, but since this guy seems to worship the word *trendy*, my bet is that the lenses are fake. *Ugh*. How I viscerally hate it when people think wearing fake glasses looks cool. It's really nothing more than a person who's not that smart trying to give the impression of intelligence which ultimately means that said person is actually quite dumb. Can't they *see* this through those gimmicky lenses?

"Hi, Sole," Gaby says, her voice overly flirtatious.

"Hi. Gaby." There's a long pause between my greeting and her name.

"You did great. Sorry about the results."

"That's okay." I can't hide the confusion.

"Anyway, I wanted to introduce you to somebody."

"Hi, I'm Somebody," the urbanite guy next to Gaby chirps, extending his hand and leaving it in the air between us.

I can tell this guy's job requires him to go through this ritualistic greeting process about a thousand times a day and that he can roll out a conversation as fast as carpenters can unravel a rug. "Hi, Somebody."

"Ha, ha, that's great!" he returns. "But really, my name is Clyde. I'm a talent rep for Premier Talent Agency."

"Talent rep?"

"I was asking around the crowd to see who knew you, and this lovely lady here came forward and said she knows you pretty well."

Gaby takes the opportunity to dip into a partial curtsy, her hand covering her mouth as if she's blushing, which she is not. This is an act.

"Pretty well?" I echo, wanting some clarity. Where does Gaby get the idea she can discard me like I was a serf in her noble kingdom and then claim to Clyde that she and I are fitted together as a sock over a foot?

"Well, I'm not here to get into that," Clyde attests.

"Do you represent Gaby?"

Clyde and Gaby turn to each other and smile. "No," Clyde says. "As much as I'd love to steal her away from her agent, I can't say I do."

Gaby adds, "But he wants to talk about, maybe, possibly, representing you."

"Really?" I quip to Clyde.

"Yep."

"But I didn't win."

Clyde is a schmoozer, and thus has a prepared answer for anything. Accompanying his prepared lines are an ultra-white, right out of the box, Crest smile. Any schmoozer worth his salt should have a great grin and quick response for any difficult question, and Clyde indeed has both.

"Winning and losing...well," Clyde jollily begins. "Those two terms don't really apply here. That's why it's important to come and watch a live performance. Hence why I came here, looking for the next comedy superstar."

"Superstar?" I repeat quizzically.

"You have a vibe on stage. A presence. A style. A thematic approach to your routine. You're a mature performer, not just telling jokes like most young hopefuls. You're sort of, I don't know, a brand waiting to happen up there. The stage is your natural habitat. The only problem is, not enough people know about you yet. That's where I come in."

"Wow. Thank you. That sounds great."

"No thanks needed," Clyde says. "That's just an observation of you and your talent. I should be thanking you."

"Okay," I say, urging him to do just as he suggested. "Go ahead."

Clyde laughs. "Thank you."

I chuckle back, letting Clyde know that I was simply making a joke about what he said. "So."

"So," Clyde spiels into a more formal tone. "Here's my card. What I want to talk to you about further is formally signing with the agency. From there, I can start getting you out to bigger and better shows, even going around the country...get you on Comedy Central, things like that. How does that sound?"

"Great. Sounds great."

"There's just one more thing. Has anyone else approached you about anything like this?" Clyde becomes somewhat possessive.

"You're my first impression of showbiz," I declare.

Clyde is relieved, putting his hand over his heart. "Wonderful. Well, okay then. Call me this week. I'd like to get you down to the office. We're in Century City, not too far from you, I believe."

I smile. "I will definitely do that."

"Excellent, Sole. Wonderful to meet you." He turns to Gaby. "And thank you for being so gracious as to find a wandering soul in need of some direction."

Gaby swats at the air, playfully being shy. "Silly man."

At that, Clyde makes his exit. It's just Gaby and I now fenced in by a galley of laughing and meandering strangers.

"So," I begin.

Gaby picks up where she left me over a year ago, except she left out the minor detail of having cast me off like a leper. "Isn't that exciting? Wow. I mean, that's big time."

"It's great." Pause. "But I..."

"You should call him. Definitely do not miss out on this opportunity."

Gaby is acting like my number one supporter right now. There's only one way to get across to her. "I don't mean to be dismissive, but the last time we talked you sort of told me..."

She cuts me off again. "I know it wasn't good. *I* wasn't good. I'm sorry."

"Okay." Then why are you still standing here? I think.

"But that's not why I'm still here right now."

That was my real question. If all she wanted to do was help me out with Clyde—great. She did that, but by the very nature of her still being here with me, I know there's clearly more.

"Let me guess," I explain. "You felt bad about what happened between us and saw an opportunity to make it up to me by making sure that Clyde got to me. It's your atonement."

She smiles, her head shaking. She's denying my accusation.

"It's not?" My legs are quivering and my body tingles, from the tips of my toes to my ears.

"I didn't just want to say I'm sorry. I...I wanted to invite you to come with me somewhere."

"Somewhere?"

"A party."

"A party?" I'm wary.

"A Stanford party. It'll be my first. How about you?" Gaby is trying to dilute the intensity that formed between us.

"Probably."

"Probably?"

"Well, I mean, I go to so many college parties every weekend, it's hard to tell. Stanford, MIT, Harvard...all the schools start to seem the same after a while." I jest back, joining her in the thinner atmosphere of playfulness.

Gaby laughs. "So you'll come?"

"When?"

"Tonight."

The heavy air encompasses us again. There is no doubt I want to be there with Gaby. No doubt.

Just then, Ava comes over, Lana winged at her side. I step away from Gaby in hopes that I can keep the parties separated. Gaby gets the hint and remains behind me where we were just standing together.

Lana and I hug and she congratulates me. Ava kisses my cheek, leaving her lipstick print on it probably. Cedro is nowhere to be found.

"Where's Cedro?" The question is for either one, but mostly Lana.

Lana takes a question she's already prepared to answer, her voice composed and lined with compassion. "You mean your dad?"

"No, I mean Cedro."

"I'm sorry, Sole, he's not here."

"I can see that. Hence my question."

"He saw your show, but then he left." Lana's features are spelling apology.

"Saw? How much of it did he see?"

"The first couple of rounds." Lana is trying to mollify my rising anger by using an over energetic vocal inflection.

"Where'd he go?" The timbre of my voice remains sterile.

"He's in Sacramento. He went to a Kings game. Apparently, their fans are into street food. He wanted to take advantage of the opportunity. He really needs the money."

I can't blame Lana for justifying Cedro's behavior. He's her love, and that's her job. I also know that Cedro does need the money since his business has never really been able to generate a profit. Nevertheless, for me, it's decision time. Should I be content *that* he came, at least for a little while? Or should I be discontented that he left and exposed himself, once again, telling me by his absence that petting his ultra-sensitive ego in this time of midlife crisis is more of a priority than his own teenage son, who is, by the way, in the crux of a young life crisis?

I choose B.

"Whatever. Chasing one opportunity means losing another. I'm done with him." Then, the moment I say it, I note the two beautiful girls around me, and that reminds me that I need to continue burying the dad issue and move on with my own.

"Congratulations again," Lana says. "Even though you didn't win, you were great."

"Hi, Lana," says Gaby, who's been standing off to the side the entire time like a good girl, and who has decided to enter this little cabal uninvited.

Why on earth did she decide to come over now?

It takes Lana a moment to recognize her. They know each other because over the course of Gaby's and my time together, she and Lana were acquainted. "Gabrielle, hi. How are you?" Lana hugs her.

"I'm great, thanks. You?"

"Doing well, thank you."

I can see Ava receding from relevancy. I try to make this a bit more comfortable for her even though it's about as possible as making a potato sack sweater feel like silk over your skin. "Ava, this is Gabrielle. Gaby for short."

Gaby does nothing. Her body offers no gesture of introduction except to mime curt coldness, as if Ava we're covered with boils, "Hi."

Ava extends her hand. "Hi, Gabrielle. I'm Ava."

"That's what Sole said."

Lana excuses herself from the very ungainly situation. "I'm going to get some fresh air." She focuses on Ava, perhaps anticipating a disastrous scenario. "Ava, find me if you need something."

Ava nods to Lana, who makes her way toward the doors. Gathering herself, Ava returns to the social brouhaha that includes the ex, the current, and me. She's undisturbed, almost wanting to laugh at Gabrielle's venomous attacks. "So, this is fun."

Gaby looks at Ava and rolls her eyes in a very conspicuous way. Then to me she says, "Think about it, Sole," and wipes off Ava's kiss print from my cheek and dots it with a print from her own glossy lips. "You have my cell." Gaby leaves it at that and pads off into the muster.

It's just Ava and I there. The whirlpool of people swirling around us doesn't close in on the two of us, but it feels like it. There's no escaping this moment.

"Um...where's Katherine?"

"She went to find Yoke. You know, you don't have to explain that whole Gaby thing," Ava says. "Ex-girlfriend. Got it."

"Really? That's it?"

"Really. That's it. "

Somehow, Ava's words are having trouble reaching me. Gaby's invitation is plastered in my mind. *Come, Sole,* the words say on the imaginary flyer floating in my head. *Come. You know you want to.*

"Sole, are you there? Hello..." Ava's head is inching closer to me, her scent filling my senses.

"Yeah, I'm sorry."

Ava tries to figure it out. "I'm sorry about your dad. Is that what's got you?"

No. "Yes," I say aloud.

"Did you really mean that?"

"Mean what?"

"When you said that you're done with him."

"Of course. I'm not one to make emotional decisions I'll regret. I make decisions based on the evidence I have."

"You think that's a good idea?" Ava is walking on eggshells with her tone, and it's sweet; it shows her concern. "Even with family?"

Right now I'm all rage and confusion—because of Cedro and the outcome of the Cashmere—while the rest of me is all lust for Gabrielle. One hundred percent of the time the conflux of those emotions rage, confusion, and lust—is always going to beat out the rational capability of a seventeen-year-old mind. Always. "A *good* idea? Nah. But it's *my* idea. And that's what counts."

"Look, I'm sorry. Maybe I shouldn't have brought it up."

231

"You're probably right," I say. Then I add some words that were better off unsaid. "Just because you had a good relationship with your dad before he passed, now you want me to hold out for the possibility of reconciliation with mine, so I can have what you had. I got it. But that's probably not in the cards for me."

The Ava I saw outside of The Laugh Factory, the one who took on Mr. Monster, a.k.a. Ryan, surfaces. "I said I was sorry and that I shouldn't have brought it up. Wasn't that enough?"

Say you're sorry, Sole. Say you're sorry. "I guess not."

"Well, like I said, I'm sorry. But you're not exactly in the best position to judge, are you?"

"Okay, Ms. Mother Teresa, God of the Universe, All Knowing Sage, tell me in your infinite wisdom why."

"No, not God, or Mother Teresa, or Wise Sage. It's just me. It's just little old me who's going to tell you something, so pay attention."

"Go ahead."

"You spend so much time thinking your dad is so self-absorbed and self-involved in his midlife crisis that you don't ever bother to try to understand why. You never try to see his point of view because you're so egotistical. You have *your* reasons for why you hate him or why you hate your mom, and that's all that matters to you—*your* reasons. Doesn't it occur to you that they might have *their* reasons?"

"Which is why I'm done with him. With them. If everyone brings their own reasons to relationships, there's no way for them to work. I'm better off without them."

"You're more like people you hate than you even know. The very person you hate your dad for being is the very person you are. The irony is, you love yourself but you hate him."

Checkmate. She's right. But I'm not confessing or surrendering. "Fortunately for me, I don't have to explain or justify myself to you."

"No you don't. You're right." After a brief pause Ava claims, "And since that's no way for relationships to work, we'd better stop before we develop a real one. I wouldn't want to bring my reasons, and you bring yours, and everything get all messy. Better to stop now while we can still part without hating each other— that is, if we haven't already reached that point."

Again, she's correct. But why don't I totally agree with her inside? My mind does, but not my heart. Do I want to live by my heart and subject myself to inevitable heartache that comes with living this way? Not really.

For whatever reason I make a weak protest. "Maybe we could still...try."

She doesn't take the offer. This time no kiss on the cheek. "Look, Sole, I'm just trying to help. Even though you don't see it that way, that's all I'm trying to do. I know you don't want things to always be like this with your dad."

I don't want your help. "I guess you know everything tonight, don't you?"

"No. That you say that tells me I don't." Ava, her brown eyes filled with sympathy for me, sighs and walks off in the direction Lana did. I'm sure Lana will take her and Katherine back to L.A.

Strike three for tonight.

Chasing one opportunity means losing another. My own words slap me around internally. Without even trying, I've already echoed Cedro's pathetic existence. By keeping to the *cajones* approach to women, by standing my ground, by living mind over heart, I've pushed my zenith away. I wonder, was my mom Cedro's zenith? Or was she his nadir?

No matter. Either way, I guess this means I'll be seeing Gaby at the party soon. Things can't be all bad now, can they?

CHAPTER TWENTY-ONE

*Sugar, whose raw power in exciting the brain
makes it perhaps the most formidable ingredient of all.*

~ *Michael Moss*

Adjoining Palo Alto is a little neighborhood dubbed The Willows. The word is that a lot of Stanford's students shack up in houses or apartments here to save on the higher rents prices that exist closer to the campus. Gaby said the party I'm supposed to meet her at is in one of those homes. Unfortunately, the reason I know the short history of The Willows is because Gaby gabbed away on the phone when I called her and told her I was coming, and that I needed to know where to meet her. Maybe it's all the skyscraping trees around these parts of California, or maybe Gaby was just that excited to be talking to me—I have no idea—but whatever's gotten Gaby so enthused about meeting up with me has definitely piqued my curiosity, not to mention my male urges. For mostly the latter, I have subjected myself to burn in a wildfire of strangers who are scorching the premises with hormones and booze amidst a clash of thumping music. If that sounds like the kind of guy who's really not into parties, then that is correct. Ironically, I am not the lover of soirées.

Real parties are nothing like movie parties. No one is King Ding here. Everyone is a singular vessel, their own looks, dress, and *twaddle*, what I call party speech, the commodities that make them valuable.

Whoever is responsible for this mayhem of self-indulgence is probably a business major. When I enter through the front door, there is no cover. However, as I traipse deeper into the muddle of partiers, I can see by the kitchen a drunken man who is about as large as one of the trees I passed on the way here. He's got a red t-shirt on that says COVERMAN on it, written in yellow across the chest. Though the shirt is fitted on this guy, it would be a gown on me. From what I can tell, the party is free, but the booze is not.

I hear him say, "Ten bucks" to a girl walking in. She reaches into the pocket of her tight jeans and hands him a bill that's folded into a rectangle.

"Unfold it," the burly guy commands.

"Sheesh. Okay. Alcohol's supposed to loosen you up, you know?" the girl voices.

"This is me loose," he returns.

"Whatever. Here," and she hands him the opened up ten dollar bill.

The burly guy extracts a snap-on band from a fanny pack strapped to his waist. Anyone who has the confidence to bring back the fanny pack has to be as lethal looking as this guy, otherwise that person would be the laughing stock of any crowd. Of course, who's going to laugh at this guy? That would be gambling with your very life.

"Happy drinking," the burly guy wishes as he wraps the girl's wrist with the band and snaps it.

I'm no business major, but I can bet that the host of this party has hired this big man to patrol the booze in the kitchen, requiring anyone who wants to drink to either pay or try to get past Mr. Fanny Pack—not a bad plan. *Party for free but drinking has fees.* Most, as I just saw, will chose to pay. At the end of the night, it's my guess that the host will give Mr. Fanny Pack a cut of the profits. It's a creative and economically constructive plan. Whoever the host is could probably get Cedro's food truck business to be more gainful and popular than it currently is. That either makes Cedro the King of Dunces when it comes to enterprise, or it makes this party's host Donald Trump in the making.

Or maybe it's a bit of both.

My phone buzzes and I quickly snag it from my front pocket. I'm expecting it to be Gaby.

ARE YOU HERE?

YES. LOOKING FOR YOU.

I'M UPSTAIRS.

Why upstairs? Then it hits me. This, or *she* rather, might be easier than I thought. My fingers jitter from expectation. At first my text reads OM XOPMIBG even though I'm trying to nervously type *I'm coming.* My phone flashes the word ON for *OM,* but it can't even suggest an autocorrect word for *XOPMIBG.* I try again.

I'M COMING UP.

SECOND ROOM ON THE RIGHT.

I'm quickly on the second story, standing at the end of the wooden stairs of this Victorian style frat house. Though I should be sprinting to the bedroom where Gaby is, I find myself congealed like hardened clay. I'm nervous, so I decide to scrutinize the décor as if I'm an interior decorator. The walls could use a fresh coat of a brighter paint color over the blunted tan tint. Whoever chose the still shots to sit in the frames must have found them in an alley dumpster where they should have stayed. Clearly these premises are occupied by guys.

After I'm done critiquing the walls, I move to count the number of bedrooms I've seen thus far since entering. Including the three downstairs rooms and the long hallway I'm staring down that is notched with one, two, three, four doorways, two on each side, that's seven bedrooms in all. That means seven smart and horny, single, emerging men shack up here, and I'm about to go into one of their rooms where Gaby is waiting.

Inhale slowly. Exhale even more slowly. My heart is still palpating like a hummingbird's at a gazillion beats a minute. There's nothing I'll be able to do to slow my pulse.

One step in front of the other, at a cautious pace, I finally reach the door. It's not entirely closed. A small slit of light indicates very little as to what's behind the wooden portal. I give one push with my right hand, letting the door ease away from the threshold.

Gaby, reclined on the bed, is using her thumb to navigate through the Web on the screen of her phone. She's posed in a ninety-degree angle, sitting upright against a pillow that cushions her back from the headboard. I follow her legs down the mattress as they're stretched out for what seems like miles. She doesn't notice me in the doorway, so I stand and steal glimpses of her for a moment. Before me is a verifiable ten. When we were together, she was a seven with the potential of being a ten, but after she put the makeover together and chiseled her body to physical perfection, she became a supreme beauty. Her ten status is now a fact, and not at all up for debate, and within my reach, and, to boot, she wants me. A little minor showbiz success and the perks start rolling. Not bad.

"Sole." Gaby looks up, having sensed me gaping at her.

"Hi," I wave as if she is across a lake a mile wide.

Most girls would feel awkward at knowing that a guy was just standing there, admiring her for how she looks. Not Gaby. This is what also makes her a ten—her confidence and comfort with being the sovereign goddess of hotness she is. She loves being adored for her beauty. That is a complete turn-on.

Ava then turns up in my mind...how demure she is, how exotic her looks are. Between the two girls, Ava's lush, brunette hair and her voluptuous lips, cheeks, and eyes—eyes that glisten and shine—give her the advantage there, but Gaby is definitely not far behind, with a beach ready freshness always about her. In a race, their looks would be a photo finish, Ava the champ by mere centimeters, at least to me. Everything else about each girl makes me crave either one just as much as the other, except in this very moment it's Gaby who's helping me make the decision a little easier and a bit more simple.

"By the looks of it, either I'm dinner or a ghost," Gaby giggles. "Sole, it's okay. I said I was sorry. I meant it. Come here." She pats the mattress.

I follow instructions and ease to the bed, sitting on it and facing her. "So you came all the way up here for...why exactly?"

"Well, you don't spend much time around our little high school campus anymore, so you wouldn't know. But, you're the talk of the town."

"You mean I'm somewhat famous at Marshall High? That's an accomplishment. Listen everyone," I mock as I'm receiving an aware in front of a crowd. "'Due to my *fame* at Marshall High, I boldly declare that I, Sole Eaby, have officially arrived in life.'"

"Stop," she lightly brushes my hand. "It's really neat to hear everyone so proud of you. They think you're going to make it—big time. Mr. Kevin was shilling for the Comedy Club and this event for the last couple of weeks, every day, loud and clear." Gaby salutes to give the full impression.

It's adorable, the way she looks when she does that.

"So is that why you're here? Because I'm the *talk*?" I ask this, wanting to know how Gaby feels about me.

Even if Gaby says that she came up here to see me just because I have a shot at fame and glory and she wants to sidle up next to an up and coming star, I think I'll still want her. Gaby is just that persuasive, or at least her ultra-hotness is anyway. *How shallow*, most girls would say about that. Well, whatever. Guys are shallow when it comes to a girl's physical appeal. That's just fact, and nothing is going to change that.

"No," Gaby justifies. "Not at all. I came all the way up here to see you."

"You can see me in L.A. You know where I live."

"I wanted to see you perform, like anybody else in the audience. I sort of wanted to know what it was like to be one of your fans...to root you on. I didn't intend to actually be here—in this room—with you right now. I just...I don't know." Gaby leans off the pillow, bringing herself closer to me. "I just saw you and I had to talk to you. It didn't feel right leaving and not...not trying to reconcile."

Reconcile. The R word. Well, right now, Gaby is the only one I will reconcile with.

"Reconcile? You mean like say I'm sorry and can we be friends?"

One curt pant escapes Gaby, coupled with the smallest of simpers. She slowly lifts her eyes to mine and reaches out to me with a hand that finds its destination on the side of my head, her fingers beginning to twist my hair. "Like this." Then she closes in on me.

I don't move. My eyes closed, I taste her glazed lips. The longer we reacquaint ourselves, the more her sugarcoated kiss seeps into my bloodstream. I'm exhilarated by her affection, in a way that I don't ever remember being.

"So, is that girl...Eva? Is she your girlfriend?"

"You mean Ava? No."

Do I feel badly or guilty about being here with Gaby? Not. At. All. Ava's the one who chose to leave.

Without thinking or plotting, I lift myself onto my feet, Gaby still seated on the edge of the bed. She's looking up at me and me down to her. We stay that way for a moment, her simper still there, somewhat shy and somewhat flaming but altogether evocative. She breaks the spell by crawling back to the middle of the mattress, and I follow.

PART 2
INTERLUDE

I associate my dad almost exclusively with that lamb roast.

~*Gabrielle Hamilton*

Definition of *paragon* according to Merriam-Webster: *A model of excellence or perfection.* In other words, paragons of anything—be they paragons of morality, like Jesus, or be they paragons of food eating contests, like Kobayashi—are standards, ideals for their respective subjects.

With that said, I hesitate to dub Cedro Eaby a paragon of anything except utter ineptness—ineptness as a father and incompetency as a business owner. I know those are harsh indictments, but, well, they're how I feel. And they're how I still feel even though...

Lana told me the news about Cedro's health, or lack of it I should say.

Cedro recently went into cardiac arrest and has been hospitalized.

Why? I don't know.

The only thing he's ever been the paragon of besides ineptness is physical fitness. There's no way this heart attack was due to his bodily health. His stellar diet (he never actually eats the goopy food he creates for the very few customers he gets. I wonder what he's been doing with all that leftover food...) and his workout regimen that includes self-defense training with the utmost of results have been nothing short of premier. There must have been a trigger. A stressor. I'll talk to him and Lana and find out what it could have been.

Despite all that, there's a clear life lesson somewhere in all of this. It could be that even paragons of elite physicality are immune to unexpected life travesties. Maybe the physical lost out in a one-on-one duel against the emotional. Maybe that's the lesson: the internal man is stronger than the physical.

Over the months since I've been living with Yoke and pursuing my stand-up career with my agent Clyde at my side, things have been going great for me. Yoke says Lana called him looking for me as I wasn't answering the phone, and her report was that Cedro and his business has gone from struggling to suffering to completely shut down, in that order. Maybe the stress of being so in debt with a failing business sacked him like a pack of wolves would a lone, helpless traveler. I thought Cedro was tougher than that. I thought he could take down financial stress like he could all of his shadow villains he would strike in the backyard. I guess I was wrong. Now that I think of it, maybe it wasn't the financial stress that caused him to tap out. Maybe it was the fact that he just couldn't take failing. He was and, most likely still is, in the throes of a midlife crisis. Maybe failing during such a time affects someone more than it normally would.

Or maybe it was something else altogether.

Maybe the guilt of him having spent my college fund on his new business that crashed and burned is what finally got to him. Maybe the fact that he betrayed his own son, even after he lived through the betrayal of his own wife and how the mother of his son betrayed them both, was what took him over.

Yeah right. I doubt that. I don't think Cedro is capable of such deep remorse.

The questions with that, however, remain: Am I just like him? Am *I* capable of such regret and remorse?

I doubt that, too.

Does that make me just like the father I loathe? If it does— whatever. That's just biology.

Nevertheless, deeper than biology is psychology. And I don't want to carry around the baggage that Ava spoke of. I don't want to regret never having forgiven Cedro and, in turn, lug around those pangs of bitterness my whole life. That would be a form of self-flagellation, and I'm not into punishing myself. So, I guess I have to do something, even the slightest thing, to prove to myself that I did enough to patch things up between us. This way I can always live with myself and look at myself in the mirror every day.

I'm eighteen now and, even if I make it to the average lifespan of seventy-two, give or take a couple of years, that's just too many years of carrying around an unnecessary grief.

CHAPTER TWENTY-TWO

It's not that my mother was a bad cook,
she simply didn't have the time.

~Marcus Samuelson

Cedro and I have been making small talk for a while, him lying in his hospital bed with an IV wormed under his skin, a mere reflection of his typical brawny and vigorous self, and me standing. He's almost deflating before my eyes, a sunken defenselessness imprinted on his face. I'm not used to seeing him this way, so delicate and fragile. I can't even be my normal, irascible and snarly self with him. When he's normal and healthy, he's fair game; but like this, there is absolutely nothing for me to gain by expressing usual snarkiness. Besides, I wouldn't want to upset him and cause him to go into cardiac arrest again.

He tries apologizing for about the fourth time. "Sole, I'm sorry. I should have been there."

I recognize this as death talk, not real talk, and I seriously do not want to engage in fraudulent conversations, so I ask, "What did the doctor say about recovering?"

"He said I should be fine, but that I have to take it easy on stressing out. Why?"

"Look, Dad, you're not dying. That means you don't have to start with all the apologies as if this is going to be our last conversation."

Cedro knows that even his dance with death could not instantly make all of our controversy go away. "You're right. If I'm honest I would probably have done the same thing again." He's referring to missing my last high school stand-up performance in favor of pursuing profit.

His truthfulness is bracing, a fresh breeze through an otherwise stale relationship. "Thank you for that honesty. I appreciate it."

"Well, you're welcome. What about you?"

"Me?"

"Don't you want to rail me with your usual attitude of contempt?"

I can't help but chuckle. "Good one. But no, not when you're like this. It would give me an unfair advantage. You can't properly defend yourself, and if you did, you could probably die. I'm a lot of things, but I'm not a murderer, intended or otherwise."

"They've got cable in here," he says.

I'm wondering where this comment is leading. "That's...good."

"I saw you the other day. You were on the Comedy Circuit channel."

"That's pretty old. It was recorded about a month ago."

"You're really funny. Even though it hurt to laugh, I did. A lot. The nurse had to come in and try to change the channel. I told her not to."

"I'm glad you liked it." I want to rub in the fact that I've been making some solid cheddar with my comedy work. I've easily made a few thousand dollars and I want to fan those bills over his scraggily, unshaven face, but I resist, of course.

"So, do you just keep doing this? How do you get to be a headliner like Kevin Smith or Louis C.K. or something?"

"Clyde says I need a second outlet."

"Clyde?"

"My agent. He says I need to get into acting or hosting media events or anything that can supplement my comedy. And he's right. Every comedian who is anybody makes it as more than just a stand-up comedian."

"Oh, like Ryan Seacrest?"

"He's not a comedian."

"I mean the hosting part."

"Oh. Right."

"So what are you trying to get into?"

"The basics right now. Film, television, and radio...but I'm willing to do Internet stuff, too."

"That's great, son."

Following a breath of silence, Lana comes in the room. We all share hugs and hello's, and then I use this opportunity to also cash in my exit card.

I ease my way to the door saying, "Well, it was really good seeing you, Dad. You too, Lana. Anyway, I'm going to get going."

"Wait," Cedro says. "Here." He reaches to his side and, from under the blankets, pulls out a wrapped box. "I almost forgot."

I amble back toward the bedside, collecting the present. "Is this a guilt offering?"

"It's your eighteenth birthday gift."

I feel badly about that last comment. "Sorry. I just forgot."

"No, I'm sorry. I'm the one who's belated here."

"Thanks. I'll open it later, okay?"

"Sure."

This time I vanish through the doorway and turn down the hallway before any last second words can reach me. I get past the nurses' station and think I'm in the clear, ready to go pick up Gaby. We're supposed to meet up and hang out, and then go back to one of her friend's house for a little VIP party.

"Sole, wait."

Caught from behind. I hear a voice and turn to see whom it belongs to. It's Lana.

"Sole, I just wanted to say it's good to see you. I'm so glad you came. He really...well it's hard for him, but he's really been wanting to see you. He feels so bad and..."

"Please, Lana. You don't have to do that. I know what's going on between him and I—or, I should say, what isn't going on. All I can say is I'm trying. I did my part."

"Did?" Lana wants to get deeper into the topic with me, but once again, she avoids soapboxing me. Instead, she sidesteps the crux of the matter. "Yes you are. And I'm sure he can see that."

I doubt it.

"There's something else I wanted to tell you."

Uh oh, I think. "What?"

"I'm pregnant."

I can feel my mouth drop. I know it's Cedro's, and that means I shouldn't care that much, but I do. That's my little brother or sister inside of her. "Congratulations."

Lana starts crying. I hold her, letting her anoint my jacket with her sorrows. Not until the tears stop do I ask, "Why aren't you happy?"

"I'm scared. The business is done. We're in scores of debt as a result and...I know he didn't tell you all this, and I wasn't going to either, but, well, he's going to have to put up the house. It's the only way."

"Where will you live?"

"My little condo."

It's a lot to absorb, but I try. It's no easy task to try not to care about something that you actually do.

"Go back to *the business is done* and the whole debt/house thing."

"Basically, with the money we can get from selling the house, that will pay off the debt he incurred from trying to maintain his dying food truck business."

"Are you selling the truck, too?"

"Everything. That will pay up the debt and give us a little time. Hopefully he can get into teaching again."

A teacher's salary and Lana's decent salary will not ever get them a mediocre house in L.A., not unless it's in the heart of gang-infested territory. Along with this, Cedro won't be getting a job at Marshall in their English department. He'll probably end up in some ghetto school teaching *Green Eggs and Ham* to illiterate sixteen-year-old thugs who can barely read but know how to pack a handgun.

"Sorry to throw that on you," Lana suggests. "I just thought you should know. He's just too proud to tell you himself."

"Of course. You're right. I should know. Thank you for telling me."

I don't tell Lana about my professional opportunity, that there's a comedy circuit touring the East Coast and that I'm practically a shoe-in for one of the full time acts, according to my agent, Clyde. The pay would be more than I've ever made in my life for doing anything, let alone something I would probably do for free.

Lana and I hug, a mechanical one as I am uncertain of how to be, feel, or think. I didn't come here to feel this way. I came to absolve myself of future guilt and walk out emotively stronger. Instead, I'm stuck pondering what I will do, feeling as if the original *bang* from the Big Bang just went off in my chest.

"You know, Lana, you could leave him."

"Leave?"

"You're not married—officially anyway. He hasn't taken the step. That means—"

"I couldn't, Sole."

"Couldn't? Wouldn't? Or Shouldn't?"

Lana kisses my cheek. "I wouldn't. I love him because I choose to, not because of what he does or doesn't do for me."

Lana's words excavate me, exposing every throb of derision I feel for Cedro. I am definitely far from loving anyone the way Lana does Cedro, but as far as the child inside of her is concerned, that's a different story. Inside her is innocence, and it deserves a chance to stay that way, despite the way Cedro has self-destructed and caused the baby to be born into a wasteland of a life.

So, there's only one way I can think of helping out Cedro, and that way includes me giving up my potential spot on the East Coast Comedy Tour. *Wonderful.*

CHAPTER TWENTY-THREE

For me, the cooking life has been a long love affair,
with moments both sublime and ridiculous.
~ *Anthony Bordain*

Crawling up Laurel Canyon Boulevard is The Curse of The Maroon. As badly as I want to get to Ava's house that hovers in the Hollywood Hills above Sunset, I find myself navigating the car without any urgency. It's been almost two months since Ava and I have spoken, and I have no idea what kind of reaction she will have once she sees me, especially because I haven't called or texted first. This will be an unannounced house call.

After passing rows of trees and obscured homes, I curl around the bend in the road and see that Ava's car is in the driveway. My heart initiates an up-tempo rock beat, causing my pores to rupture and let nervous moisture drain out, and tingly chills flicker over my skin and atop my head. This should be a happy occasion, but my body is telling me it's more intense than that.

I park along the road and turn off the ignition, sighing to myself and sitting back. There's no rush to exit the vehicle.

As I ponder, my phone vibrates. Even though I have a strong idea who the text is from, I check anyway. GABRIELLE. Her complete name flares on the screen, and under that is her message. WHERE ARE YOU?!?!

I was supposed to have already nabbed her from her house where we would have then grabbed something to eat and, from there, trudged off to her friend's house where there's a party going on. Instead, I'm sitting in my car like some eerie schizoid who's having a delusional episode and can't decide which of his many mind voices to listen to.

Gaby will have to wait.

To dip my toes in the proverbial waters of uncertainty, I try dialing Ava's number. No text or something impersonal. I'll go old school on this one. After four rings and no answer, it's official that she doesn't want to talk to me. It's now time to go dramatic.

I walk up the steps and to the front door of her Spanish style home that her father bought when he was alive. He clearly was a well-employed man.

With dusk approaching, my imagination begins to arise, and I start to pick up the pace of my gait, thinking that the ghost of Ava's father will knife through the trees and haunt me. Maybe, if his ghost is able, it may materialize and taunt me with long-winded, spooky phrases like, "How...dare...you... Ooh..." But there is no ghost.

I knock on the door.

A moment later, a lithe, petite woman greets me. "Sole, hi, what a surprise. How are you?" It's Ava's mother. I only met her once before, but her tone suggests that Ava hasn't mentioned anything about how she and I haven't spoken at all.

"I'm good, thank you, Ms. Rozen."

"That's so good." Ms. Rozen is dressed in a blouse with a pair of blue leggings, having no problems at all convincing anyone that she can pull off young lady's attire. "I'll get Ava."

"I'll wait here, thank you."

"Okay."

Perhaps her not insisting that I come in means that Ava has explained the distance between us after all. With this, I don't know how to position myself. Should I pace back and forth? Should I sit in the chair? Figuring that there is no right pose, I decide to check the news on my phone until she comes out.

"Hi, Sole," Ava's soft, warm tone calls in a way that indicates she is not angry or much of anything toward me. In fact, she's neutral. I could be a sponge salesman to her and this is what I would get. Maybe anger would have been better in this case. At least I would have known she thought of me over the past few weeks.

I play the diplomatic card, too. "Hey."

Ava isn't offering any more of herself than her distant politeness. The uncomfortable silence rises to its feet and dances over me in mockery, all the while Ava is as composed as the song playing through her phone. She softly hums the melody in that syrupy tone of hers.

"I didn't mean to disturb you," I suggest.

"I was just downloading some songs." She continues to use her finger to scroll up and down on her screen.

"I called you before I knocked."

"I know. I just didn't answer."

Now that that's out there, I have no reason to be coy. "I know you don't want to talk to me, and I can understand."

"So why are you here?"

"To say sorry."

"Okay. So say it."

"Sorry."

"Okay, now tell me why you're really here."

"Do you accept my apology?"

Ava ponders, her gaze still fixed on the phone's screen. "I do."

"Thank you."

"Will you please tell me why you're really here now? Because if it was just to say *sorry*, we'd be done."

"I need your help."

"I'm sorry to say, but there isn't help for your condition. Misanthropy and jerkishness are not curable by medicine. It's more of a change-of-heart-and-mind thing."

"I thought you said you weren't upset about any of this."

"I'm not. I'm upset that I'm still dealing with you after I thought I wouldn't have to deal with you anymore."

"Fair enough," I sigh. "So, will you hear me out?"

"Do I have a choice?"

"If you tell me to leave right now, I will."

Ava sets her phone into her pocket. She's thinking. Suddenly, her eyes soften. "Go ahead. What do you need?"

I fill her in on Cedro's situation, not failing to leave out the part about Lana's pregnancy. "It's my dad's, in case you're wondering," I jape.

Ava is holding back a smile that wants to expand across her luscious cheeks. "I wasn't wondering. But thank you."

"So, with all that said, I have a plan."

"A plan?"

"And it includes you."

"How so?"

"Will you come with me somewhere?" Ava's left brow crawls up her forehead. "I have to show you. But you can drive and follow me if you want."

After she inhales and exhales the breath slowly, she surmises, "Fine. And I will follow you."

*

I'm leaning against The Curse of the Maroon that is parked along the curb, sipping from the java I stopped to get along the way between mine and Ava's house. Ava is next to me, but her car is stalled behind mine. We're gazing at what was once the house I called home. What was once the house where Cedro, my mom (God be with her pathetic soul wherever she is) and an infant-to-toddler me lived. The blue paint and white trim shading the panels adorns this family structure ever so perfectly. It cries out for a DNA-bonded unit of people to grow up and old together in as it looms over a lush, manicured lawn.

Wait. What?

"He's letting the lawn die." I walk to the hose that's attached to the house near the humble porch and turn it on high. It's cool right now, a wintery L.A. dusk. I watch the water sluice from the rubber tube, splashing onto the rusting lawn.

Ava strolls to where I am on the porch and reminds me of why Cedro hasn't been able to tender the grass. "He's been sick, you know?"

"Yeah, I know. It's just that I'm not used to seeing it this way. No matter what's happened *inside* the house, the *outside* has always looked great. I don't want to see that go away."

"You're just your everyday cover-up artist, aren't you?"

"It's like how I'm always joking. You know how Nietzsche said 'Wit is the epitaph of emotion'?" Well, that's how it is.

Humor is the outside of the house, the epitaph, masking anything that may have died inside."

"Even this house is a metaphor for your life. Interesting."

"Which is why I just can't stand to see it this way."

Ava ponders for a moment while I finish spraying the grass and rolling up the hose. She finally notices what I brought her to see. "Did you notice the sign?"

She's talking about the sign staked into the grass that reads FOR SALE. I did notice, but I didn't want to acknowledge it out loud. Talking about it just makes it too real.

"Come on inside," I say. "Maybe my dad didn't throw out my stash of coffee. We can refill." Ava's got that untrusting look on her again. To allay her doubts I add, "I'll explain over another warm cup."

Ava follows me inside.

Sifting through the cabinets, I find that my stash of ground coffee beans are still there. "Yes. He didn't throw them." I take the bag of blueberry grind and place it in the coffeemaker. Then I fill the pot with water and pour that into the dispenser. "Okay. In a couple of minutes—heaven."

"So what's this plan of yours?"

When the coffee is ready, I add the sweetener and powder creamer, just the way she and I like our Joe, and lead us to the backyard patio. I turn on the tube of lights bordering the awnings, to add a moody effect. In the ottoman are blankets, and I take one out for Ava and offer it to her. "Thanks." She receives my offering, and we sit on the cushioned furniture. As for me, I'm just fine in my Henley and leather jacket.

Over the next cup of coffee, I detail the information Lana told me about and how I'm thinking of cancelling my spot on the East Coast Comedy Tour to stick around and help Cedro and

Lana get on their feet again, financially—for my soon-to-be brother or sister's sake.

"You know, it's not like they're going to be homeless or anything," Ava suggests.

"It's not that. It's just that it *shouldn't* be that way—at least, not for the little guy. It doesn't *have* to be that way."

"I say the same thing every time I think about my dad."

I set my cup down. "I'm not trying to compare situations. I know my situation doesn't compete—at all—with losing someone."

"No. It's fine. All I'm saying is that I understand you." There's that silence again, the one that keeps popping up in my conversations lately. That means only one thing: there are some serious issues occurring in my life.

"Is that how you feel about how things worked out for you?" Ava breaks the spell of quietude. "And that's why you want to rescue the baby."

There are two ways to answer a probing psychological question. The first is direct and honest, which tends to saw off the edge of emotion that wants to show itself, and I certainly don't want any tears or heaviness to rise in me right now. The second way to answer is to get close to the issue, whaps all serious and deep and reach into my soul to explain the pain and hurt I've experienced because of everything—wah, wah, wah. I'm not going to do that.

Like I said, direct and honest is the best way to staunch emotion. "Naturally, I admit I'm a bit bummed that my dad was too busy trying to figure himself out that he sort of left his son to filter through the growing up process by himself, without someone really there to explain things to him. To make sure he came out on top."

Ava responds in her soft tone as if she's a shrink on the armchair and I'm lying on the sofa. "At least he didn't leave. Like your mom."

"Yeah. You're right. *'At least.'*"

"Well," Ava draws us back to the point, not taking the bait to start a who's-had-it-harder war. "You told me the plan. You haven't told me about how it involves me."

"I've saved the best part for last."

"Oh no. I'll be the judge of what's best, thank you very much."

Standing up, I discharge my ideas like an automatic machine gun does a magazine of bullets. After I do, I summarize, probably for the gazillioneth time, my main point. "The thing is, my dad has no concept of branding. If he wants his little mobile enterprise to stand a chance, he's got make it a brand. All that I can do. What I can't do is make the brand go viral."

This is the part where Ava clearly understands her role in my scheme. "Are you planning on paying me a flat fee or giving a percentage of royalties?"

I'm caught off guard. "Uh...umm..."

"I'm kidding. We'll worry about that later."

"Oh. Phew." I sit back down across from her. I want to sit next to her, but she's given me no indication that this would be a good idea, and I don't want to ruin any rapport I've built. "I'm glad. I—"

"Look, I'm only considering this because I think it's great. I think the sacrifice you're making for your family is...well, I can say I didn't see it coming."

I'm fairly certain that Ava is suggesting I am showing myself to be a compassionate human being who actually possesses a genuine love for people other than himself. My face, I am also certain of, is showing how astonished I am that someone would actually think this about me. "So you'll do it?"

"What are you thinking? Website? Social media?"

"That's just for starters. I want to go big. By the time we're done, I want Food Network to be crawling to us. I was thinking of, like, posting videos of the company. Sort of like a documentary of running a mobile food business. We'll call it a Truckumentary."

"Like a reality show concept?"

"Exactly. And you make apps, right?"

Ava is offended, her face curling back as if she's just smelled a raccoon's rear end.

"I'll take that as a yes," I declare.

"So, is that all?"

"I'm going to rename it."

"Is your dad okay with that?"

"He destroyed his company. He should be thankful I'm taking the initiative on all of this. He'll thank me later."

"You're pretty sure of yourself, aren't you?"

I shrug. "Well, how do I answer that without sounding—"

"Like an egotistical, misogynistic scrotum sack?"

"See what I mean?" I confirm, wearing my I-hope-you-think-I'm-as-irresistible-as-I-think-you-are-right-now face. *I regret letting her go.* It's showing.

"Well, maybe this will make you a bit unsure: I will help you." My smile is as wide as the United States from east to west. She continues. "But we're only friends." Smile gone. "*Only* friends." Now it's like she's ripped the happy from my face, thrown it to the tile floor—hard—and is stomping on it in a ritualistic way, maybe the way the Native Americans dance around and trample for their deities. "Can you deal with that?"

261

Of course, I won't let her know my heart is falling like confetti from my chest down through my body. "Can I? Can *you?*"

Ava laughs, the joke covering up any discomfort lurking around the patio. Ava brings her cup to her lips with two hands and sips—so cute. She sets the cup back down on the table. "I think it's really great what you're doing."

"And I think it's really great that you're helping."

Just when a small connection is sparked, my phone buzzes. *Gee. Who could that be?*

*

After Ava has left, I'm now stranded and free to wonder what to do about Gaby, alone, in the living room of the house. Even though Ava isn't back in my life "like that," I don't feel like I can see Gaby right now. I must be crazy turning down a night with a ten when, really, I have no other plans or anything on the old agenda tonight.

I've lost my mind. I resign myself to this thought when I text Gaby.

CHANGE OF PLANS. STAYING WITH MY DAD IN THE HOSPITAL. SORRY. CALL YOU AS SOON AS THINGS CLEAR UP.

OK. SORRY TO SEEM PUSHY. TAKE THE TIME YOU NEED. MIND IF I GO TO THE PARY WITHOUT YOU?

GO HAVE FUN…WELL, G-RATED ANWAY.

OF COURSE. YOU'RE THE BEST!

Gaby can be so sweet when she wants to be. That's the girl I knew before she turned into the Gaby she is. The ironic thing is, the Sole I know does not dislike either Gaby. However, the Sole I'm finding myself becoming, this weird and strange version of myself who is willing to do things for people without expecting anything in return...this is the Sole that somehow can't register with Gaby.

There definitely must be something wrong with me.

As far as girls go, it doesn't get any better than Gaby, at least physically. She's a universal ten, and U-tens can register with any male of the human species. Except for me right now.

Now I know there definitely must be something wrong with me. I put my hand on my forehead. No temperature.

The one thing I haven't done is open the present Cedro gave me. It's still in my car. I rise, gather my keys and jacket, and head outside, locking the door to the house behind me. I don't intend on returning tonight.

The gift offers me a distraction, even if for a few seconds. I settle myself in the driver's seat and reach over to the passenger's side. The sun is all but sunken in its celestial chambers for the night, leaving beams from a lamppost and a few glints of natural horizon light to illuminate the interior of the car.

Unwrapping the gift, I can see it's a box that is meant to encase a watch. Judging from the care and design put into the box, I gather the watch wasn't cheap. Seeing the words INVICTA scrawled on the top, I know this watch wasn't cheap.

I lift the top half of the case.

The silver rim is glistening, and the dials are just as lustrous. The black straps are thick and sturdy. I don't know what *chronograph* means as it applies to the watch, but as it applies to me, it means *really cool*.

It's a touching offering, one I'll accept.

CHAPTER TWENTY-FOUR

I'm not in this to make people feel bad about themselves...
I never had a lot of that nurturing element when I was a chef...
sometimes it just comes across as a little bit of tough love.
~Scott Conant

A couple of days later, things are starting to roll. What's gotten some of these things tumbling forward are my recent earnings from my comedy gigs. *Teeth cringing.* That's right: I've had to ante up my own bankroll to fund the *restructuring* of Eaby Baby's Edible Crazies. Since it's my stash of cash that's funding Project Relaunch, the first order of business was to change the name.

"Here she is," Cruz says, his accent coming through.

Cruz is part owner of Miguel's Body and Paint on Pico Blvd. in West L.A. The reason Cruz has just earned two grand of my own, hard earned cheddar is because if it were anyone else, I would have had to pony no less than five G's for the custom makeover that the food truck just received. Cruz happens to be one of Leo's—freshman Comedy Club member at Marshall High—cousins. Leo threw in a good word for me and so—lo and behold!—a three thousand dollar discount which just means I'm two thousand poorer. This is quite an act of contrition. I hope heaven is taking notice of my generosity toward Cedro, despite his track record as a father.

"It looks amazing." I take a picture of the newly named words stenciled on the truck's side: STREET FOOD & LOVE.

Surrounding the words are no longer the pastels and bright vomit colors from Crayola's Reject Department. These are fresh, modern tones, artistically woven together in contemporary fashion. The white backdrop is boldly contrasted with a multi-colored, jagged heart that's broken in multiple places and spread throughout the sidewall, adding much needed color over the simple base. The words STREET FOOD & LOVE are swelling as if they are about to burst in various chromatic color schemes. The edges of the words are sharply cut in some places and rounded in the other. It seems to represent the different forms and definition that people have when the word *love* is spoken. For such a short and simple word, a million different images and ideas spring up in people's minds when they hear it. Everyone has their own idea of what love is. In relationships, it's no wonder why they don't work. People realize at some point that their definition will never match their partner's, so they split. For STREET FOOD & LOVE the meaning is singular and clear: *love* means *scrumptious food*.

"Thanks, Cruz. It's awesome."

"My pleasure," Cruz says, standing by my side and admiring his work the same way I am. "You got my cousin something to go to school for. He's always had trouble with his grades. Now, he sees that being smart will only help his comedy."

"I'm glad."

Breaking our moment of admiration and reflection is a commotion of horns blaring on the street. A sheeny, white BMW is pulling into the parking lot, leaving a morass of agitated drivers on Pico Boulevard in its wake.

Oh no. I know that car, and I know whom the ash blonde hair behind the wheel belongs to.

"Great," I say.

"You know that crazy chick?"

"She's sort of my girlfriend."

Cruz slaps his hand on my shoulder. "I used to play baseball. When I saw a fastball coming straight for my head, I used to get out of the way. I suggest you do the same with that one," Cruz forecasts and doesn't waste another beat standing next to me. He walks back into the shop.

Gaby parks the car—well, it's more like halts the car, like police officers do when pulling up to an emergency crime scene—at an angle, taking up two slots. Not even giving me a chance to catch up to the speed at which all of this is occurring, Gaby is out of her vehicle and stomping toward me. That's not the oddest part of all this. Her Samsung Galaxy S4 is in her hand, and its sheer size makes it as conspicuous as if she were carrying a block of cheese.

"Hey," I say, hoping that these next moments won't go as badly as the events up to now presage.

I'm wrong.

Gaby holds the screen up to me. "I found your little *Truckumentary* on YouTube. By the way, pretty shrill on coining the new genre—Truckumentary. I like it."

"Thanks—" I'm confused. She's angry, but she just complimented me.

"But that's not why I'm here."

Come to think of it, I never told her what I was doing today. In fact, I haven't spoken to her much in a couple of days. That means she's found the link and page Ava created for the documentary portion I envisioned. That means she knows about Ava.

As part of a marketing campaign, I decided to catalog the events of relaunching the business by posting videos of some of the major moments. My only point for this is to try and create a following, to create a fan base. With Ava having set up the page, all I have to do is shoot some video through my phone and upload it to the site. Apparently, Gaby found the site and saw yesterday's post which was a segment of me pulling up to Miguel's Body & Paint with the truck just before it went into the garage for a makeover—sort of a before and after effect.

"Why didn't you tell me about this? All you've been saying is, 'I've had to take care of my dad.'" Gaby uses a whiny voice to imitate me.

"I didn't say it like that."

"That's not the point."

"If you want to get technical, I actually have been taking care of my dad."

"How is that?"

"This truck is his business. I'm helping him out since he can't exactly do it himself."

The stunned silence engraved on Gaby's face is priceless. I realize that my motives for helping Cedro out are anything but altruistic, but still, no one knows. Besides, Gaby's the one who came roaring in here like a tsunami gone wild, crashing angrily on me like a fifty-foot wave. If she hadn't done that, maybe I wouldn't have had to play the, *I'm-such-a-loving-son-who's-trying-to-help-out-his-ailing-father card.*

"Sorry." Gaby admits her fault.

"Even if you didn't know that, it's not like I was doing anything behind your back."

I forgot about the first video I posted two days ago after Ava agreed to help.

Gaby remembers at the same time I do. She pushes some things around on the phone's face and then flashes me the screen. It's the first video of Ava posting the first live links of the website.

"So is that you filming this girl?" Gaby notes, her question more of a dare as in *I dare you to prove me wrong.*

"Yes."

"Okay. So you're filming this girl uploading the website and I'm just supposed to think, '*Oh, how cute. It's Sole filming a web designer*—' a very pretty web designer I might add. And a very familiar one. I remember her, Sole." I stand silent, waiting for Gaby to do all the talking since she seemingly knows all the answers. "She's the girl from up north. What's her name—Eva? She's the one you were seeing before I poached you from her."

"You didn't poach me."

"Oh, I didn't? Then how did you end up with me later that night when you went up there with her?"

Well, moment of truce. Or truth. Or whichever. Of the two, I decide I'm going to choose truth, and that means that I'm going to lose out on any more skintimate moments with Gaby and her perfectly perfect body. This is not normal for me, which seems to be the theme right now. Normal is no longer what it was. A new normal is being defined, and, God help me, I'm going to go with it.

"I ended up with you because she and I had an argument. It was more about me running *from* her than me running *to* you."

This is only offensive to Gaby because of her U-Ten status. U-Tens tend to be narcissistic and, even when rejected, would rather have someone say something condemning about them personally. This way a U-Ten can snuff her nose up at you and say something like, "*Too bad. Your loss. There's a line of guys who'll appreciate me,*" or something like that. They never want to hear that they were a second choice because then it's not all about them.

"So what are you saying?" Gaby asks, completely blindsided now because I have pretty much said that I would have chosen Ava over her if given the chance.

"I'm not saying anything. You're the one who came here. Remember?"

Gaby considers everything. "Aren't you supposed to be headed back East?"

"I was. But I'm doing this now."

"What do you mean, 'I'm doing this now'? You're giving up comedy?"

"No, I'm not giving up comedy. It's just on hold right now. I gotta help out my people. Family."

"But you hate your dad."

I shrug, not expecting Gaby to understand.

Gaby tries a different route with me, a sensitive one. "But this was a big break for you. You're just giving it up? Just like that?" Gaby moves in, planting air kisses around my neck. After a few of those, she lets her lush, glossy lips glaze over my cheeks and my mouth.

I get it now, just right now, as Gaby's lips are causing my body to swell. The reason my comedy tour was so important to her was not because of any personal meaning it had for me. Like I said, tens have this code they live by: *Everything revolves around me;*

that which does not revolve around me makes no sense. Gaby is making it clear that she wants me only as long as I'm on the up and up. That's why she showed up at the Cashmere and invited me back into her life. That's why she's been here the past couple of months. Not that I am rubbish or anything, but girls like Gaby don't just go for *who* the guy is. It's just as much about *what* he has to offer.

"Is this whole comedy thing more important to you than me?" I ask.

Gaby's head draws back in faux shock. "What? No. Of course not. I just know that it means so much to you. I'd hate for you to regret it."

"I'd regret not doing this more. I'll have more opportunities for comedy."

"That's not how the industry works. You know that. You have to take the opps when they come or there may not be another chance."

"Clyde's still my agent. I've told him about it. Yes, he gave me the same spiel, but in the end he respected my decision. He said to let him know when I'm ready to go back on gigs. He assured me that my talent is still talent and that he intends to capitalize on it as much as I want to." I say it in a way that implies, *Top that, bee-witch!*

Gaby's affection falls limp, short-circuiting as if someone could just unplug all her desire for me in an instant. She backs away, leaving a couple of feet between us. I can still smell her perfume, Touch of Pink. *Lord, I'm going to miss the scent of her skin.*

"You don't seem to feel the same way Clyde does about me," I tally more points of contention.

"I'm sure he's right. And I know you'll succeed." Gaby feigns an amalgam of kindness and sympathy, her hands folded in front of her in a praying form. *This is the universal body language for I'm sorry.* "You need to be able to focus on all this right now." Gaby's hands make wax-on wax-off circles in front of her. "I'd just be a distraction anyway."

"You wouldn't be a distraction. You'd just have to support me. That's all." I mean what I say, but I know it's no use.

"No, really. It's better this way. Call me when...you know...all this is clear. Okay?"

"Sure, Gabs."

"I hope your dad gets better soon. I really do." Gaby, the classic ten, strides back to her white BMW, slips on her oversized Poncherello sunglasses, and joins the flow of automobiles along Pico.

I'll definitely not post this in the Truckumentary.

CHAPTER TWENTY-FIVE

My mom made two dishes: Take it or Leave it.

~ Stephen Wright

Project Relaunch's headquarters are at Cedro's house. He's still in sickbay, so this is the best place to operate from since it has the least amount of distractions.

In the living room, I have an easel set up that has a sheet of poster paper plastered on it for everyone to see. It's the master list, a guide of things to do that Ava, Lana, Yoke, and I can focus on. And, seeing that we've almost checked off all the have-to's before we can finally get Cedro's mobile enterprise out on the streets the right way, creates a little buzz in the atmosphere.

Helping with this are the sounds fusing through the surround sound speakers. The selected songs are from a playlist of someone's registered account on Spotify with the tag VILLAGEWESTLA. Drums and lead guitars behind throaty vocals are the common threads in each song, and they've been enough to keep us motivated and working for the last couple of hours. *Way to go VILLAGEWESTLA, whoever you are. Your taste in music is shrill.*

I check the poster paper on the easel again:

> Business Website (Ava) ✔
> All Social Media Sites (Ava) ✔
> Tracking App (Ava) ✔
> YouTube Page for Truckumentary (Ava/Sole) ✔
> Facelift/Paintjob (Sole) ✔
> Rename Company (Sole) ✔
> New Menu (Lana)
> Selling Route/Locations (Sole, et al)

"What does *et al* mean?" Yoke asks.

"It means go get me a soda from the fridge," I jeer. "How's it going in the kitchen?" I call out to Lana.

Lana sips from a glass of water she poured for herself then sets the glass down. In the past, the glass would have been filled with wine, but since Baby Eaby is in her, water is the way to go. She writes down the ingredients to the recipes that will be on the final menu and tastes each item and sauce as she goes. It's important to know exact amounts and measurements so that each dish can be replicated. "Just about done," Lana calls out.

"So what *adult* libations does my dad carry in here to drinkee?" I ask, holding up an empty glass to insinuate that I want her to fill it with something strong and toxic.

"Nice try." Lana reads from her notes, ignoring my pitch for some alcohol. "Well, signature dish number one is guisado—chicken, beef, pork, *et al.*"[16]

"What the freak, man?" Yoke peals, standing up yet again to get something from the fridge since he thinks *et al* means *get me*

---

[16] *Guisado* is the name for a type of base that can be used as the foundation for any type of meat. Its core ingredients are tomato/tomato sauce, garlic, and onion sautéed so that there is a thick broth created for the meat to wade in. Moisture is pivotal for the success of this dish.

something to drink. "You guys keep using that phrase. Couldn't you just say, 'Will you please get me something to drink?'"

"Actually, yes," I attest, holding my stomach because I'm busting up in fits at Yoke, who's got his head inside the refrigerator, looking for water.

"You're such a pebble puke," Yoke gibes.

"*Et al* means *the list goes on,*" Ava defines from the kitchen table as she is tapping away at the keys on her laptop. "Sorry. I just couldn't keep seeing Yoke do that popping up and down thing anymore." Ava's index finger is modeling the up and down motion.

"You're such a liar," Yoke pulls his head out of the fridge and blares, scowling at me, pretending to throw the bottled water that he's holding. "Thank you, Ava. See, Sole, Ava just modeled the humane thing to do: telling the truth."

"I guess I'm a savage," I shrug.

Lana continues as if nothing else was said. "All guisados are served with either a griddled flatbread or a buttered and grilled roll. Dish two is—"

"Wait," I interrupt. "Come up here, and write it down." I flip the main checklist over the top of the easel so that a blank page is showing.

My only requirement for Lana when designing the menu was that the food has to be thematically connected. That's what makes it a *brand*. People want to go to food trucks because that truck sells a certain kind of food, like Land Rover dealers sell Land Rovers and not Toyotas. It's got to be exclusive. Surely[17]

---

[17] *Surely* is the proper way to say *sure* here. Cedro, once English teacher extraordinaire, drummed that into me. It sounds pretentious when I say *surely,* but I can't help it. It's habit. I've been saying it for so long.

that, by definition, eliminates the possibility of all customers wanting that truck, but that's fine. That's the way it works in the street food culture, that is, if the plan is to actually bring in the big jack, the mean green. It's all about the branding of your menu.

Lana brings her notepad into the living room which flows seamlessly from the kitchen. I hand her the marker and wave her toward the blank page.

Ava, Yoke, and I watch Lana as she scrawls in lovely swirls across the white paper. Behind Lana, I make pirouettes and pretend to write in the air to the tunes of The Airborne Toxic Event as if I am entranced like Mickey Mouse in *Fantasia*.

"Sole's lost it," Yoke asserts.

Ava giggles, enjoying the mania and momentum of the moment.

Before the song can end, Lana backs away from the easel. "There it is."

1. Guisado served with protein (pork, chicken, beef, et al) and carbohydrate (Hawaiian bun or griddled flatbread); Sauce (guisado is wet as is)

2. The Burgeneggtor with various ground proteins (pork, chicken, beef, et al) all topped with mozzarella and cheddar are served between grilled Hawaiian bun or griddled flatbread; sauce (sunny side up egg inside—yolk)

3. Shrimp burrito wrapped in griddled flatbread and topped with shredded cheese; sauce (freshly made salsa and garlic cream sauce)

4. Smoked and roasted pork shoulder or sirloin tip pulled and topped with shredded mozzarella and cheddar mix and served as a sandwich between Hawaiian bun or griddled flatbread as a

burrito; sauce (freshly made salsa or jalapeno honey barbecue sauce)

"Tada!" Lana turns around when she's done.

I hate to do this to Lana, but it's a must. I have to see if Lana can truly see the brand, the theory behind the food. It's strange, but that's what the customers are going to want. To me, food is intake, like gas for a car. But that's not necessarily the case with people who frequent food trucks. Food is philosophy to truckies, and they're going to expect that we have some esoteric meaning behind what we're going to serve.

"Huddle," I clamor, waving Ava from the table and urging Yoke to read what Lana wrote. Ava comes and sits on the cushion beside me. "So what do you see?"

"Words. A list." Yoke begins to describe.

"No, you literal dolt. I mean thematically. How does this menu directly suggest Street Food and Love?"

We're all quietly pondering for a moment.

"All the proteins are wrapped," Ava speaks slowly, conjuring the thoughts one at a time and carefully. "That's the way people want to be when they're loved. Just wrapped in it."

Lana nods. "Exactly."

I take this as a cue to give Ava that look, that coded gaze of admiration that lovers share. Except, I'm reminded that we are not in love.

"I mean theoretically, of course," Ava defines loud and clear.

"And you get to choose how you're wrapped—bun or flatbread. Just like people get to choose who they will let love them," Yoke rubs his philosophy into the grind.

"Pretty good, Yoke-a-Doodle-Do."

"There's one thing that I think we haven't said. And I think it's perfect." I look at Lana when I'm saying this.

"Everything has some kind of sauce." Lana smiles proudly.

"Exactly," I reinforce, still trying to entreat a flow, a connection between Ava and I.

Trying but failing.

"Every love affair needs some '*sauce*,'" says Ava making quotation marks at her side with her fingers.

"It needs to be moistened with attention and affection," I add, looking at Ava when I say this.

She turns away.

"Maybe she was thinking of a different kind of sauce," Yoke inauspiciously concludes.

Fortunately, Ava has adjusted to Yoke's debauched humor already. "Not really."

I place my hands together in a reverent manner of worship. "Lord, please...I pray for Yoke in his time of plight. May his depraved mind be made whole. Amen."

We're all laughing, even Yoke. When the billow of laughter recedes, a what-happens-now silence emerges. To break the wonderment, I rise from the sofa and walk up to the easel.

"May I?" I ask Lana, holding out my open palm up. Lana places the marker in it. I turn the page back to the checklist of items on the previous page, remove the cap from the blue marker and place a checkmark next to NW MENU (LANA) so that it now reads:

New Menu (Lana) ✓

Underneath that I add one item to the remaining, unchecked one.

Selling Route/Locations (Sole, et al)

Name menu items (?)

The question mark means one of us has to be assigned the task.

"Ooh, I'll do it," Yoke rises and waves his arms.

"Is this your orangutan mating dance?" I ask.

"The one you taught me? Yes," Yoke bites back.

"Well, good. Because I hope it didn't mean you weren't actually volunteering to come up with names for our menu items."

"Aw, come on, Sole."

"Uh, no. Absolutely, categorically not. As sure as Tiger *Woods'* name fits his personal profile—no way."

"Let's think about it and write some stuff down tonight, then tomorrow we'll decide," Lana suggests.

"Sounds good," Ava agrees.

Yoke digs through his backpack and extracts a notepad and a pen, his thoughts blazed in ink in a flurry across the page.

"I have one more item to add," Ava adds. Except for Yoke, who's in the zone right now as he acts like God Himself is divining through his hands, Lana and I are gawking at Ava, waiting to hear her idea. "Why don't we throw a relaunch party? Your dad gets out the day after tomorrow, Sole. We could have some legit flyers made and do a street blast. I'll update the Internet. And Lana, can you make a sampling of the items?"

"Sure?" Lana is hesitant, thinking what I am.

"We're in this to make money. Isn't this thing going to put us in the negative right off the bat?" I query.

"You have to put in a little money in to get a lot out of it. Trust me, this will create a nice whir out there. It'll get 'em talking. It'll help bring in the peeps."

I shrug. Lana gives a soft, tacit approval of her own.

"Relaunch fiesta it is," I declare.

"Ooh, I got it," Yoke blurts. "Check this out."

I take his notepad and read off his suggestions for what he thinks we should name each menu item. "Okay, ladies and gentleman, for your dining pleasure we first have the *Dragon Gui Wrap.*" I cough, almost choking, not believing an intelligent life form actually put thought into this. "Yoke, is this supposed to be the guisado?"

"Yep," he confirms proudly. "As in *gui*-sado."

"But why *dragon*? It's not like we're serving dragon meat."

"No, subterranean slime, it's *gui* as in what the Chinese women wear. *Dragon* is because it just goes with all things Chinese."

Ava and Lana are covering their mouths, hiding their grins. I try to be as kind as I can under the hilarious circumstances Yoke has set up. "There's nothing Chinese about the menu."

"Oh, yeah." Yoke is truly stunned at his oversight.

"I'm not sure about this one, buddy."

"Well, what about the next?" Yoke asks.

"Lana already named it *The Burgeneggtor.* Remember?"

"Okay, skip that. Go to the next."

I read Yoke's third effort. "*The Shh-Quiet-Now Wrap.*" I'm at a loss. "Is this the shrimp flatbread burrito?"

"Yes it is."

"Why is it called The Shh-Quiet-Now Wrap?"

"Because, dunderhead, don't you hear the *shh* in *shh*-rimp?"

"And that would explain the *Quiet-Now* part?"

"Now you're on my wavelength," Yoke beams.

"Well, I think we'll just hold on to these ideas until tomorrow," I announce, trying to stealthily sneak away from the topic. "Why don't we try the menu now?"

The four of us schlep to the kitchen, waiting to sink our teeth into the food we've been talking about, the food that Lana has been slaving over for a few hours. I reach into the refrigerator and hand out water and soda. The playlist still rumbling through the house has us closing a long night to the crows of All At Once, a perfect musical conclusion.

"All the shrimp wrap needs is bacon," I surmise, my mouth stuffed.

"Bacon would be perfect," Ava agrees.

Lana scribbles that down on her notepad.

I hold up my soda can in the midst of us, our mouths all still full. "To Project Relaunch," I force through the flavors and textures of Lana's eats symphonically beating on my tongue.

With equally jammed mouths, Ava, Lana, and Yoke push their water bottles and soda cans toward mine, all meeting in the center of our circle. "To Project Relaunch!"

CHAPTER TWENTY-SIX

The way you cut your meat reflects the way you live.

~ Confucius

"Surprise!" an agglomeration of random strangers says when Cedro walks through the double doors of the entrance to Lot 613, an event venue in the Arts District in Downtown L.A.

Stark black and white shock covers Cedro's angled and gaunt face. He genuinely was not expecting this. Lana whispers into his ear, probably explaining what all this is about.

Lot 613 can hold up to a thousand people, although maybe a third of that max occupancy has shown up—not a bad turnout. After the initial hoorah, the guests immediately return to doing what they were doing a few minutes ago, just before I had the music silenced so we could all greet Cedro. Street Food & Love's launch party is officially underway even though it unofficially has been vibing for over an hour. Those on the dance floor look around the air as if the music is just going to come from nowhere. I nod to the DJ from where I am, and he resumes driving resonant beats into the sound system so that the rhythms drill through the crowd's skin the same way it does in a club.

The colored lights—red, violet, yellow, green, and blue in various sequences—splash around the wooden beams threading the ceiling and the rusted, metal staircase that twines up to the second level. This gala feels like a movie star was hosting it. Ava and Lana did a fantastic job.

The tables set strategically in the outside patio area, away from the entrance, are filled with small, disposable plates, each containing plated portions of the items the truck will specialize in. There are four tables, one for each of the main dishes that will be the staples of Street Food & Love. The purpose of the sampling area being staged here is so that people have to actually delve into the deep end of the party to taste, uh-hum, *greatness*; the guests can't just eat and sneak out. Assigned as the Tasting Monitor is none other than Yoke. He has been tasked with ensuring that each person who samples a plate fills out a survey card.

Here are the card's questions: 1) What would you change about the plate? Be specific. 2) What would make the plate even more irresistible? Be specific. 3) Would you be willing to go out of your way to purchase food from the vendor of this dish? If so, please "like" this vendor on Facebook.

Once someone fills out the survey card and consequently hands it over to Yoke, he then gives them a Street Food & Love business card that has all the sites and links listed where Street Food & Love can be found on the Internet.

To make sure things are going as planned, I waddle over to the outdoor patio area.

Ropes of mood lighting sag from the rooftops, each spotted with dimly lit bulbs.

"How are things going?" I ask Yoke.

Yoke is wearing a trendy little get-up—fitted jeans, a plaid shirt with a solid tie, and a light blazer over that. He seems poised, not his usually diffident self. "Would you like to try the—?"

"Yoke, it's me. Hello?" I wave, interrupting his invitation.

"Or maybe I could interest you in—"

"Stop it. What are you doing?"

"Just rehearsing," he smiles, enjoying that he's like a little splinter under my skin right now.

"Well?"

"Well what?"

"What's the word? How do you think people are liking the plates?"

"Let's see," Yoke cups an elbow with the palm of his other arm, tapping his finger at his temple. "A lot of '*Oh yeah. That's good.*'" He says it like someone deeply yearning for something.

"They said it just like that?" I ask.

"Well, maybe it was more like, '*Ooh yeah. That's good.*'"

"You said it the same way," I remark dryly, not entertained.

"No, I didn't. I added the extra 'ooh.' In any case," Yoke urges, a tincture of frustration now settling in him, "people seem to like it. Except one person suggested we should put guacamole into the *Éros* wrap."

"Hmm. That's a great idea. Can't believe we missed that. We'll definitely do that."

I read the signs rising from the center of the tables, the new names for each dish gaudily flying over the food like a flag on a castle. What we decided to do was name each of the four plates a type of love as defined in the Greek dialect which has the most definitive articulations of love on the planet.[18]

The burger plate has been named *The Storge* which is the Greek word for love meaning *affection*. It's the base, simplest form of love experienced, like ground meat is the base and simplest form of food we carry.

The guisado plate is named *Philia*, which means *brotherly love*. The way guisado is sort of a Spanish gumbo and a dish that people prepare when they want to be hospitable to unexpected guests seems to match the meaning of brotherly love, so we just went with it.

The shrimp in griddled flatbread is called *Éros* because *eros* is the word to express a passionate, sensual, and lustful love. Shrimp with shredded cabbage, cheese, salsa, a cream sauce and, per the guests recommendation, guacamole, seems to be a sexy plate, so we let this plate take on the name. I realize shrimp isn't really sexy, but we need to brand our food and this is the best we could do.

Finally, the pulled tri tip and pork plates are called *Agápe* because this is the highest form of love, the sacrificial love where you love without expecting anything in return. In turn, the effort and time needed to successfully prepare the tender fall-off-the-bone tri tip or pork shoulder is pure sacrifice, hence the name *agápe*.

---

[18] For example, when Americans use English to express love, they use the same word every time. "I love cats. I love to ski. I love pizza." These are all ways to express a favorite animal, hobby, or food. We also use *love* to try to convey our deepest passion for a person: "I love you." The word love here is diminished because of how it's used over and over in lesser way. This is not so in Greek.

"Well, well, well," a voice says beside me. When the arm belonging to that voice slings itself over my shoulders, I know who it is.

"Hey, Dad."

"Son, this is amazing. I can't believe it. I'm...I..."

"Lana told me about the baby."

"She did, did she?"

"Yep."

"Yeah, she sort of 'fessed up to me the other day." Following a moment of silence, Cedro says what he came to say. "You didn't have to do this."

I could get all sentimental and sog up my crisp new duds that I bought for this shindig—tan corduroys, a checkered blue shirt under a pastel pink and blue tie, all under a fitted sports coat—but I won't. "I did, actually." I turn to face Cedro. "I know what it takes to make the business successful. If that gives my little brother or sister a chance to grow up in our house that you put on the market and have a semi-normal upbringing...then yes, I have to."

"What do you mean '*semi-normal*'? You don't blame me for your mother leaving, do you?" Cedro's tone is incredulous, not believing such thoughts would cross a rational human being's mind.

"Nope. But I do blame you for all this." My arms make the motion to the song "He's Got the Whole World In his Hands."

"I never asked you—"

"I mean the reason all this has happened. I mean why couldn't you just stay a teacher? We could have been normal. You work, and I go to school, and we hang out with each other, like a father and son. Then I go off to college and admire you for being such a great dad. But no. You spent most of my life searching for yourself, doing all these things and making all the weird decisions—all the while I'm just orbiting around you on the outside. Watching."

Boom. Now it's my turn to drop the nuke.

Cedro is cloaked in the fallout of the aftermath of my heartache—years of pent up frustration deployed in an instant.

"I never knew you felt that way."

"You mean you don't *remember* I felt that way. And wait, it's not *felt*. It's *feel*. I *feel* that way," I state.

"Son, you don't understand. It's hard for a man to realize he might never be whom he always wanted."

"That's called sacrifice, Dad. It's called parenting. It means your time's expired."

"I guess that's the way you've always seen it. One day you'll understand. Or not. I hope it's *not* and that you get all you wanted the first time around."

"I hope so," I double his words over, not knowing why.

"Look," Cedro begins. "We can't do this right now."

I sigh. "You're right."

"I just came to say thank you. So, thank you."

There's nothing else for me to say. If I continue, I'll make it worse. "You're welcome."

"So, what's next?"

"You let me call the shots for the business." Cedro offers me a look of pure skepticism. "You're not even supposed to be working anyway. Doctor's orders."

"How do you know?"

"Who do you think?"

"Lovely, lovely Lana."

"It's because she cares."

"I know."

Cedro thinks about it. "Okay, son. I trust you with this."

I trust you with this. I'm touched, but again, I won't show it. "Okay. Sounds good." I extend my hand.

Cedro pushes away my formal gesture and hugs me. "Okay then," he murmurs then walks toward the inside where the main space is, where the party is happening.

"Thanks for the watch." I call out.

Cedro turns and smiles, a sincere one, one I haven't seen much of. "It's the least I could do." He walks through the doors, the crowd ingesting him.

A few moments later, I take my turn at the mayhem inside the main area. Strolling around, I decide to walk up the stairs to the mezzanine level. There's no one here whom I know, which is a good thing. We want unknown people to come and share the news about the company. The more, the better.

Suddenly, someone taps me on the shoulder from behind. I turn.

"Hi." It's Gaby.

I can't hide my astonishment.

"I know. I'm the last person you expected."

"What are you doing here?"

"I read about this on your Web page. Thought I'd check it out. It's really amazing. This turned out shrill."

"Thanks."

"You're really going for this, aren't you?"

"I told you, it's something I have to do."

"And you never do anything halfway."

"You are correct. You know me well enough to know that about me."

Gaby inhales and lets out the breath slowly. "I miss you well enough, too."

"What?"

"I thought about it and…it was stupid. I was stupid. I…"

"Hey," a chipper, familiar voice joins us. It's Ava. "Hi—Gabrielle is it?"

"*Eva* is it?" Gaby mocks.

"Okay, okay. Let's not—"

"Honey, it's okay. I understand," Ava explains. "No worries." Then Ava presses a silky, ripe kiss on me. She's stunned me and knows it, so she lets her lips dangle over mine until I kiss her back. I take full advantage of the opportunity, sucking every bit of her luscious lips. When we separate, I absorb Ava, her dark, accented eyes reflecting any light in the vicinity. "I just wanted to say I'll be right over there," she says and walks away.

"So, are you guys *back*?" Gaby inquires like a puppy asking if anyone has seen her owner.

What do I do? What do I say? We're not back together. And if I say yes, then I'll be without any girl. If I say no, at least I'll have a U-Ten again. But at the expense of what? If I return to Gaby, I know I'll get distracted and forget about all this, the very reason I am here tonight.

"Uh, yeah. Yep," I declare unconvincingly.

"Are you sure?" Gaby giggles.

"Uh, yeah. Yep. Back together." I join my hands together a couple of times, mimicking the *together* motion.

"I guess this is goodbye then?" Gaby expects me to change my mind.

She's almost a fortuneteller because every surge in my body is urging me to take back what I just told her. "I guess so," I stutter the words, forcing them out, defying my male instincts.

Gaby bites her bottom lip, knowing that she still makes being a guy difficult. Knowing that she is every guy's desire. "Okay then." She kisses my cheek and then whispers, "I could have been yours."

Gaby, a tight green dress snaked over her, struts off.

After I get over my paralysis, I walk over to Ava, who's looking over the edge of the mezzanine rails.

"Don't get any ideas," she says. "I was just saving you from a big regret."

"Regret?"

"You know as well as I do that if you went back with her all of this, all that you're doing—nada. Gone. You'll forget about it."

"Isn't that my choice to make?"

"*Was* your choice. Until you brought us all into it."

"So I'm like your Captain Spock now? Your Commander in Chief? Your almighty leader?"

"Exactly. You can't just lead us out to the battlefield and then say, 'Okay, troops. Good luck. I'll be back at home pulling for you.' It's not how it works."

Ava is spot on. There's no use fighting her. "I hear you."

Ava turns to me, looking sensuously ripe in her own snaky, shortcut dress. "You're actually agreeing with me that fast? That's got to be record time."

"When you're right, you're right."

Ava feels my forehead. "Hmm. Maybe change is possible."

I grab Ava's hand and place it over my heart. "Not maybe. It is."

"See," Ava pulls her hand back. "Just when I was starting to believe." She laughs at her own joke.

I join her with laughter of my own. "So you and me?"

"Plutonic. Plu. Ton. Ic. Capital P." She tries to make a P shape using both of her hands.

"That doesn't look like a P," I jest.

"Close enough."

CHAPTER TWENTY-SEVEN

Never eat more than you can lift.

~ Miss Piggy

"I put us up on TruxMap," Ava notes from the passenger's seat in the truck. "And sent out blasts on Twitter, email accounts, Facebook, Instagram, *et al.*"

Ava and I laugh because of the way she stresses the phrase, *et al.* She's playing on how I told Yoke *et al* meant to go get me something from the refrigerator and how he kept popping up and down from his chair every time he heard the word. Aww... Memories.

TruxMap, by the way, is a live, in-real-time, virtual map that shows where all registered food trucks can be found that day in Southern Cal.

"Awesome. Thanks for doing that," I say, steering the beast toward South Harbor Boulevard, which is technically in the greater L.A. Basin but specifically in a little coastal spot called San Pedro where the vessels The Queen Mary and Spruce Goose are stationed.

There's a dinner event here every third Thursday night of the month called Just Too Much Thursdays. I'm prepared for there to be some stiff competition as over twenty-five food vendors will be on hand.

But we're ready. I hope.

We've not only prepped well, we have people coming out to this exploit tonight just to buy from us. At the Relaunch Party, we made a special announcement that generated quite a whir.

Ava and I had spent some time brainstorming the business after the little Gaby affair, and we decided to tell the guests during our impromptu broadcast that if they Tweet something laudatory—well, we used the words *shrill* and *cool*—about the food and the company, or if they can get five friends to "*like*" us on Facebook—all this of course has to be verifiable—they'll receive two dollars off their purchase the next time they stop by the truck. That was followed by some hoots and hollers.

In anticipated response to that pronouncement, I've given Yoke a special job tonight. He'll be standing by the truck, checking phones of people who are willing to prove they're discount worthy. If they verifiably are, Yoke will give them a card that we had printed for this special offer. Customers will then be able to redeem the coupon at the window. It's a nice way to create anticipation and make our prices just a bit lower than those around us.

There's also another secret weapon on standby. I had Yoke borrow the P.A. system from Mr. K so that, in case I had to do some open-air comedy, I'd be prepared.

"Everybody set?" I ask

Ava and Lana call out, "Affirmative" from the can.

When Yoke doesn't respond, I repeat, "Yoke, are you ready?"

Yoke is standing just to the side of the truck's front end, a few paces from where I am which is right under the serving bay. "You mean you're asking me, too?"

"Uh, yeah. Why not?"

"Oh, because, I don't know...once again I've been given the most irrelevant job this side of Europe, and I didn't think it actually counted as being an official task."

"You know, if you need your diaper changed, you could just ask—but not me. I'm not going anywhere near your stash."

"Well, who says I want you near my stash?"

"Dude, you'll take anyone near your stash. Don't act like it's not true."

Taking a quick inspection of the parking lot and the bottlenecking in the streets, I gather that this gala will make Harbor City of San Pedro the place to be. Car after car, person after person ranges along the asphalt and sidewalk eager to steal away the evening by tasting fatty foods from their favorite mobile caterers. All the stops are out. Trucks from fourteen feet long that looked like they've been resurrected from the automotive graveyard all the way to thirty-foot monstrosities that are meant to be driven by Goliath himself are humming along, their kitchens hot and eager as if they were sprinters in the starting blocks.

That's when I notice a face in the oncoming flow of people, one I know quite well and one I was not expecting.

"Hey," I greet Cedro. "Did Lana forget something?" I'm referring to the backpack slung over his shoulder.

Cedro is amused. "No, no. I came to help."

"Doc said you're out of commission for a few weeks."

"Yeah, doctors say a lot of things."

"That's what they get paid for. It's their job. They're sort of supposed to tell you their professional advice as it pertains to small issues, such as your heart and your very physical existence."

"I feel fine."

"So do sociopaths. They feel great, even when they're slicing and dicing away."

Cedro isn't just trying to be patient. He truly isn't bothered with my onslaught of snarkiness. Could it be? Is he changing a bit, too?

This is weird.

Cedro and I might be coming to life altering revelations around the same time. We could both be trying to become better men, better humans. This should be a discovery worth celebrating, like the Rosetta Stone or Dead Sea Scrolls or something, but it's not. Not to me. Why? Because Cedro is a forty-plus, almost fifty-year-old grown man. He should *already* be the guy I am—and I still don't know what's gotten into me— becoming.

"Look," Cedro compromises with his explanation. "I just came to help. I didn't want to miss it, you know?"

You've spent your whole life missing things that pertain to me. Why don't you just continue doing what you've been doing? "It's understandable. But still, you're not supposed to."

"Sole, it's my business, you know?"

"Cedro, it's your business that you couldn't run, you know?"

Here is where Cedro will prove his mettle. I've markedly disrespected him by a) using his name when I addressed him and b) tongue lashing him with raw, unbridled rancor.

Cedro takes the atmosphere into his lungs and blows it out. This must be a diffusing technique.

Now, there's something worth noting here. If Cedro were to ever cross the line, he could obliterate me rather quickly. He knows how to tactically fight and, well, I don't. I have a mouth, but have yet to prove I can back it up. Come to think of it, there doesn't need to be any proving: *Let the records show that I can't back it up.*

A calm, controlled Cedro says, "I'm here. I'm staying. Tell me how I can help."

When he speaks like that, it makes me put the metaphorical gun down that was ready and aimed at him. Reluctantly I add, "You can be a rover."

"What's a *rover* do?"

"He roves."

"Of course. What a silly thing for me to ask," Cedro deflects my sarcasm in a disappointed manner. Maybe he was expecting kindness from me. "Seriously, Sole, I'm here to help."

"Seriously, Cedro, doctor said you're not even supposed to be here."

"Yeah, well..." Cedro flexes and kisses his wilting biceps, "I feel great."

I shake my head in disbelief. "Look, just fill in and make sure the guests are fine. If they need something, get it for them. Make sure they don't have an excuse to not buy from us."

"I can do better than that," Cedro boasts, slyly slipping his sunglasses over his eyes. "I'll draw them in."

"Please don't," I implore.

Cedro discounts my advice, turns, and beams toward the sound system. I can see him finishing the setup, plugging chords in the right places and such. The flow of the masses whorls around him like a current, but he remains undeterred. He's as naively excited as a newly badged CIA agent who's just been dispatched into the field for the very first time.

"It's almost dark, you know!" I bellow to Cedro, trying to get him to take off the shades since the sky is dressing itself in its evening wear—pinks, purples, reds, and oranges canvassing the heavens.

He doesn't care. He rises, microphone held inches from his mouth, and begins to speak. "Come on over to Street Food and Love!"

*

It's almost ten o'clock and all the families, couples, and children have fled the area. The Street Food & Love crew is in clean up mode as are the other trucks still parked all around. The night turned out to be a success. And it was a good thing Cedro showed up. There were a lot of technical issues we ran into— how to operate the oven, what to do when this machine does this or that and all that good stuff.

"Completely sold out," Lana says.

"It's a really good menu," Cedro notes, sinking his teeth into the *Éros*, which is the shrimp flatbread wrap plugged with a cream sauce, cheese, guacamole, cabbage, and salsa.

As a crew, we've decided that each of us gets a meal off the menu following the shift. Just one. That's pretty standard for food industry workers. As a result, each of us takes a moment here and there to step aside from cleaning up and bite off a portion of dinner. I'm enjoying the seductive textures of my *Agápe*, the name of the pork shoulder wrap that is succulent and moist and practically melts in my mouth. The honey barbecue sauce and salsa combo make the flatbread slide effortlessly down my throat and I'm enjoying it all the more.

"Hey," a girl says, not just to me, but to all of us.

I turn. Standing there all perky as if she hasn't just spent the last four hours inside the guts of a piping hot truck, serving ravenous and sometimes annoying foodies who think they "really know what good eats are," is a smokin' hot young woman, maybe early twenties, who's wearing a pink shirt with the words BABY'S BODACIOUS BURGERS printed in black across the chest. I have to shake my head to make sure I am seeing the word *burgers* and not *boobers*.

I take the initiative on this. "Hi. What's going on?"

"I just—well, we wanted," the young woman says, turning back towards the pink truck with the same words that are written on her shirt stenciled on the sidewalls of their snazzy food truck, "to say that you guys are solid."

"Thank you..." I leave room for her to fill in the thought with her name, the beam across my face indicating to this young woman that I am flirting.

"Julie."

"Thank you, Julie."

"So, hey, Angela from El Vagón Fusión said you're pretty cool."

Angela reminds me of Christie. I pause at the altar of Christie set up in my mind. I never called her, but maybe if things go south with Ava, I just might. "Angie's down."

"Yeah, she is. Hope you guys are, too. I'm sure we'll be seeing you around."

"Where are you guys going to be next?" This is an established food truck business, and I want to pick her brain for the best selling spots.

"Fiesta in February Food Truck Night in Westchester."

"I bet I know why they call it that," I jape.

Now when I say something like that, there are two directions someone will go with this. If this girl from Baby's Bodacious Burgers asks me *"Why is that?"* then she's flirting and I can ask for her number[19]. If the smile suddenly evaporates from her face and she says something like *"Wow. That's awfully Sherlock Holmes of you to figure out"* then she's suggesting to me that coming over here may have been the biggest mistake of her life.

"Oh, really. Why is that, Sherlock Holmes?" Julie asks, combining my two predictions, which would be confusing if she didn't have that flirty look on her face.

"Because it's February." I wink.

"Are all of you who work your truck this smart?" Julie asks.

"Nope. I'm at the top, and the intelligence level declines from there." I'm clearly joking so that Yoke, Ava, Lana, or Cedro don't take it the wrong way, in case they're listening.

"Great," Julie remarks. "Then I don't have to worry about you being our competition." At that Julie walks away, her skinny jeans framing her body so well that she moves up from a nine-plus to a clear ten.

Ava comes up to me. She pretends to be a pitcher, throwing a ball to a hitter. Then she jogs a few paces ahead as if she is now the batter. She sets her arms as if she had a bat in her hands and mimes the swinging motion. The batter she's pretending to be has obviously whiffed on this pitch. "Strike three," she declares softly. "You're outta there."

Cedro's the next one to come up to me. "Don't say it," I urge.

---

[19] Ava isn't my girl, by the way, so she has no leverage on me. Plus, it might be nice to make her jealous. This Julie chck is a solid eight, almost a nine.

"I don't care about that," he says. "I heard what she said about that event, the Fiesta in February thing. Is that on the map?"

I pull out my phone from my pocket and move some things around until the calendar of events I have scheduled for Street Food & Love comes up. I start to type the information in. "It is now."

"Good," Cedro says.

"Why?" I'm flummoxed by Cedro's positivity.

Cedro approaches me and slings his arm around my shoulder. We're side by side, looking at the house lights spotting the hills. "Oh, Young Jedi, you must learn something..."

I laugh, humored with his hyperbolic tone, and don't move because I like his gesture. I do. I really do. I miss this. What son wouldn't like his father chumming up with him? Though I won't admit it or return the *manfection*,[20] but I do like it.

Cedro continues. "Even a beautiful woman can make herself an enemy. Did you ever see Jennifer Aniston in *Derailed*?"

"That's not a true story."

"No, but it should be. Most guys I know would fall into the same position as Clive Owen's character did."

I nod in agreement.

"So," Cedro declares, "from what I heard, that girl just declared war with us." I look at Cedro, understanding slowly forming on my face. "Eh?" he spurs.

I get it. "It's on," I say. "It's so on."

---

[20] Soleism #5: *Manfection* is the combination of *man* and *affection*. It's my words for a socially legal and legitimate form of affection two males display. For the record, there is absolutely wrong with a little *manfection*. In fact, it's healthy. At the very least, it means the two guys involved are confident with their manhood.

CHAPTER TWENTY-EIGHT

My doctor told me to stop having intimate dinners
for four unless there are three other people present.
~ *Orson Welles*

Street Food & Love's crew of five—Yoke, Lana, Ava, Cedro, and me—not only has considered it a personal war to best Baby's Bodacious Burgers, we've considered it our personal crusade to out-earn and out-sell any other truck that dares try to peddle their grub in the same city as we do.

Our caravan arrangement is as such: either Cedro or I will drive the truck and there will be one car following—Cedro's Jeep Rubicon—if the sell site is more than two hours away (to save on gas), and two cars if the site is within a two hour drive. The second car will be Lana's or Ava's, depending on who wants to be behind the wheel.

A couple of days after the San Pedro smash, we're in Diamond Bar at a bowling alley, in the parking lot. The plan is to hawk as much of our menu as possible before we close up there, and then stop at a pub around midnight to dump the rest of our supply. Drunks make great customers because they always want something savory to settle the effects of the brew.

Ava stays with Lana and prepares the food. Yoke is their sous-chef of sorts, on standby and ready to do whatever it is they need.

"For once. Just once I'd like to do something meaningful."

"I didn't bring the Huggies, Yoke, so you can't wet yourself today. You're just going to have to tough this one out."

"I'm serious, Sole. This is my last trip if you don't let me—"

"Okay, okay," I patronize. Not that we need Yoke for the business to succeed. We don't. But as a friend, Yoke's important, even as eccentric and odd as he is. That's why I work with him. "Why don't you come in with us?"

"Inside the bowling alley? With you and your dad?"

"We're going to...how can I say this? We're going to *gather a customer base.*" The way I say it makes it sounds like Cedro and I are going to do something illicit.

"Be specific," Yoke directs.

I take a few moments to ponder how I'm going to pitch the plan to Yoke. Cedro and I don't exactly have an outline. We're going to go inside the alley and work the crowd, hand out our cards and steer people away from the gaseous alley food that's more like nuclear waste and encourage them to eat at the truck instead.

"I think I can handle that," Yoke attests.

"Fine. Come on."

As the three of us get ready to troop inside, a car pulls up next to the food truck. Getting out of the vehicle is Katherine. She might officially become crew member number six. Shrill.

"Hey, Yoke, check it out." Yoke turns around. He's speechless. "What's up with you two?"

"Nothing," returns Yoke.

"Why not? I thought you two were hitting it off that time we went up north."

"If you thought that was hitting it off, then you clearly don't know the definition of *hitting it off*."

No matter what Yoke says, he can't deny his maleness, his attraction to the first girl he's ever gotten past the word "hi" with before she stalked away in primal fear. He's not doing a good job of concealing this desire either as he's gawking at Katherine.

"So why you don't you go talk to her?"

"What do I say?" Yoke asks, scared.

I think for a second. "Well, first thing is, you don't have to be scared. She's not a homicidal alien who's studying the human race to find their weaknesses so she can transmit that information to her superiors whereby they can then quickly eliminate the entire human population. She's a girl. So make it simple: ask her a question."

"About what?"

Geez, Yoke. No wonder girls are afraid of you. "Something interesting."

"Like what?"

I think about this tactically. "Ask her, 'If you were going to try and sell food from a truck, where would you go?'"

"That's pretty good."

"Yeah, I know. But I'm also serious. Pick her brain. A, it will give you something to talk about, and B, you two will be genuinely helping out the business. Isn't that what you wanted—a *meaningful* task?"

I watch Yoke rehearse exactly how he's going to say what I told him. "Wait, one more time. What do I ask?"

"Ask her where she would pitch the truck if she were going to sell food from it."

"That's not what you said," Yoke combats.

"It's the gist, not the exact words, dink brain. You can add your own flavor to it."

"Oh, okay. Got it." Yoke doesn't bite back because he is in deep thought, trying to hold onto the one whole sentence he has to put together for Katherine.

"We're going to go inside and work the crowd. Why don't you stay here and...well, you figure it out," I advise.

"Sounds good," Yoke agrees and makes his way to Katherine.

Cedro and I each take in a deep breath, eye each other and nod, then brave through the double doors, toward the bowlers inside.

"I'll get the bar and work my way back to the lanes," Cedro said.

"I'll start at the arcade and snack stand, then work my way back to the middle of the lanes," I affirm. "We'll meet there and, by then, should have canvassed the whole place."

Without wasting another breath, we get to work.

With the muddle of teenagers and nothing-else-to-do-tonight twenty-somethings in the arcade, I have to take a few moments with each one. The whole *"Can I have your attention please?"* spiel won't work because it'll just chafe them more than anything, and they'll definitely not come and eat out of sheer spite. It's not cool to interrupt someone in the middle of a video game.

"Hey, you're crushing it," I spiel to a kid and give him a two-dollar off coupon so that he'll come and eat. Most likely, these kids need to hear the word *discount* if I'm going to get them to the truck as their minds will wrestle with the question, *"Do I use my last few bucks on food or a few more games?"*

"Do double-left, diagonal-right, up-up-up, down-down for a killer move," I say to a what-looks-like-a-thirty-year-old man who's playing a guy my age.

"Aw, that freaking sucks," the my-age guy says after my suggested move destroys him. He's not a threat because he looks like a bunch of celery stalks tied together with dental floss at the joints.

"It's cool." I hand him a coupon. "Grab a bite afterward. It'll take the edge off. We're right outside."

When I walk out of the arcade room, I scope out the wide alley of forty lanes, gathering myself and trying to locate the snack bar. I spot this dink of a kid thinking he's funny by tossing the ball down the lane of the bowler next to him. Bad move. The guy next to him is serious about his bowling and doesn't think it all undiplomatic to slap the kid across the face, grab him by the back of the neck, and walk him to the bench behind the scoring table. Not even this boy's parents are bothered. The dad stands over the heh-heh-I-think-I'm-really-funny boy and points at him, giving him a lecture, the crushing of plastic and urethane of the balls and pins resounding all around.

Locating the snack area, I turn toward it and hear a break in the usual alley noise. A chorus of laughter is coming from the lounge. That's where Cedro's territory is.

What I see at the bar is a group of people cluttered around someone, whom I can't see from my angle; but I can hear the voice. It's Cedro. He's telling jokes to a group of middle-aged misfits, all of whom are at the bowling alley tonight because it is apparent they have no other thing to do in this entire world.

I guess I do take after Cedro in some ways. I can't remember ever seeing Cedro be this social or gallant, this attention-getting extrovert. I didn't know he had it in him.

By the time we finish canvassing the alley and we walk outside to the truck, a line is crawling around Street Food & Love. Our campaigning worked. Off to the side are Yoke and Katherine, milling through the crowd—together—and making sure the customers have everything they need.

"Aw. That's cute. Yoke didn't scare Katherine off this time."

"Good for him," Cedro concurs, holding out his fist so that I can pound it. "We make a pretty good team."

I pound his fist. "I have to admit, it's true."

"Too bad we didn't see it before."

"Too bad *you* didn't see it before," I counter, still not ready to forgive and embrace.

"Okay" Cedro accepts my rebuttal humbly, apology in his eyes. "It's too bad *I* didn't see it before."

CHAPTER TWENTY-NINE

Health food may be good for the conscience,
but Oreos taste a hell of a lot better.
~ Robert Redford

The schedule for the next few weeks is set up to be busy and brutal, but together the crew of five is ready to be the best new food truck business to hit the springtime streets.

One of our stops is the Garden Crescent Convalescent Home. We've arranged to blow in during the afternoon lunch hour which is practically dinner for these seniors. It's difficult to tell which meal is which, that's why the hospital's administrator who permitted us to come said we should arrive for a midweek serving from 1-4 PM.

Surprisingly, this stop on our food truck tour was the brain craft of Yoke and Katherine. The two of them spent the entire evening at the bowling alley, and afterward, at the pub, conjuring up best places to include on our route.

When the crowd is slow to come, Cedro and I find each other, knowing what has to be done.

"Well?" I ask.

"Let's do this," Cedro charges.

Inside, Cedro talks to the receptionist and, a moment later, the administrator who arranged this with us comes out. "Gentlemen, how's it going out there?"

"It's not," I say.

"We were wondering if we could, I don't know, talk to some of your residents, maybe entice them a little," Cedro proposes.

"You know, we take good care of our residents. I know that sounds strange to say, but unfortunately, that's not the reality of assisted living. But here it is. Our reputation is *elevated standards* and *personal attention*. If you look at the smile on most of our residents' faces, you'll note the difference."

Cedro ingests the word of warning. "We wouldn't dare violate that. We actually want to just...*add* to it."

The administrator slips his hands into the pocket of his slacks, considering the proposition. Skepticism melts into a trust across his smooth, manicured face. "Okay. No problem." He and Cedro shake hands and the administrator walks down hallway.

"What are you thinking?" I ask, standing eye level to Cedro.

"Come on."

Cedro leads me down a hallway, to the cafeteria. Even though the room is chalked full of gray-hairs and pruned-skins, it's eerily still and quiet. I note the way these elderly citizens, who move so slowly it's like they have invisible weights strapped to their limbs, are staring at their plates—literally—as if the mush pile on it is going to stand and walk into their mouths.

"I'm not sure why most are not eating," I whisper.

"You don't have to whisper," Cedro says, his voice at a normal volume and then goes into a whisper. "They can't hear you anyway."

I laugh, an authentic one that causes me to close my eyes just to get through it so that the entire room doesn't notice. When I open my eyes, I realize I'm standing here alone.

"May I have your attention please?" Cedro says from the middle of the room. "If anyone can identify what that pile was before it was a pile, I will give you a free lunch from Street Food & Love. In case you don't know what that is, it's our food truck outside that has real meat and real cheese and real bread on it—just for you!"

"A baby's Hershey squirts," a man, his face creased more than a crumpled piece of paper, bawls out his explanation of what his plate of mush was before it was mush.

The room is filled with laughter. Cedro rambles over to this man, who's smiling as if he's been waiting to say that for years. "Congratulations, sir. Here you go." Cedro hands him a coupon.

A nurse sashays from out of nowhere. "Oh, umm, that's not a good idea," she conveys. "He's um...let's just say he can't eat that."

"No you can't, Jim. You know that," the nurse reminds the elderly man, Jim, as if she's talking to a child.

Jim is annoyed. "Why not?"

"Oh, Jim, you know why." The nurse has patience for miles.

"It's a conspiracy," Jim protests.

"Everything's a conspiracy," the petite nurse whispers to us. "He says that America's involvement in the Vietnam War was a depopulation effort of U.S. men because they didn't finish the job during the post-World War II era."

"Eugenics," Cedro buttresses the nurse's thoughts.

"Smart old guy," I murmur.

The nurse nods and escorts Jim away.

All around, disgruntled and curious senior citizens are rumbling, wondering exactly what they can do to eat some food that is anything but the *baby's Hershey squirts* in front of them.

I whisper to Cedro. "I think you just set off a bomb."

"Only this bomb doesn't destroy. It employs," he winks. "Come on, let's go around and help them out to the truck."

"You do that," I say. "I'm going to go to the nurses and find out which residents are not allowed to eat from the truck. We don't want anyone dying on us—lawsuits and all that."

"Good idea."

At the nurses' station is a heavyset lady in blue scrubs who is practically her own continent, her skin being the land in this comparison and her outfit the ocean. *Yikes, she's big.* Because she is swallowing the chair underneath her, it appears from my angle that she is levitating in a squatting position. I desperately want to walk around and verify that I am not dealing with preternatural powers at work here. The irony is so *heavy* (pun intended) that I want to break out in fits: a nurse, the supposed icon of health in this building, turns out to be the epitome of self-sabotage.

"May I help you?" she asks with a stuffed mouth, pushing aside her plate of slopping beans, rice, and a mauled burrito on the desk so as to seem more professional, which is not really possible under the circumstances.

"Yes," I say, and I explain to her what's going on.

As if she just realized where a glut of buried treasure lies, the elephantine nurse gladly tells me to hold on. She then relays something into the P.A. system and, within seconds, a hive of RN's and LVN's is swarming the counter. The head nurse briefs her colleagues and dispatches them to the truck outside. She then advises me, "As long as you guys get the go ahead from the nurses, you're fine. They know their residents' conditions and will clear them. If they say *yes*, the old grays can eat. If they say *no*, they can't. No matter what those little seniors say—no. It's a life and death sort of thing, got it?

"Got it."

"So," the porcine health worker starts, leaning in and raising her brows as if she is going to—*ugh, gross*—flirt with me, "what's in this for me?"

She's either talking about a rendezvous with me later on—*ugh, gross, part two, the sequel*—or...and I remember the half-eaten lunch that's spoiling next to her. "Well, you did just save us from a landslide of lawsuits."

She chuckles, her paunchy cheek vibrating. "Yes I did."

"How about a discount on a plate?"

"Discount?" When she tightens her face, her lips almost disappear.

Ugh, gross, part three, the trilogy. "A free plate?"

She holds up two fingers and rubs the rolls on her belly.

"One and half." There's no such thing as a *half a plate*, but I refuse to not get the last word on negotiations.

"Deal." Her face is undulating again.

Ugh, gross, part four, the—oh, just make it stop!

By the time I get outside, Street Food & Love is flanked thickly with a hoard of society's aged elite, most supporting themselves with walkers that have tennis balls covering the bottom nobs. The nurses are calling out to Lana and Ava, who are inside the truck. Lana is working the kitchen while Ava and Katherine are at the windows taking and handing out orders. Yoke is roving, this time never having complained about his insignificant role because Katherine has decided to join the team whenever she has some free time, and he doesn't want to appear to be a whining toddler about it.

An idea comes to me.

I walk over to Cedro's Rubicon, take the P.A system out of the back and set up the speakers facing the crowd. Connecting my iPod to the mixer which is obviously connected to the speakers, I am able to blare some music.

"What are you doing?" Yoke asks.

"Just watch."

It's like caterpillars trying to wriggle out of a cocoon watching the residents of Garden Crescent jitter to the rhythms of Glenn Miller, Jimmy Dorsey, Harry James, and others of their era. The most some can handle are a couple of quick knee bends and an arm thrust, but to them they're dancing, probably feeling like they did half a century ago.

"That's freaking hilarious," Yoke says.

"No, that is," I say when I see Cedro right in there with a white-haired woman. He's grinding her, in an innocent, playful way, from behind.

From the window I see Ava laughing, her white smile and exotic face beautiful. She stops and catches me. There's commotion all around, but right now it's just Ava and me. Neither of us turns away. She said this was going to be plutonic, but her wordless gaze is saying to me, *"Maybe. We'll see."*

Cedro's words interrupt the moment. "Look." He points.

There's a shopping center across the street and, leaking out from its premises are droves of people. They're coming over to the truck.

"Jackpot," I say.

"Sha-bing!"

I stare at Cedro. "Are you trying to bring that one back?" He laughs a quick, shotgun gut chuckle. "So," I think out loud as it hits me, "how are we going to collect from these seniors?"

"Already took care of it," Cedro regards. "It's going to be charged to their account."

"Huh. Pretty good arrangement. I missed that one."

"Like I said, son, we make a pretty good team."

CHAPTER THIRTY

Jesus said I am the Way, the Truth, and the Light.
Was He talking about calories?
Does that mean I'll be skinny in heaven?

The trail Street Food & Love has blazed across the Southland is quite remarkable:

Three high school lunches (Lord knows I don't miss these institutions of catastrophe at all), including one band tournament where we raked in a heavy haul of mazuma. Midway through the day, we went out and bought a second supply of ingredients and sold out of those after the tournament. Instead of going out to dinner, parents and students gathered around the truck, bought some grub, ate, and chatted.

Four business luncheons (stiff but steady income).

L.A.s Farmer's Market just off of Fairfax (a couple of celebrities bought from the truck as they often frequent this scene on weekend mornings).

Six college campuses: UCLA, USC, Cal State Fullerton, Loyola Marymount, East L.A. City, and Occidental (the girl gazing was monumental that day).

An endless number of bars, pubs, and random stops at nightlife hotspots.

Two RV parks, The Dunes just off PCH and Malibu Beach Park (the atmosphere is family friendly, and the sales were solid).

Every weekday and weekend for the past seven weeks has been work. Rewarding work? Yes. Exhausting work? I had no idea it would be like this. Pure adrenaline has kept us going.

About a month ago all of us decided that it just wasn't feasible for the entire crew to make every single event. We were burning ourselves out, and it could have been devastating to the company. So Lana stayed home on this one, which was a fortuitous decision. With her being almost five months pregnant, the schedule was fraying her nerves. She needed the R and R. This meant that Cedro retook the reigns that were once his. He returned as the cook, the man behind the menu, the *new* menu that is since it's been drastically renovated from his old one which consisted of mainly meat melts.

On a Sunday in March, the last day of Audltcon, which is a convention honoring achievement in the adult film industry, the day begins slowly[21]. Of course, Baby's Bodacious Burgers is also here, and their M.O. is clearly depicted. The girls have taken a page form the Hooter's playbook and have exchanged their usual tight T's and jeans to painted-on tanks and hiked-up Daisy Dukes, and every five minutes at least one of the girls keeps coming out and is trying to lure in customers. Being obscured in the can all day makes it difficult to get guys to see what they want them to see: their bodies.

---

[21] By the way, what kind of *achievements* are we talking about? For the guys is it "Longest Duration Without Orgasm" or "Longest Streak of Film Sex Shooting Without Acquiring an STD"? How about for the girls? Is it "Most Likely to Be Able to Have a Family and Lead Normal Motherly Existence After Porn Career"?

Ava and Katherine can't stand it.

"Hmm," Ava says and looks at Katherine. "Come on. Two can play here. We'll be back." At that, Ava takes Katherine in her car and they head off the grounds.

"What's up?" Yoke asks.

"Don't know. But let's keep prepping."

Yoke and I continue to get our meats and sauces ready for the crush of customers expected (For the record, it's really hard to say *meats* and *sauces* as it pertains to Yoke and I with a straight face, and it's even more trying when considering where we are.).

Within an hour, the girls return. They walk into the truck looking a little *different*. Well, not *different*. *Upgraded*.

"What do you think?" they ask simultaneously.

Ava and Katherine are strutting around in halter tops that halt just below their hoobies and a pair of hot pants that don't quite make it over the intersection of rear end and back of thigh.[22]

Yoke and I watch, speechless.

"Can you guys handle the prep still?" Ava asks.

We nod, unable to use primitive words such as *yes* and *no*.

"Great. Get ready for a crowd."

The girls walk down the truck steps and out to the vast lot, sun beaming down.

"Ava is...I mean," Yoke begins noting Ava's goddessness.

"Yeah, no kidding," I say.

---

[22] I think I've mentioned Ava is a ten. Even Katherine has been losing some of that extra density she's been carrying. She's deflated from a solid size seven to a four or five. She's got the Scarlett Johansson look. It's pretty hot.

"Do you think there's any chance that Ava and Katherine get in a mud wrestling match with those girls from the burger truck?"

My right eyebrow spikes up to my hairline. "Now that would be something. But I have a better idea. I'll be back. Can you handle this?"

Yoke beams, knowing that prep is important, and that he's doing some significant work. "Don't worry about a thing."

I dart from the truck and catch up to Ava, who is being smothered by three guys.

"Dude, we're talking to the lady," one of the dark-haired, Middle Eastern guys says.

"He's with me, boys," Ava rebuts, and the guys back off.

"What is it?" Ava asks me in a surreptitious tone as if we're talking strictly confidential.

Part of this plan is selfish, motivated by pure hormones, and the other is tactical, an entrepreneurial effort. I whisper the idea into her ear. I have no inkling of hope that Ava will actually do this, but I have to give it a try. If Ava agrees, my eyes will be able to witness something that they might not ever get to see again. It is to be the apex of experiences.

Ava listens to me reel off a detailed plan in a matter of seconds. She nods at all key points. When I'm done, I pull away and watch her face as she mulls over what I just said. Slowly a smile creases on her face. This is the universal sign for *yes. She agrees! Oh yeah!*

"Great!" I express and, without wasting another moment and before Ava can change her mind, I run into the convention center.

The atmosphere is lusty and licentious. I can tell who is who in this fiasco of pornography because those dressed in more clothing are nothing more than sex-itchy fans who've paid to get it while those (ladies) in scantily clad attire are working professionals in the porn industry. The directors and actors are walking in pressed and fitted shirts wearing tight expressions that seems to suggest, *"F-you, jerk. I'm awesome because I work with hot chicks who take their clothes off for me every day."* I can't deny these men this.

Scouring through this crowd, I start to ask anyone around for what I need. Porn stars, both guys and girls, directors, managers, and mere patrons are all up for grabs.

"I'm looking for a bikini," I say to a man who looks at me and laughs.

"Oh, drag. Yeah, that's not this convention," he corrects. "Check online. They're probably doing that one in Florida."

I walk away, thinking how I have to rephrase my solicitation. At different spots in the convention center, there are stages set up where interviews are being done live and run through a P.A. system. The women being interviewed are wearing bikinis. I figure that if I explain to someone that I am working with one of these ladies, they might direct me to where I might find a *costume* i.e. bikini.

"My girl needs to get dressed for an interview, but she had an accident—can't really go into that right now. Anyways, I need a suit for her."

The man I ask, a porn actor probably, as I can tell by the *cocky* (no pun intended) expression on his face, one that seems to be counting the women he's slept with the same way an insomniac might count sheep—*"415, 416...no wait, 423. Yeah, that's it. 423 women."*—tells me, "Ask Rachel. She had the same problem."

"Who's Rachel?" That question just told this *movie* star that I really don't work in the industry. "I meant *where's* Rachel," I stress. "But never mind. I'll find her."

I don't know who Rachel is, but my bet is that she's hot and makes money by servicing men. With that understanding, this should be simple. I won't look for Rachel, I'll ask any woman who fits the description of Rachel.

I hit up the next Rachel I see, and I don't think she is really Rachel.

The woman responds positively. "Follow me." She leads me to a makeshift dressing room that is curtained off. "So, you're looking for a replacement bikini. What size is she?" she asks.

"Who?"

"The girl you need it for, silly."

"Good question. What size is *totally hot*? Is there a numeric equivalent for that?"

The woman strips off her clothes and is in her lingerie. I suppose my mouth drops open because she laughs. "Don't get the wrong idea. I'm just trying to get you see how she compares to me so we can get an idea."

This sensually hot woman, not an ounce of fat on her, with tones and lines of leanness tracing her body in all the right places, is twisting her hips, letting me size her up. She is about two inches taller than Ava, but just as tiny. "I'm a perfect zero, obviously," she guffaws at her own statement, obviously proud of her physique. "In letters that's an extra-extra small. In waist it's a twenty-three or twenty-four, if there is no twenty-three."

"I need two your size and two about a size or two bigger."

"Okay," she says, glad to help.

She doesn't even reach for her clothes. Instead she opens up a Tupperware container and pulls out some bikini sets of various colors and styles, all wrapped in plastic.

"Thank you," I say, choking on my words because I was short of breath.

She kisses me on the cheek. "I'd love to work with you someday. You should get in the industry. You'd be a star. Girls like me would clamber to work with you." I watch her get dressed. "Ta Ta." She flips her hand to me and leaves me in the curtained room.

It takes me a moment before I start the very conscious effort of breathing—in, out, in, out—and gather myself.

When I do, I race back outside to Ava, who already has two of the four girls from Baby's Bodacious Burgers ready. I give them their bags.

"You're going down," Julie says, and the girls from the burger truck head into their unit to change.

Ava and Katherine strut off and do the same in our vehicle. While they were doing that, I set up the P.A. system and prepare to make an announcement.

"Bikini contest happening..." I tap the mike to make a beating, drumroll sound. "Right now."

The rules are as such. The girls will each come out, one at a time, and model their...*gifts*. I'm going to play host, asking each of them interview questions. Then after each has their turn, all four are going to stand next to each other, a foot apart, facing the audience. The guys in the audience have agreed to buy from the truck that is represented by the girl they choose.

"And now, please welcome Juicy Julie!" I say.

First Julie, from Baby's Bodacious, comes out to a reception of squawking men.

I wait for the cheers to abate. "So, Julie, how important is IQ to you in a relationship?"

"Very," she said. "If you don't have the brains, then you don't have the game. At least for me."

The crowd of over a hundred and growing erupts.

"Thank you, Juicy Julie," I say.

When Ava comes, I have to try to focus. She looks astonishing in her brightly colored bikini, cut so that not one inch of her curves is hidden. This I've never seen before. Her stomach, perfectly flat, and her hips, hued by an angel, are so desirous under her humble breasts.

"Uh," I stammer. "Please welcome, Alluring Ava."

The men are silent, taking her in. Then they applaud, their clapping delayed. Ava just has that Bathsheba Effect on all males[23].

I ask the same question as each *contestant* has a fair chance to respond.

"You're thinking of intelligence quotient," Ava gapes into the mike, adding cuteness to her spiel. It's fake and effected girlishness and not the usual Ava, but she surely is pulling it off. "When I hear IQ as it applies to a relationship, intelligence is

---

[23] *The Bathsheba Effect* is taken from the Biblical account of David on the rooftop. He was a king, chilling one evening, scoping out his kingdom and probably thinking, "Dang, I am awesome." Then he saw something even more awesome: A naked girl bathing on her rooftop. David, no doubt, stood in awe for a moment. Apparently scholars want us to think that rooftop bathing was a customary practice back then. Yeah. Whatever. This lady, Bathsheba, was a sten and she was doing something extraordinary, something that only tens do, and that is to flaunt themselves. A ten who's utterly hot and knows it and doesn't hide it, brings herself up to an eleven. In short, David, the king, summonsed this lady to his bedroom and basically said, "The king—that'd be me—wants you for a fling." David's initial response when he saw her, the moment he laid eyes on the most beautiful thing he'd ever seen, is The Bathsheba Effect.

overrated. I'm looking for *intimacy* quotient." She embellishes the word *intimacy* and it consequently turns every guy on.

"I got a lot of that, baby!" Random roars surge out.

Julie's coworker, Samantha, strides up to the mike, and she goes through the interview. "I stands for *intensity*. Q stands for *quality*. I'm looking for some *quality intensity*."

One man calls through the cheers, "That's backwards, sweetie. It's IQ not QI."

"Shut up, durge donk!" another voice from the morass of men bellows. "This isn't a spelling bee."

Laughter follows.

Katherine is next.

"So, Killer Katherine, tell us your theory behind IQ as it pertains to love."

I watch Yoke, whose world has momentarily stopped.

"Well, I've always been shy because, let's just say, I'm not exactly a size zero."

"It's okay, honey. They're just numbers," some man yells, and more laughter follows.

"Exactly," Katherine announces into the mike. "That's why I is for *immediate* and Q is for *qualified*. In other words, take me as I am now. If not, don't expect me to be a zero later."

"You're qualified!" a flurry of men screams.

The girls go through two more rounds of questioning. On the last round, a few guys bring out buckets of water and set them at my feet.

"What's this?" I ask, the questioning echoing in the air.

"If you don't know, you shouldn't be hosting," the bearded, burly man says for all to hear. Of course, he gets his intended response from the mob: roars.

I look at the contestants and they smile. They're game.

325

Four brawny guys carry the buckets of water and set them down in front of each girl. "Ready?" I ask. When the guys are ready and armed with the buckets in hand, I start to count. "One. Two. Three."

All the girls are soaked and probably the mob of men, too.

By the time the competition is done and I direct the men to make a line in front of their choice, Ava's line is unquestionably the longest.

"And your winner," I pronounce. "Alluring Ava! She'll be signing autographs, too, by the way. All you have to do is order a drink, and she'll take a Sharpie to the shirt on your back."

I turn to Ava, who's cringing at me since I just added this feature into the bikini contest. *Her face is so cute like that.*

Julie, as irascible as she can be, has no right to be a sour sport about this. She agreed to it and, besides, it's not like she isn't going to make some good profit. Her line is evidence of that. From a distance Julie nods to me and I nod back. Bad blood has just morphed into clean competition and a symbiotic business connect.

CHAPTER THIRTY-ONE

By the time they had diminished from 50 to 8,
the other dwarves began to suspect 'Hungry'...
~Gary Larson

SOLE, DO YOU KNOW WHERE YOUR DAD IS? Lana texts.

ISN'T HE WITH YOU? AT THE HOSPITAL?!

NO. THAT'S THE PROBLEM. WE HAVE OUR SONOGRAM APPT. HE WAS SUPPOSED TO HAVE ALREADY BEEN HERE.

I'LL TEXT HIM.

NO. IT'S NO USE. CAN YOU DO ME A FAVOR?

SURE.

Of course I can do Lana a favor. Like I've mentioned, she's a surrogate mother to me. I'd do a favor for her the same way any son who respects and adores his own, biological mother.

CAN YOU COME AND MEET ME?

Cedro's absence is untimely and, admittedly, unexpected. He's spent the last months constructing a scaffold of trust, of respectability, of responsibility, and of sincerity—all the things I can't ever remember him showing. Though I never said it, over these past weeks I was starting to develop a certain belief in him, the way I always wanted to. Until now, I thought relaunching the food truck business was one of the best decisions I've ever made. But in one moment, in a repeat of the old Cedro, all that was being made new is now disintegrated. It's neither new nor old. It's just nothing.

I'LL BE THERE IN TWENTY MINUTES.

When I finish my text, I put my phone in the back pocket of my Levi's. "Thanks, Mr. T-Rez. It's been a crazy time. This extension has been more necessary than you can know."

"No problem, Sole. Good news is you're officially done," T-Rez advertises. "That means you can drop the *mister* bit. From now on it's just T-Rez to you."

"Pretty shrill of you to offer that. It's sort of like we're on the same level now," I retort.

"Uh, no. It's nothing like that," T-Rez delineates, pointing to his forehead. "You got some major cognating to do before you catch up to the millenniums of wisdom stored up here."

I laugh. "I'll you give you that."

T-Rez sticks out his hand. "Sole, it's been a pleasure. I can't wait to catch your acts. I have no doubt you're going to make it."

"That means a lot." I firmly shake his hand. "You're a class act, T-Rez. You have my number. We gotta chill sometime. Grab a drink, perhaps." T-Rez displays a sideways glance at me, not sure if I'm kidding. "Okay, maybe just some lunch then," I amend.

"I'll have to take you up on that. Being seen next to a celebrity can only increase my status among the ladies."

"Still not married?"

"Never will be. But that doesn't mean I don't want friends."

"Yeah, sure, T-Rez. *Friends.* I got you. Well," I close, "see you at graduation."

For the last time, I walk out of the single classroom door that belongs to T-Rez. No more packets or papers to turn in. Even though what I just submitted should have been in months ago, T-Rez's generosity was a saving grace.

On the way to my car, there are no other activities. It's late morning, not quite noon, and classes are in session. Marshall High is pacific, and I suppose this is the way I'll remember it. So many other life things have occurred that high school seems more like day care, a place I long left in the rear view mirror.

*

I walk into the ultrasound room where Lana is seated. I don't know if she's crying. Her hair is down over her face that is revering the floor. If Lana is teary-eyed, I have no idea what to do or say. I've never known her to be a weeper.

"Lana?"

She looks up, eyes ringed with red but dry at least. "Sole. Thanks for doing this."

"Of course." I take a seat next to her. "You did tell them I was your..."

"Stepson. Is that okay?"

"Phew. Yeah. As long as they didn't think...well, you know."

Lana laughs through the teary remnants tracing her features. "Give it up for the queen of cougars." She holds up her hand to receive a high five.

I high five her. "There you go."

"Well, Ms. Averil, we've stalled as long as we can. It's time. Or we can reschedule," a female nurse says as she enters.

Lana looks at me, wanting advice. "Do you think your dad will get mad? I mean I'm going to know the baby's sex."

"I don't mean this in the wrong way," I answer. "But he's not exactly here. What he thinks right now is sort of irrelevant."

Lana hugs me. "This is sort of your life with him, isn't it?" I don't say anything. I need all my strength to retain any possible torrent that wants to flow from my eyes, but it's hard. It's like trying to patch up a cracking damn that has no chance of detaining what's behind it. "You're good, Sole. You're strong."

When Lana pulls back and gathers herself, she tells the nurse to go ahead with the ultrasound.

I witness it all as the technician pours the water soluble jelly onto Lana's hill/belly and uses the probe to spread it around. Suddenly, she starts narrating, her face not looking at us but in the direction of the display. "Head circumference looks good. Abdominal circumference...same. Good. Heartbeat...well, listen." The technician raises the volume.

Du-dum-du-dum-du-dum, the baby's rhythm is steady and quick.

Tears scud down Lana's cheeks.

"Okay, Ms. Averil, are you ready?"

Lana gapes at me. I nod. "Yes," Lana affirms.

"Okay. Do you see those three lines?"

"Uh huh. Yes."

"Well, let me disclaim, the prediction is not a hundred percent accurate, but we're pretty good at this. So you can almost bet the likelihood is high that the sex of the baby is..." The technician makes sure to look at Lana when she says this. "A girl. Congratulations."

A sister. Holy cow.

Lana embraces me, and I comfort her. "Congratulations."

*

Shortly after the technician has left and printed the pictures, Lana and I are leaving the room. A small commotion rumbles down the hall. Someone is jogging toward us.

"Hey, guys. I'm so sorry I'm late," Cedro apologizes.

"Late is for something that is still going on. You're past late," Lana says stiffly.

Cedro tries me. "Thanks for coming here with her."

I don't say anything.

"I'm sorry," Cedro implores, gingerly moving a step close to Lana. "But I have some really good news. Trust me."

Moment of truth here: Both Lana and Cedro have good news now. If Cedro has changed and he is genuinely sorry and has a good reason, then he'll insist on Lana's good news first. Why? Because it's his kid—well, his daughter, actually—that Lana has photos of. It's between a life he created and something else. That something else could be important, granted, but not as important as that life. He never figured this out with me, but I hope he can for *her*.

"But you first," Cedro softly prattles to Lana. "You have the news of a lifetime. No offense, buddy," Cedro jests with me, holding out his fist for me to pound.

I don't leave him hanging. "None taken."

Leo Tolstoy said, *Everyone thinks of changing the world, but no one thinks of changing himself.* He was wrong about Cedro. *I* was wrong about him. And I could not be more overjoyed to admit that and witness a more selfless and honest Cedro.

Lana takes the photos of the out of her purse and holds them for Cedro to see. "See these three lines?" she asks.

"Uh huh," Cedro nods, stupefied as a lumberjack with an axe in Times Square.

"Do you know what they mean?"

Cedro shakes his head.

"They mean she's a girl."

Following the hug and tear fest—again!—Lana asks Cedro, "So, what is your good news?"

CHAPTER THIRTY-TWO

Give me liberty or... OOOooo... A jelly donut!

~ Homer Simpson

Cedro wants to share his astounding news over a home cooked dinner at his house. I, of course, invited Ava.

It's been a couple of days since we've seen each other or spoken. Street Food & Love took a much needed sabbatical so that its *staff* could regroup. Stepping away from each other was the perfect remedy after a long run.

"What do you think it's about?" Ava asks from the passenger's seat of The Curse of the Maroon.

On my iPod I have The Kooks set, the song "Junk of the Heart (Happy)" serenading us.

After I called Ava to ask her to accompany me, she agreed to not only come, but to also let me pick her up. From her house even. But she insisted that her agreeing to come, in no way, constituted a date. "Moral support. Friendship fortifying. Emotion sustentation. These are what I'm subscribing myself to. That's the deal." These were her exact words.

I've never actually heard anyone use the word *sustentation* before, so I was cornered. I had to consent to her stipulation.

"I don't know. Maybe he got a teaching gig somewhere. Maybe even his old job," I answer her question.

"Really?" Ava remarks with enthusiasm. "That would be great, no?"

"It would have been great, but now I don't know. The business is doing great. They could make a lot of money."

"But the work. It's just them, now. I mean you're not going to do that full time, are you?"

"Pfff. No way."

"See."

"Well, they still have you, don't they?" I wink at her.

"Pfff. No way," she repeats. "I was just seasonal help."

A few minutes later, we pull up to Cedro's house, Street Food & Love hibernating cozily in the corner of the drive. Without saying much, we disembark my car and careen to the door. I have a key, so I don't knock.

"Welcome! Welcome!" Cedro exhibits bona fide felicity. "Enter, please."

"One step ahead of you," I hail.

Ava punches my arm, not hard, but just to let me know to ease off the snark pedal.

"Okay. Sorry," I whisper to her.

"Sit down, please. It's ready," insists Cedro.

Before we take our seats, Ava and I exchange hugs and niceties with Lana.

"Congratulations," Ava tells Lana.

"Oh, thank you, Ava. Thank you so much." Lana hangs onto Ava as if they haven't seen each other in years. "And I don't just mean for your words. You've done so much. So much. Thank you."

Even Ava can't refrain from sharing a slight sob with Lana. "It's been my pleasure."

Practicing a bit of old school courtliness, I hold out the seat for Ava. She looks back at me, confused.

"Chivalry is alive and well?" I ask.

"You're such a dork," she plays. "But it's cute. Thank you."

When Ava is situating herself in the chair, Lana catches my attention. She points at me, a threat really, jabbing her finger as if there were a five-foot iron prod extending from it that she is enjoying thrusting into my thorax. It's a gesture that means, *"Don't you ruin it with her this time."*

"Okay, okay," I mouth, no volume to my words.

We watch Cedro serve us a gourmet meal of scallops and strips of rib eye (surf and turf), sided with cheesy au gratin potatoes and a medley of vegetables. "This sure is a nice alternative from the food truck, ay?" Cedro motions.

"Ay," I approve.

"Ay," Ava and Lana are united in their agreement.

With some acoustic instrumental music drawing through the house, like a low tide current, we all begin eating. There's something larger than an invisible elephant in the room. It's more like an entire newly discovered solar system has integrated itself into this very house and, until Cedro says what's on his mind, this cosmological structure has no intention of melting away.

"Well, do you want the good news or the good news first?" Cedro ruefully inquires.

Lana can't contain her pleasure. She obviously already knows.

"Does that mean you have two times the good news but only one headline for us? Or does that literally mean you have two bits of information for us?" asks Ava.

"Aw, smart," Cedro counters, cutting a bite of rib eye, stabbing it with his fork, and inserting it into his mouth. "It's actually two bits of info."

He chews, swallows, and sets his fork down. "This is absolutely wild. But, next week, *Eat St.* is going to film Street Food & Love in action and air it on the Cooking Channel."

"No way. That's amazing," Ava claps.

All eyes are now on me. "That's pretty shrill. Really. There's no stopping Street Food & Love now." All eyes are still on me. I cobble some faux buoyancy together. "So what's the other news?"

"We've been voted best new mobile enterprise for this year, and we're being spotlighted at Southern California's biggest festival: The L.A Vendy Awards. They want to *bestow an award upon us.*" Cedro says this last part with a British accent.

"That's really great," is all I can muster.

A weighty silence takes over, muzzling each of us. Cedro eyes Lana and reaches for her shoulder. She nods and Cedro takes this as a cue. He rises from the table. "Be right back." He and Lana no doubt spoke about this sequence before Ava and I arrived.

A moment later, Cedro reenters the room, the silence still reigning, save for a hollow clang of a fork and plate here and there.

"Here you go." Cedro is standing next to me, an envelope extended to me.

"What's this?" I ask.

"*Check* it out."

I accept the overture and, without hesitation, open its contents. If it's biological warfare, I'll die because I haven't bothered to pull the envelope away from my face. Inside I see no powder and breathe no toxins. It's a rectangular slip of paper, a check. I pull it out and read the details.

PAY TO THE ORDER OF: SOLE EABY. FOR: FORTY THOUSAND DOLLARS. SIGNED: CEDRO EABY.

"Uh..." My voice is flickering, and it's not because I'm holding forty G's in my hand addressed to me. I know what this is.

Cedro bends down beside me, his humility full tilt. "I am so sorry, son. I know...I know there's nothing I can say or do to redo our lives. And that regret is mine. And yours. I won't deny you that. I know I've created deep regret." He regroups. There's more to say, and I let him take his time. I want to hear this. "This money is yours. I saved it for you and gave it to you. I shouldn't have taken it and used it."

"You gambled and won," I say.

"No, son. That's not the way it went at all. And I want to say this before all of us—all of us who are Street Food & Love: I gambled and lost. But you are my wild card. You're my ace up the sleeve. Thank you, Sole."

Waterworks. I'm gushing, a deluge of emotion cascading over my face. Everything is blurry. I don't even try to harness the tears. They've wanted to come out for some time now. Tonight the dam is broken and the body of water it was framing is getting its chance to run down like a rapid escaping down river.

Cedro hugs me, and I hold him back. I hold him so tightly, every inch of my arm a year of my life that I felt I lost with him, a moment lost to his midlife crisis that I want back so badly I think I can squeeze it out of him.

"I love you, son. I'm so sorry."

337

"I love you, too, Dad. And I'm sorry, too."

Around us, unequivocally, Lana and Ava are moistened around the eyes as well. For the next minutes, the house is filled with four criers. But at least the pinch in the air is gone. We're no longer surrounded by unspoken strongholds. In a sense, we're free. Midlife crisis. Young life crisis. It's all transformed to, well, like Ava once said: *hope.*

"Keep the money," I offer. "The baby and all. That's my sister. No way can I take it."

My dad insists. "Sole, you have no idea what you've done with that truck. No idea." My dad's smile is so large it's like a kayak has docked on his face. It means that money is not only not a problem anymore, a total reversal has occurred. Money is now a power, a force in their lives.

"Glad I could help."

"Sole, have you thought of majoring in business?" Lana asks. "What you did...the vision, the leadership you displayed...none of us had any idea what we were doing and you just saw it and ran with it."

I start laughing hard, and it takes me a moment to recover. "I didn't really know what I tried would work. I just sort of had these ideas in my head." I look at my dad. "For a *long* time."

"A long time, huh?" my dad asks. "Like long enough that you could have spared me all this grief and said something before?"

I shrug.

My dad beams. "I was such a dunce," he says.

"Can't disagree with that," I play back.

"Oh, hey, Sole, there's one more thing," my dad gestures to the door with his hand. "Over there. Go check it out."

"Okay," I say. "But isn't this the *third* bit of news? You said *two.* Does this mean it's bad news?"

"There is no more bad news," Cedro assures. "Go open it."

I rise and amble to the front door. Cautiously I peer out of the peephole. There's nothing there. I look back to the table, all three—Ava, Lana, and Cedro—gaping at me with huge smiles.

When I open the door, the FOR SALE sign falls toward me. It hits my leg and I reach for it, clasping it in my hands. I bring it in the house and lightly set it down on the living room floor.

"That belongs in the trash," Cedro celebrates.

This is when Yoke enters. He must have placed the sign by the door and was waiting for his cue before entering. "So do you sometimes," Yoke jests.

"I don't know. It's good advertising for me, don't you think?" I ponder aloud to everyone. Then I direct my words at Ava. "Unless, of course, you want to take me off the market."

EPILOGUE

We won.

Street Food & Love took home the Bon Appétit Award. It was a great experience, not just because of the accolade and high mantle the business now stands on, but because the award was received in the presence—no, let me amend that: in the *face!*—of all our competitors. On stage, where Cedro, Lana, Ava, Yoke, and I stood to accept our endowment, I could see Julie and the girls form Baby's Bodacious Burgers. They were none less happy that we took home this prestigious award than we were.

Atop this recognition, Street Food & Love also raked in the Best New Mobile Business for that year and was named the L.A Vendy champion. But this wasn't the best part.

I won, too.

During Cedro's speech, on the stage set up at Pan Pacific Park which is right off main artery Beverly Boulevard and adjacent to The Grove amphitheater, Cedro received a secondary prize, well, not exactly secondary, but more like a parallel prize: Best New Chef.

Astonished, Cedro, in a fitted t-shirt that displayed his Return to Muscular Status body and the ink splashing down his arms, took a moment before spieling into the microphone. The judges were few but potent, in terms of the clout they wheeled.

James Cunningham, whom we had met when he hosted us on a segment for his nationally syndicated show, *Eat St.*, was front and center on the panel.

Lee Anne Wong from the show *Top Chef* was all dazzled in spiffy attire, her sharp looks making it unclear if the voting was actually unanimous or if she was the sole dissenter.

Hadley Tomicki from *GrubStreet LA* casually waved and gave us a thumbs up from his post.

And Bryant Ng from *Spice Table* smiled like a banana was pressed over his lips. That's how much pleasure he took in seeing a nobody from out of nowhere take in these prestigious laudations.

"I'd just like to say that, first of all, Street Food & Love is a team effort. It's a unity thing. Literally, love is what made this business exist." Cedro looked at me when he said this next part. "Love is what resurrected this business that, at one point, was underneath and left for dead. Come here, son."

The thousands in shorts and warm weather attire who were blanketing the park cheered under the Los Angeles sun. Cedro and I hugged tightly, as men sometimes do, as individuals who deeply respected each other.

When we separated and regained our own space on stage, Cedro boasted. "This Best New Chef award, though my name is on it, has to be shared with my lovely lady, Lana."

Lana, a stomach revealing the cargo inside, sidled up next to my dad. He kissed her, rousing the audience to excitement. Then he dropped to a knee and, well, she said yes.

Lana retook her position next to Ava and Yoke onstage, and my dad railed on. "And with my son, who is better than the man I'd always wanted him to become. He is the man I hope I can be." Applause, again, then, in the wake of the cheers, my dad continued. "With that said, ladies and gentlemen, let's hear the heart and *soul* behind Street Food & Love, my son, Sole Eaby."

I grabbed the microphone and, of course, embroidered my speech with my customary humor. "Thank you, thank you," I began after the applause. "I have to say—you all are funny. You do know that you're applauding because, as Best New Chef, we've greatly contributed to the obesity epidemic in this nation..."

A chorus of laughter resounded.

"I'm actually serious. We have to round to the nearest thousand for calorie count. And fat grams—forget it. You've heard of Botox, right? Well, now—screw that. We've commercialized our product and redistributed to the cosmetic industry as Fatox. Apparently rolls and jiggles are the new look."

When the crowd calmed from this joke, I added. "Okay, on the count of three, everyone, grab some flesh roll." I pulled skin from my stomach region to model what I mean. From the stage, I witnessed a band of people, standing shoulder to shoulder, grab their fat rolls around their waists. "One. Two. Three. Pull and jiggle!" We all pulled and jiggled.

"Seriously, though, I have to say something," I continued. "As my father has passed the praise to me, I must admit, too, that there is absolutely no way I can stand here and take credit for this. No way. See, there's this girl. And she taught me the meaning of two words: *hope* and *reconciliation*. She taught me that relationships either thrive or die with them. They need both. They need what I call *hopeanciliation*[24].

"We are all standing here, right now, on this stage, because of this word...because we opened ourselves to each other and kept

---

[24] Soleism #6: *Hopeanciliation* is a position of the heart. It means that a person must continue to keep their heart open to the idea that people just might change and that when they do, you must be ready to forgive and reconcile with them so that the relationship that was once damaged can be restored.

our hope alive in each other. Because relationships that were once crushed were restored."

The audience extolled the poignant speech that was, uniquely, from the heart, from *my* heart.

Such a weird sensation.

The verdict is still out on this one. I don't know if I truly like this vulnerable position, this laying it out there stuff.

"In short, ladies and gentlemen, I stand here before you, ennobling the girl with the biggest heart I know." I turned and faced Ava. "Ava Rozen, will you please step forward and accept your reward. Street Food & Love is because of you. You were right all along about my dad...about me. Thank you for helping me see that. You are the inspiration for all this. You truly are *my* inspiration."

Ava confidently gaited toward me and took the mike. "Did you actually think this little spiel was going to work?"

The crowd gushed with laughter.

"It did," Ava boomed into the sound system and wrapped her arms around me, the cordless microphone still in her hand. She inched up on her toes and I embraced her. Right there, in front of a thousand city goers, we kissed.

ABOUT THE AUTHOR

H.A.'s love for all things caffeinated is what keeps him awake so that he can pursue that glorious tyrant called Nostalgia. And after all, isn't that what provokes most adult authors to write stories about the teenage years they long ago left behind? When he isn't writing, H.A. can be found quaffing coffee (Yes, he might be addicted—don't judge) reading, snapping photos, making music and, on rare occasions, attempting to discover the elusive, and maybe impossible, secret to time travel. *Street Food and Love* is H.A.'s first novel.